BLACKFEET TALES
FROM
APIKUNI'S WORLD

BLACKFEET
TALES
FROM
APIKUNI'S
WORLD

By James Willard Schultz

Edited by David C. Andrews

University of Oklahoma Press • Norman

This book is published with the generous assistance of The McCasland Foundation, Duncan, Oklahoma.

ALSO BY JAMES WILLARD SCHULTZ

Blackjeet and Buffalo: Memories of Life among the Indians (edited by Keith C. Seele) (Norman, 1962)

Why Gone Those Times? Blackfoot Tales (edited by Eugene Lee Silliman) (Norman, 1974)

Floating on the Missouri (edited by Eugene Lee Silliman) (Norman, 1979)

Many Strange Characters: Montana Frontier Tales (edited by Eugene Lee Silliman) (Norman, 1982)

LIBRARY OF CONGRESS CATALOGING-IN-PUBLICATION DATA

Schultz, James Willard, 1859–1947
 Blackfeet tales from Apikuni's world / by James Willard Schultz; edited by David C. Andrews,
     p. cm.
 Includes bibliographical references.
 ISBN 978-0-8061-5975-1 (paper)
 1. Siksika Indians—Social life and customs. 2. Frontier and pioneer life—Great Plains. I. Andrews, David C. (David Chisholm), 1924– II. Tide.
E99.S54 S279 2002
978.004'973—dc21   2002019045

The paper in this book meets the guidelines for permanence and durability of the Committee on Production Guidelines for Book Longevity of the Council on Library Resources, Inc. ∞

For Janet,
My "sits-beside-me" woman
with my love and thanks
for more than a half-century
of patience and understanding

And then Tom he talked along and talked along, and says, le's all three slide out of here one of these nights and get an outfit, and go for howling adventures amongst the Injuns, over in the Territory. . . .

The Adventures of Huckleberry Finn

Contents

Illustrations

Acknowledgments

I owe thanks—and sometimes much more than that—to many people for their help and encouragement in seeing this collection into book form.

For many years, the loyal members of the James Willard Schultz Society urged and encouraged me to get this book done. They are largely responsible for its finally being completed.

E. Lee Silliman, of Deer Lodge, Montana, who has compiled three of the seven posthumous Schultz collections, offered many suggestions and much support. The late Warren L. Hanna, Apikuni's biographer, was convinced that this collection was a good idea and that I should do it. And that goes for the late Wilbur W. Betts, of Seattle, Washington, who completed the writing of *Bear Chief's War Shirt*, the manuscript Schultz was working on when he died. I regret that Hanna and Betts are no longer here to share in the enjoyment of this achievement.

Special thanks are due to at least three people. Bob Eldredge, of Monkton, Maryland, not only designed the beautiful masthead for *The Piegan Storyteller*, the quarterly journal of the Schultz Society, but also prepared an outstanding map of Schultz country in Montana that he titled *Apikuni's World*. That was originally to have been the title of this volume, but Edward A. Shaw, a long-time society member who read the manuscript and offered helpful suggestions, noted that the present title would be better, since many readers might not be familiar enough with the name "Apikuni" to associate it with James Willard Schultz and the Blackfeet. Finally, over the twenty-one years we enjoyed as a society devoted to Schultz's life, times, and works, Dean G. Combs, of Winnetka, California, served unselfishly as the publisher of *The Piegan Storyteller*. I rejoice to count these three and so many others I came to know during the years of our society as dear friends.

My sincere thanks to all the good folks at the Museum of the Rockies and the Special Collections section of the Renne Library at Montana State University in Bozeman, Montana. Numerous visits there, as well as countless letters requesting copies and a huge amount of information, were handled with pleasantness and good cheer. Not once was I refused assistance.

I also thank the staff of the University of Oklahoma Press. Kimberley Wiar, senior editor (now retired), and John N. Drayton, director, were most helpful in the preparation of the manuscript, and Daniel Simon, acquisitions editor, polished the editor's introduction. Karen C. Wieder, editorial assistant, offered timely advice and counseled patience throughout the publishing process. They are no doubt among many who make dealing with the University of Oklahoma Press so rewarding.

My greatest thanks must go to Janet Andrews, my wife of fifty-six years, who put up with my escapes from chores to work on this and other Schultz-related projects over all that time. Her understanding and loving support—and all the wonderful adventures we shared—have meant a great deal.

Finally, a bow to Apikuni himself, whose writings have brought so many of us together for the better part of a century. May you have found peace and comfort in the Sand Hills.

Editor's Introduction

In the summer of 1877, James Willard Schultz, a seventeen-year-old lad from Boonville, New York, leaped from the deck of the steamboat *Benton* to the levee at Fort Benton, Montana Territory. This day marked the beginning of Schultz's long love affair with the West, with Montana, and with the Blackfeet Indians. Only after seventy years, following Schultz's death in 1947, did the relationship end.

Young Schultz, or Apikuni, as he quickly became known to the Indians,[1] arrived eager to hunt buffalo, to experience Indian life, and, later, to recount some of the drama and mystery of the changing frontier West. He lived among the Blackfeet, married into the tribe, became fluent in their language, and was accepted as a tribal member.

Schultz was born on August 26, 1859, to Philander Bushrod Schults and Frances (Joslin) Shults (as it was spelled at the time). His father was a prosperous merchant, dealing mainly in produce, and James grew up in relative affluence. His mother hailed from nearby Jefferson County.

In his early years, as James developed a deep love for the outdoors, the forests and waterways of the Adirondack Mountains became a second home for him. He never completely accepted the confinement of classrooms, and his school days were checkered with boyish pranks, absenteeism, and various discipline problems. There is little doubt that his parents had their hands full in his formative years. He even ran away once or twice but always returned to the safety and comfort of the family home at 153 Schuyler Street. That home still stands and, since October 1976, has been designated a New York state landmark.[2]

Philander hired two area woodsmen to train his son in the ways of the wilderness; thanks to them, Schultz became skilled in camping, hunting, and fishing—pursuits that would be most useful to him in his later years out West. It was the silence and solitude of his beloved mountains that enchanted him the most, and he could be found more often than not out in those deep woods.

His father was an accomplished violinist, and he supervised James's lessons on that instrument and encouraged him to love good music, a devotion that would stay with him for the rest of his days. The family often traveled to New York City by rail for concerts by the New York and Brooklyn Philharmonic Orchestras as well as performances at the opera. James's passion for opera would grow throughout his life.

An early influence on him was C. Hart Merriam, who lived in nearby Locust Grove. They shared a common love for the outdoors and, though Merriam was four years older than James, they never allowed that difference to interfere with their friendship. Later, James would name his son after his boyhood chum. Hart Merriam Schultz, as he would be known in English, became a noted Blackfeet artist, using his Indian name, Lone Wolf.[3]

As a youngster, James also had his difficulties with formal religion. He was rebellious in Sunday school, often questioning the teachings of his Presbyterian instructors. The story of Jonah and the whale, argued James, was a fairy tale. It was physically impossible for a whale to swallow a man; its throat simply could not open that wide. Eventually, he gave up attending Sunday school at all, no doubt greatly disappointing his good Christian mother.

When James was about fifteen, his father died unexpectedly. It was a hard blow for the young fellow to accept, and he shocked family and friends by taking his fishing pole and disappearing for the rest of the day. He said later that he just had to be alone for a while. After this sad event, James's guardians decided that he should attend a military school, where he would have much stricter discipline. They selected

Peekskill Military Academy on the lower Hudson River, and hoped he might be encouraged to make a career for himself at West Point.

It was a vain hope. His school days at Peekskill were hardly any more successful than they had been in Boonville. The pranks and mischief continued: often he would disappear, taking a train to New York City for the opera or a concert. On the final day of his junior year, he fired off a cannon, breaking several dormitory windows.

Summer was approaching and, when it was suggested that James go to St. Louis and visit his uncle, Ben Stickney, who managed the Planters Hotel there, he eagerly agreed. The trip and the experience would change his life.

The hotel was close to the Missouri River waterfront, and its lobby was a gathering place for trappers, traders, and frontiersmen going to and returning from the edges of western America. The young easterner quickly discovered that simply by hanging around this lobby, he could see and talk with an assortment of colorful western characters and hear some fantastic stories of buffalo hunting and adventures with Indians. He made up his mind that he had to go West and see some of these things for himself. He wrote home and asked for a loan of $500 so he could take a steamboat upriver and learn what life was like beyond the frontier.

No doubt with a good deal of reluctance, his mother and guardians agreed, extracting a promise from James that he would return home in the fall to complete his education and pursue a budding military career. Of course, James promised to do so—but he likely knew then that he could never keep such a promise. In fact, he only returned home two or three times after that. We know he was there in 1878 because the upstairs bathroom window has "J. Schultz, 1878" crudely scratched into one pane. On the stairway wall going up to the attic there remains a crayon sketch of an Indian done by James' younger brother, Freddie. In his first book, the semi-autobiographical *My Life As an Indian*, he tells about another trip back home, but he refers to the place as "the little New England town where was my home."[4]

And so, in the midsummer of 1877, the intrepid young Schultz boarded a steamboat for the trip upriver. A dream was about to be realized. Arriving at Fort Benton, the head of navigation on the Missouri, Schultz soon fell in with Joe Kipp, a mixed-blood trader whom the Indians knew as Berry. Not long after, he would happily accept an opportunity to live with the Blackfeet, hunt with them, and almost literally become one of them. By the time he received his Indian name—Apikuni—the mundane ways of eastern life had become a thing of the past.

Schultz began recording what he saw, heard, and experienced almost from the day he stepped ashore. He often refers to his "notes," but few have ever been found.[5] He was blessed with a marvelous memory for detail and was soon penning articles and reminiscences that would become the basis for his thirty-seven published books about Indian life and culture. For example, some of his earliest pieces were published in George Bird Grinnell's *Forest & Stream* under the title "In the Lodges of the Blackfeet," and they would be a major part of his first volume, *My Life As an Indian.*

Schultz and his writings have been the subject of much controversy over the years. There are those who insist that his works are completely fictitious. There is little doubt that a great deal of each book was dredged up out of memory and his rich imagination. Yet he did actually experience many of the situations about which he wrote. As a storyteller, he combined countless tales he had heard around campfires, incidents in which he had taken part, and legends from many sources. Indians frequently embellish their tales from the past, just as all other people do. Schultz doubtless added many touches of his own. Regardless of what was truth and what was fiction, no one can deny that he was first and foremost a teller of tales, one of the best America's youth ever had.

Schultz's work, like that of many creative writers, is partly autobiographical. Although it is virtually impossible to draw a line between fiction and truth, it is clear that he wrote with authority about his world, based heavily on his first-hand knowledge and personal experiences. He provides a rare glimpse and marvelous perspective of a passing parade—of the fur trade, of trappers and mountain men, of Indians and whites moving between two cultures, but mostly of Indian life and times.

This emphasis in Schultz's work—on the daily lives of the Black-feet and of other tribes—deals mainly with the hunt, with warfare, and with cultural and character clashes. Those subjects and his way of dealing with them were probably responsible for some of his work being classified as juvenile, and some of it is, in the same way that some of Mark Twain's writing is juvenile. The hunt, for example, represented a part of the constant and often desperate search for food. Warfare, especially between hostile tribes and against increasing intrusions by whites, was a way of life. The cultural and character clashes in his work reveal the frontier white, the half-blood, and the full-blood, each with flaws and strengths, in a world in rapid and sometimes deadly transition.

That world—Apikuni's world—was presented in a voluminous body of published works: forty-four books, thirty-seven of which were in print before his death. The seven posthumous books, including this one, are primarily collections of short stories, reprinted in book form with two exceptions: when he died in 1947, Schultz had been laboring on *Bear Chief's War Shirt*, but had completed just sixty-two manuscript pages. Schultz's good friend, the late Wilbur Ward Betts of Seattle, Washington, would complete the manuscript and arrange for its publication.[6]

The other exception was *Floating on the Missouri*, edited by Eugene Lee Silliman, a poignant memoir of a boat trip Schultz and his Blackfeet wife, Natahki, took in the fall of 1901.[7] It was to be her final trip with him; shortly thereafter, she developed a serious heart condition and passed away. A heartbroken Schultz felt that his life was over. Such was not to be the case. There followed a job at the *Los Angeles Times*, some years in Arizona, numerous returns to Montana and the Glacier Park region, guiding trips, and, of course, continued serious writing.

A wealth of Schultz's short stories and articles appeared in many periodicals from the 1880s well into the 1940s. Among the publications that printed them were Grinnell's *Forest & Stream*, *American Boy Magazine*, *The Youth's Companion*, and the *Great Falls (Montana) Tribune*.

Shortly after the death of Natahki, Schultz, now battling depression, was contacted by Ralph Pulitzer, son of Joseph Pulitzer, who established the journalism prizes. Young Pulitzer wanted to go hunting in Glacier Park. At that time, no other white man knew the park as well as Schultz, so he was a natural choice for a guide. Schultz accepted the job, perhaps believing it might help get his mind off the loss of his beloved wife.

Pulitzer wanted desperately to get a bighorn sheep. Even though they were not in season, Schultz agreed to help him and, in June of 1903, Pulitzer shocked Schultz and the others in the party by shooting not just one but four bighorn rams. Schultz protested when Pulitzer kept on firing but his arguments fell on deaf ears. Photos were taken of the multiple kill and later were spotted in a Great Falls photo shop by game warden Jack Hall. Another warden, a man named Green, located Schultz alone on a boat on the Missouri River. Pulitzer and a companion were off hunting. Green confiscated the head of a ram as evidence then, oddly, departed, not waiting for the two hunters to return to the boat. Not for another month, when Pulitzer returned to Montana, did Green catch up to him. Pulitzer eventually was allowed to plead guilty and was fined five hundred dollars.

Meanwhile, Schultz fled the country to avoid prosecution and did not come back for eleven years. During this period he worked at the *Los Angeles Times*, spent much time in Arizona, and also wrote for Grinnell's *Forest & Stream*. When Louis Hill asked Schultz to return to Montana in 1915, the latter learned that the case against him had at last been dropped. That summer, he wrote *Friends of My Life As an Indian*. The poaching incident must have had some lasting effects on Schultz; never again did he have troubles with the law. Yet this very likely did taint him in the eyes of his critics.[8]

Many of Schultz's later articles and stories would concentrate on the Indians of the Southwest, where he and Lone Wolf would live in their Arizona years. During this period, Schultz wrote a series of articles for *Forest & Stream*. Titled simply "In Arizona," these ten articles are primarily a reminiscence of Schultz's years there, describing adventures he had and telling about some of the great characters he met and knew in southern Arizona and northern Mexico. Schultz had just completed an unhappy stint as literary critic of the *Los Angeles Times*. The lure of hunting some wild turkeys drew him to

Arizona, where he found two kindred spirits in a couple of men whom he calls the "Old-Timer" and "Sonora."[9] *In Arizona* has recently been published by Butterfly Lodge Museum, Greer, Arizona.

In the mid-1970s, a small group of Schultz aficionados and students of his writings formed a society to preserve his memory and to promote his works. Called simply The James Willard Schultz Society, the group included Mrs. Jessica D. Schultz Graham, Schultz's fourth and last wife. Her welcome assistance helped create a quarterly newsletter, *The Piegan Storyteller*, which began life in January 1976.[10]

The society grew and flourished for almost twenty-one years. Forty-four states and about a dozen foreign lands were represented in the membership. The total of more than 1,500 members over the years included individuals, schools and colleges, libraries, and other institutions. When publication ceased in mid-1996, thirty-five of the original members were still active.[11]

The controversy over whether or not Schultz was truthful in his writings—or whether they were all simply figments of his active imagination—led to the writing of an essay for the final issue of the *Storyteller*. Many members had been asking that we explore this question, and we felt that it had better be done in this final issue. The essay was titled "Who Was James Willard Schultz?" and in it evidence was introduced to support our own contention that much of what he wrote did really happen and that he did participate in some of those adventures:

> It is surprising these days to go into a second-hand book store almost anywhere and ask if they happen to have anything by James Willard Schultz. About 80 to 90 percent of the people who operate these shops have never even heard of him.
>
> And so the question, "Who Was James Willard Schultz?" is not all that unfair, for so many people born in the second half of this twentieth century were never blessed with the opportunity to grow up with his wonderful stories. . . .
>
> The emphasis here must be on that word "stories," for that is primarily what he wrote: fiction or semi-

fiction for young readers about Indian life. Apikuni, to use his Blackfeet Indian name, never pretended to be a historian or, by any stretch of the imagination, an ethnologist. Yet his books are crammed with history and his descriptions of the daily lives, the customs and culture of the Native Americans are an ethnological treasure. It is more than likely that he never realized this fact. He was not trained in either field; in fact, he never completed high school to the best of our knowledge.[12]

The anthologist Keith C. Seele supported this conclusion. In his introduction to what would be the first of the seven posthumous collections of Schultz material by five different writers, Dr. Seele says: "He was a storyteller, but he never set himself up to be a historian or a scientist."[13]

Another anthologist, Lee Silliman, concurred, as does the eminent George Bird Grinnell. The latter, the most learned ethnologist of his day, praised Schultz in glowing terms for his deep understanding of the people about whom he wrote. He referred to Schultz as "sympathetic and convincing" in his portrayals and also gave him credit for seeing the Indians as human beings in every sense.[14]

Too many early writers would often picture any Indians as wild and savage, completely lacking in humanity, and little more than beasts in their treatment of the white man. Schultz, with his intimate knowledge of Indian ways, especially those of the Blackfeet, was able to penetrate their thoughts and thus give his readers a far truer look at these Native Americans.

Silliman's superb memoir, *Floating on the Missouri*, celebrates a time that both Schultz and Natahki could see slipping away. He describes this float trip in nostalgic terms, with Schultz and his wife revisiting places they knew from the past and reminiscing fondly about those good times. Silliman pays particular attention to the scenic beauty of the Missouri valley and speculates on what lies ahead, not just for Natahki and her husband, but for all Indians. It is a touching look back at a most memorable time in their lives.[15]

With three of the seven posthumous collections to his credit, Lee

Silliman is likely the most well-read of all the Schultz scholars. He understood his subject better than anyone else who ever wrote about him. He and Grinnell and Seele, however, all recognized that Schultz sometimes played fast and loose with the facts. This surely was not done purposely but probably was due to carelessness or forgetfulness. Seele never viewed Schultz as infallible but as subject to occasional exaggerations. Yes, says Seele, he did take some liberties, but he actually lived much of the history he relates in his books.[16] Both Silliman and Grinnell were critical in the same way but both felt that his stories more than made up for his failings.

In 1984 the late Warren L. Hanna, of Kensington, California, took over the task of writing the definitive biography of James Willard Schultz. Several chapters had already been written two years earlier by the late Harry James, a close personal friend of Schultz. But James, a well-known author of a number of books dealing mainly with western subject matter, was ailing and did not complete the work. For several years the manuscript was in the Schultz papers at Renne Library, Montana State University in Bozeman. Hanna, a member of the Schultz Society, a noted expert in compensation law and author of dozens of volumes in the legal field as well as others, worked more than two years to complete this biography. His research took him to numerous sources, leading to the discovery of some unknown Schultz writings. Hanna, too, concluded in his introduction to the biography that Schultz should "be remembered . . . as a storywriter who seldom let facts get in the way of a good story."[17]

In the last issue of *The Piegan Storyteller*, I wrote:

> In the rush to judgment on James Willard Schultz, it seems clear that many did not care to give him his rightful place in life as a master storyteller; rather, it suited them better to dwell on his faults almost to the exclusion of what he had achieved with his numerous fine tales of Indian life. That achievement stands him in very good stead among American authors of books for younger readers and assures believers that if those superb books could be reprinted, a new and enthusiastic generation of Schultz readers and fans would be born.[18]

Among his countless Blackfeet friends, Apikuni was honored and respected as an interpreter of their oral traditions. In a society where stories, legends, and history were passed from one generation to another by word of mouth, Schultz had a reputation as a man of honor who kept those traditions alive through his "thick writings." Often one finds that phrase in those of his works that were not fictionalized accounts of some exciting adventure but, rather, detailed tribal legends or stories that described some of their long history. One example is the book he wrote when he came home to Montana after the Pulitzer incident had cooled down: *Friends of My Life As an Indian.*

When the late Warren L. Hanna had completed work on his biography of Schultz, his vast collection of notes compiled during his research contained a number of articles left over that had originally appeared in *Forest & Stream.* His widow, Frances Hanna, later put these together for another volume entitled *Recently Discovered Tales of Life Among the Indians.* Following this, she also had published a series of a dozen or so short biographical sketches titled *Stars over Montana: Men Who Made Glacier National Park History.* Included in the latter are sketches of both Schultz and his son, Lone Wolf.[19]

Hanna's papers were all turned over to the James Willard Schultz Society after his death. Today those papers, as well as all of the society's remaining materials, are housed at the Schwinden Library in Fort Benton, Montana. It is most fitting that they are kept there, where Schultz first landed in Montana. Like the huge quantity of Schultz memorabilia in the Special Collections Library at Montana State University, all of this is available to scholars and researchers.

Much of the material in *Recently Discovered Tales of Life Among the Indians* and several of the sketches in *Stars over Montana* were reprinted in the pages of *The Piegan Storyteller.* Reprints of pertinent stories and articles were offered to the membership as were regular features. The latter included "The Camp Crier" (society news and notes), letters from members and others, original writings, and many photos and maps. The publication became a grand resource, pulling together material from magazines, newspapers, and memoirs from a great many old-timers.

One much-heralded story that appeared in its pages was a serialized article about the late Angus Monroe, grandson of the noted Rising Wolf or Hugh Monroe. Gordon L. Pouliot of West Glacier, Montana, did the research and wrote this fine article, which ran in three consecutive issues. Rising Wolf had been the subject of one of Schultz's most famous books. Angus was ninety years old at the time of our first society meeting in 1978 at Glacier National Park. He and his wife, Lily, attended and even gave members a tour of noted places in the Park. What was most surprising about this is that Angus was by then totally blind but had a memory as sharp as if he had been a young man.

Another person who penned several articles for the *Storyteller* was Dorothy Floerchinger of Conrad. Known as a famed local historian, she was noted in Montana educational circles as well. Dorothy Hamaker, of Shelby, Montana, was a third contributor to our journal.

The society also published three Schultz book-length tales that had never been issued in book form. They were *The Peace Trail, The Man in the Wooden Mask,* and *The Sacred Buffalo Hunt.* All had been published as serials in *American Boy Magazine* and were serialized in five consecutive issues of *The Piegan Storyteller.* One other Schultz work is as yet unpublished: "The Wolfers, or, Woodhawking on the Upper Missouri."

It was in the pages of *The Youth's Companion,* an old family weekly, that young readers of earlier times found many Schultz short stories and serials. Twenty-three short stories in all and eight serials were first published there. The first short story appeared in the issue for November 3, 1910, the last in the July 7, 1927, issue. By that time *The Youth's Companion* was on the verge of combining with *American Boy Magazine.*

Five of the original twenty-three short stories had already been published in two anthologies: "Puh-Poom" (July 5, 1923) was selected for inclusion in *Blackfeet and Buffalo: Memories of Life among the Indians;* "The Buffalo Hunt" (November 3, 1910), "Laugher, the Tale of a Tame Wolf" (December 2, 1926), "Medicine Fly" (May 19, 1927), and "A Bad Medicine Hunt" (July 7, 1927) were all reprinted in *Why Gone Those Times? Blackfoot Tales.* With one minor exception, those five have been omitted from this collection. I have used the opening five paragraphs of "The Buffalo Hunt" as the author's introduction to this volume.

Seven of the stories presented here appeared originally under the topical title of "Memoirs of a White Indian," perhaps with the idea of later reprinting them in book form with that title. Those seven are noted, but are not in chronological order. The order of these stories has been altered slightly but is basically progressive for continuity and narrative development.

To the best of my knowledge, these Schultz tales are the last of his short stories to appear in hardcover. In spite of the time gaps— several years in places—between the publication dates of the stories, the collection has special merit in its easy flow and progression.

We meet Schultz shortly after his arrival in Montana Territory, when he is still a boy, and we follow him through the kind of experiences that would initiate a young warrior. Apikuni plays a role in many of these stories, usually identified as Spotted Robe. Whether these accounts are fact or fiction, we cannot tell for sure. It is likely that much of each one is completely fictitious.

The other four posthumous Schultz volumes contain different subjects. *Floating on the Missouri*, as indicated, was a memoir; *Many Strange Characters: Montana Frontier Tales* was Lee Silliman's collection of Schultz's "white man" stories; the two others are *Bear Chief's War Shirt* and *Recently Discovered Tales of Life Among the Indians*.

Other excellent books about this colorful era in American and western history are Walter McClintock's *The Old North Trail* and *Old Indian Trails*; Warren L. Hanna's *Stars Over Montana* (described previously); and two special classics: George Bird Grinnell's *Blackfoot Lodge Tales* and John C. Ewers's *The Blackfeet: Raiders on the Northwestern Plains*.[20]

These books will provide historical and cultural background for the stories about Schultz's world contained in this volume. Readers will find that, in the telling of these eighteen exciting tales, Schultz has proved once again that he was a master storyteller, regardless of whatever failings he may have had attributed to him. Like all of us, he was human, with most of our frailties and basic weaknesses. We ought to judge the man on what he achieved in his lifetime instead of condemning him for those smaller faults.

In his last years at Lander, Wyoming, Schultz suffered a series of debilitating illnesses and hospitalization. He did almost no writing after 1940. He died at Lander on June 11, 1947, and was buried on a hillside overlooking Two Medicine Valley, near Browning, Montana.

Notes

1. An earlier version of his Blackfeet name is Ap-pe-kun-ny. That name and a translation of it—Spotted Robe—are used in some of these stories. He is also known as Far-off White Robe. Some even claim that his name was Huck Finn.

2. Matthew J. Conway of nearby Woodgate was the moving force behind efforts to commemorate the Schultz homestead. The house today is owned by Mr. and Mrs. Roland Larrivey.

3. For many years, until about 1993, it was believed that Lone Wolf was the only child that Schultz ever fathered. But in the course of some research at the Mansfield Library of the University of Montana in Missoula, Nancy Hubble of Columbia Falls, Montana, discovered that there had been a second child born to him and Natahki, his Blackfeet wife. It was while they were ranching at Midvale (now East Glacier Park) that a second youngster (not identified as to sex) was reported to have been eaten by a bear while playing in the front yard. In the September 14, 1893, issue of *The Columbian*, a story detailed what had happened. No remains were ever found, just some shreds of the child's clothing. Schultz never mentioned this tragedy. Later, other newspapers picked up the story.

4. James Willard Schultz, *My Life As an Indian: The Story of a Red Woman and a White Man in the Lodges of the Blackfeet* (New York, Doubleday, Page, 1907). The quotation comes from a reprint (New York: Beaufort books, 1983), p. 134.

5. When Schultz died in 1947, his files were crammed with information, including much material for future works. Today, most of what remains will be found in Special Collections, Renne Library at Montana State University in Bozeman, Montana. But there are no notebooks there, even though he was said to have written many notes on legends and stories he had heard in such journals.

6. *Bear Chief's War Shirt*, started by Schultz and completed, much later, by Wilbur Ward Betts, published by Mountain Press Publishing Company, Missoula, Montana, 1983.

7. James Willard Schultz, *Floating on the Missouri*, ed. Eugene Lee Silliman, University of Oklahoma Press, Norman, 1979.

8. Warren L. Hanna, *The Life and Times of James Willard Schultz (Apikuni)*, University of Oklahoma Press, 1986. Chapter 20 details the Pulitzer poaching case.

9. Today the small cabin Schultz and Lone Wolf erected near Greer in the White Mountains is owned by the Greer Property Owners Association and houses a museum and gift shop. The restored historic structure is devoted to Schultz and his son. It was acquired several years ago from the U.S. Forest Service, which had been using the building for storage. Mr. and Mrs. Sam Applewhite III of Scottsdale, Arizona, were instrumental in the acquisition of the property. Karen Applewhite and several volunteers run the museum and shop, which are open to the public from Memorial Day through Labor Day.

10. Mrs. Graham, then well into her eighties, died unexpectedly in June of 1976, following an unfortunate fall. Her broken hip was healing nicely, but complications set in and her health failed.

11. Eighty-two issues of the *Storyteller* were published in that span, including a special memorial issue after Mrs. Graham's death and a special forty-page final issue in the spring of 1996. I served as editor of this small magazine, and Dean G. Combs of Canoga Park, California (known today as Winnetka), was its publisher. It was a happy collaboration and might still be going on today if health problems had not forced me to retire in 1996. Failure to find someone else who could assume the position of editor led to the magazine's demise. Starting in the summer of 1978, we held seven triennial meetings, six at Glacier National Park. The 1990 gathering was held at Fort Benton, where Schultz had first set foot in Montana. In 1981 the society successfully had the proper Indian name of Running Eagle Falls restored to a noted park feature previously known as "Trick Falls." We tried twice, without success, to have the original set of thirty-seven books reprinted.

12. Permission to quote from this essay was granted by The Schwinden Library, Fort Benton, Montana.

13. Keith C. Seele, *Blackfeet and Buffalo: Memories of Life Among the Indians*, University of Oklahoma Press, 1962, p. ix.

14. Quoted in Silliman's *Floating on the Missouri*, p. x.

15. Silliman, *Floating on the Missouri*, p. xvi.

16. Seele, *Blackfeet and Buffalo*, p. xi.

17. Hanna, *Life and Times*, p. xvi.

18. *The Piegan Storyteller*, volume 21, spring 1996, p. 38.

19. James Willard Schultz, *Recently Discovered Tales of Life Among the Indians*, compiled and edited by Warren L. Hanna, Mountain Press Publishing Company, Missoula, Montana, 1988; also Warren L. Hanna, *Stars over Montana: Men Who Made Glacier National Park History*, Glacier Natural History Association, West Glacier, Montana, 1988.

20. Walter McClintock, *The Old North Trail, or Life, Legends, and Religion of the Blackfeet Indians* (London, Macmillan, 1910; reprint, Lincoln: University of Nebraska Press, 1999); McClintock, *Old Indian Trails* (Boston: Houghton Mifflin Company, 1923; reprint, 1992); George Bird Grinnell, *Blackfoot Lodge Tales: The Story of a Prairie People* (New York, Scribner, 1892; reprint, Lincoln: University of Nebraska Press, 1962); John C. Ewers, *The Blackfeet: Raiders on the Northwestern Plains* (Norman, University of Oklahoma Press, 1958).

Author's Introduction

James Willard Schultz

[This introduction is taken verbatim from the start of Schultz's story "The Buffalo Hunt," one of the five stories not appearing in this collection. It was included in *Why Gone Those Times? Blackfoot Tales*, edited by Eugene Lee Silliman (Norman: University of Oklahoma Press, 1974).]

My people said that of all the professions, that of war was best suited to one of my temperament, and I agreed with them. Therefore it was intended that I should go to a military school, preparatory to entering West Point.

But my lungs were not so sound as they should have been, and our family physician said that I must go west and live on the high, dry plains for a time. I went, well provided with letters to the members of a great fur-trading company at Fort Benton, Montana. One of them, dear old Kipp—or Berry, as the Indians called him—was appointed my guardian.

I was to stay on the frontier a year. I remained there, except for occasional visits east, for so many years that I do not like to count them. I went [in 1877], a boy of seventeen. I am white-haired and wrinkled now.

There were no railways in Montana in those early days. Except Fort Benton, there was no settlement save Helena, Virginia City, and one or two other mining camps in the mountains. On the Great Plains were various tribes of Indians and millions of buffalo and other game.

My friend and guardian, Berry, followed the buffalo with the Blackfeet, here one year, there another, as was determined by the shifting of the herds, and his trade with the people amounted to thousands of fine buffalo robes, beaver skins, and other pelts. Through him I came to know the Blackfeet and to love them. I learned their language, lived with them, hunted and warred with them against other tribes, and was adopted as a member of the tribe. So I do not write of those old buffalo days from hearsay, but from actual experience.

BLACKFEET TALES
FROM
APIKUNI'S WORLD

1

An Adventure with Ap-si

Originally published under the topical title "Memoirs of a White Indian" in *The Youth's Companion*, November 24, 1910.

The women were busy tanning buffalo hides for new lodges. First they stretched and dried them, then with an elk-horn, iron-tipped hoe, they scraped off the hair and a portion of the inner side of the skin. Lastly, with a mixture of brains and liver, they removed the glue and put them through a strenuous course of rubbing, see-sawing them on a heavy rawhide thong. The result was a beautiful leather, creamy white and as soft as buckskin.

Girls of fourteen or so helped their mothers with the lighter part of this work, and provided the wood and water for the lodge; but for the greater part of the time, except in berry season, they played and romped to their hearts' content. They had dolls of stuffed buckskin, which they carried about on their backs, and talked to, and made miniature lodges for. A favorite pastime of both boys and girls was making clay images. Often fifty or sixty of them would gather at the

3

WHAT COULD TWO BOYS DO AGAINST TWENTY-NINE ENEMIES?

edge of a stream where there was a bank of good clay, and soon the
shore would be strewn with miniature buffalo, deer, elk, wolves,
horses, and men.

Three great runs of buffalo had been made, and as every family
had secured enough hides for new lodges, the rule against independent hunting was relaxed. I was at just that age when a youth enjoys
both the pastimes of the young and the more serious pursuits of his
elders. Thus one day I would risk life and limb on a buffalo run with
Running Crane, and on the next afternoon I could be seen making
clay animals with the children. I must confess that my work was very
inferior to theirs.

My favorite young friend was a boy of about seventeen, named
Ap-si (Arrow). He was strikingly good-looking, very high-spirited,
and everything he did at work or play was done with a vim. His

mother was a widow, and he had a sister a couple of years younger than he.

The family was quite poor, owning not more than a dozen horses, and none of them were swift enough for running buffalo.

Ap-si had no gun, and seldom hunted with his bow, for the returns were too small. By herding horses for one or another of the great men of the camp he managed to keep his home from want, for he was given quantities of meat in return for his services.

For three winters his mother had been storing away a buffalo robe whenever she could toward the purchase of a rifle for him. At that time the traders asked twenty good robes—worth one hundred dollars—for such a weapon as he wished. Already the self-sacrificing mother had saved fifteen robes. By the end of the next season the number would be complete, and then the little family would be independent. Instead of herding horses for others, Ap-si would become a hunter, and go to war, to return—if the gods favored him—with a record of brave deeds, and many horses of the enemy.

"But why go to war?" I asked Ap-si more than once. "I do not think it right that you should. And then, think of the danger—you might be killed. Who then would care for your mother and sister?"

"Ap-pe-kun-ny, my friend, listen!" he would reply. "From that far north river Saskatchewan, south to the Yellowstone, and from the Backbone-of-the World [the Rocky Mountains] eastward to the plains, where the snow lies deep, all that land of wide plains and high mountains, of many rivers and much game, all that belongs to the Blackfeet. When Old Man made the world and created people he gave us this land and everything on it. At once we were envied by the other tribes, and they tried to take it away from us. They still try to do so, and thus it is that we are at war with them."

I did not argue further. Of what use would it be? What right had I to do so, I asked myself, whose ancestors had wrested nearly all America from its red owners, and except here in the one buffalo country left, caused them such suffering, such misery and want.

"Come, my friend, Ap-pe-kun-ny," said Ap-si to me one morning, "take your fast-shooting gun, I will take my bow, and we will go with my mother and sister after berries."

"Do not go very far from camp," Running Crane cautioned me. "I don't want you to run into any prowling war party."

I promised, and we started, mounting our horses and riding away up the valley of the Musselshell, Ap-Si and I side by side, where the trail was broad, the woman and the girl following. Ap-si wore an antelope hunting-cap, or headdress, which gave him a very grotesque appearance. It was the horns and headskin of a buck antelope, nostrils, ears, and all, dried in a life-like manner and well fitted to his head. He made me one later, and most of the hunters wore them when they went hunting.

With such a headdress, one could look over the edge of a ridge, the rim of a valley, or steal through the low brush of the bottoms without much risk of alarming any game which might be in sight, and which he wished to approach.

It was particularly effective in antelope hunting. With the possible exception of the bighorn, these are the keenest-eyed, the most wary of American game animals, but they are also endowed with considerable curiosity, and the males love to fight one another at certain seasons of the year. So when the antelope-capped hunter saw a band away out on a level plain, or basin, where it would be impossible to creep up within range, he had but to show his head a few times, and the quarry would come to him.

The serviceberry bushes were loaded with fruit that season, but all the camp was gathering and drying it for winter use, and we rode to thicket after thicket, only to find it stripped. After traveling three or four miles, we began to pass a number of berrying parties, but we kept on and on until we had left them all, and then we found a large patch of bushes fairly drooping with the burden of ripe, purple fruit.

The women picketed their ponies and began to fill their sacks. Ap-si and I ate our fill of the berries, had a drink of river water, and then, remounting our horses, rode on up the valley in search of game.

About three miles from where we left the women, a solitary bull elk, alarmed at our approach, broke from a grove of cottonwoods and trotted rapidly off up the side of the valley, toward a deep coulee, in which was a dense growth of bull pines. The animal had not winded us, and when about three hundred yards distant it stopped and looked back, wondering, probably, what manner of creatures we were that had disturbed his rest, and if it were really worthwhile to keep on climbing the steep hill on such a hot day.

"Oh, let me have a shot at him with your gun!" said Ap-si, sliding down off his horse. "See how fat he is; and I want some fresh meat for our lodge."

I should have liked the shot for myself, but Ap-si was so eager for it, he so seldom had an opportunity to kill game with a rifle, that I passed the weapon down to him. "Aim for the top of its back, it is a long way off," I cautioned him, knowing that the bullet would fall about a foot in that distance.

He sat down on the ground, rested his elbow on his knee, and with a quick sight, pulled the trigger. Following the report, I heard the bullet thud against the elk; but he only flinched, and then sprang away up the hill, head straight out, his great velvet-covered, many-tined antlers laid flat back parallel with his spine.

Ap-si sat watching him, never thinking that he had a repeating rifle in his hands and could reload and fire many times. And there was such an expression of incredulous surprise on his face that, much as I knew it would mortify him, I could not help laughing.

"O Spotted Robe!" he cried. "Oh, do not laugh! I am shamed enough! And I have wasted one of your precious bullets! Oh, how could I have missed such a big animal, and standing still, too!"

"But you did not miss," I said. "I heard the bullet thud into him, and—why, look at him! He is wobbling, he cannot go far."

The elk had ceased trotting, and was now walking with unsteady legs and drooping head, occasionally stumbling, almost falling before it could regain its balance. Ap-si mounted his horse, and we followed it as fast as we could, but it disappeared in the pine coulee before we were halfway up the hill. A few minutes later, we also gained the timber, and only a few yards from the edge on the brown needles lay the noble animal, dead. We dismounted, tethered our horses, and sharpening our knives, removed the hide and cut the meat in convenient portions to fasten on our saddles.

Before starting homeward we decided to build a fire and roast the

tongue and a rib or two of the elk. I sat down and began to cut some
shavings, when Ap-si came hurrying to me, and from the wild look
in his eyes I knew that something was wrong, even before he spoke.

"O Spotted Robe!" he whispered. "The enemy! A big war party
of them! Come and look!"

I sprang up and followed him, my heart beating fast. At the edge
of the timber Ap-si stopped behind a low scrub pine and pointed
down into the valley. I peered through the branches and saw a number of horsemen riding in single file down one of the big buffalo
trails that skirted the river. I counted them. There were twenty-seven
in the party, and two more who were riding a half mile ahead, as
scouts. They were at least a half-mile from us, but for all that I whispered instead of spoke. "Maybe they are our own people, Ap-si?"

He shook his head. "No, we have only one war party out, and
they have gone far north against the Crees."

Although I felt it was as he said, still I argued. I wanted to put off
mentioning the terrible thought that had come into my mind as
soon as I saw them. "Most likely, then, they are some of our own
hunters returning home."

"O Spotted Robe!" he exclaimed, impatiently. "Where are your
eyes? Don't you see that there is no meat, nor fresh, drooping hides
suspended from their saddles? And would our hunters be returning
home without all their horses could carry? O my mother! O my sister! What shall I do? What can I do to save them?"

He had spoken my thought, but I could not answer. I had no
plan, I could think of none, and I felt utterly helpless. What could
two boys do against twenty-nine enemies?

"O sun! O all ye above people!" Ap-si prayed, lifting his hands
entreatingly toward the sky, "Help me, show me the way to save
those I love."

He was silent then for a moment, thinking deeply. I was not trying to think of something to do. I felt utterly powerless. My only
feeling was one of resentment. Why should there be war parties? I
asked myself. By what right did they come marauding through the
country to destroy the lives of peaceful hunters and berry-pickers? It
seemed terribly unjust.

"Spotted Robe, may I take your gun just for a little while?" Ap-si asked.

I handed it to him.

"Listen," he continued. "I am going just outside of the timber to fire a few shots at them. Then I will return the gun to you, get on my horse, and ride up the valley in plain sight of them. They will follow me, I think. If they do, then as soon as they are out of sight, ride as fast as you can to where we left my mother and sister, and hurry them toward camp. Warn all the people you pass. Ride on to camp and arouse the men; they will come to save me, or avenge me if I am dead."

I said nothing. I had nothing to say, and I watched the war party as Ap-si ran out of the timber. At the first shot he fired, they stopped and looked our way. He held the rifle at an elevation of many degrees, and the second bullet must have struck close to them, for they broke for the cover of a small grove. The two scouts came back at a swift lope and joined them. It was as if the earth had swallowed them; not even a horse remained in sight.

Ap-si came back, handed the gun to me. "Take courage, take courage!" (*i-kak-i-mat*) he said, as he mounted his horse, quirted it smartly, and bursting out of the timber, sped quartering down the hill and up the valley.

With straining eyes, I watched the little grove. How innocent, how peaceful it looked! Across the river from it a band of buffalo was filing down into the bottom for water, all unaware of what was hidden in the green foliage.

Suddenly the buffalo turned and rushed back up the hill; two horsemen were crossing the river. As soon as they reached the other side they rode swiftly away up the bottom. A moment later five more of them came out of the grove and pursued Ap-si, and still later twenty came riding straight for the timber where I stood watching them. How I wished then that I had taken my friend Berry's advice and remained safe with him at the trading post on the Judith.

I waited a moment to see if the remaining two of the enemy would come out of the grove, but they did not appear. I then ran to my horse, and climbing into the saddle, rode up the coulee through the timber a little way, then out of it and up on to the level plain, where I made the animal "burn the ground."

I kept looking back at almost every jump, expecting every moment to see the enemy on my trail, but I had covered more than a mile before I saw them coming hot upon it. I was riding parallel with the river, and was well past the grove, where two men still remained. So I swung toward the valley, and when I arrived at the rim of it, rode obliquely down into it. When I reached the bottom, and the game trail we had followed in the morning, I was not more than a mile, I thought, from the berry-pickers. Looking back, I saw my pursuers just coming into the valley. They did not seem to have gained any ground, but to have lost some.

I was encouraged. I could surely reach the women and hurry them down to where there were other berrying parties, including some men who had come as a sort of bodyguard, I thought, and they could at least hold the strangers at a distance until help could be got from camp. And then the two horsemen I thought still in the grove appeared suddenly out of the bed of the shallow river, and shouting their battle-cry, came charging across the flat!

They were about two hundred yards off to my right, and the foremost fired at me. I had then practiced but little in shooting from the left shoulder, and the position was still awkward; but I raised my rifle and did my best, firing four shots in rapid succession, aiming as well as I could at the man with the gun. The other, I was sure, had only a bow.

My bullets went wide of the mark, but they had a good effect. Realizing that I had a repeating rifle, the two slackened their pace considerably and kept three or four hundred yards behind.

Try as I would, I could not increase that distance between us. And behind them came the rest of the party, save those who had ridden up the valley after Ap-si.

As I neared the place where I expected to find the woman and the girl, I felt that my time on this earth was growing short. I could never get them on their ponies and in flight before the whole crowd would be upon us. I turned in the saddle and fired three more shots at intervals, occasionally shouting as loudly as I could, "*As-to so-oh-iks!*" (A war party is coming.)

I came to the berry patch, but saw neither the women nor their ponies. Beside the trail was a heap of freshly stripped serviceberry bushes, and in it fresh pony tracks pointing campward. They had started back then. I hoped that they had long since arrived home.

A mile farther on, the trail passed through a large grove. Looking back at my pursuers, I did not notice what was ahead, and before I was aware of it I rode into a lot of horsemen who were gathered on each side of the trail!

Such a shock as the sight of them gave me I have seldom experienced. And then I saw that they were my own people, not enemies, and foremost of them Running Crane himself.

"Go on! Go on!" he cried, with an emphatic motion of his hand.

I understood, and kept on, but now I looked back with a different feeling. My fear was gone; in place of it I had an absorbing desire to see what would happen to those riders so relentlessly trailing me.

I saw, away in advance of the main party, the two come as heedlessly into the grove as I had done. Then suddenly they pitched headlong out of their saddles, a dense smoke-cloud filled the space between the trees, and there was the boom of many guns. I pulled up my horse and turned to go back and then I shuddered. No, I did not want to see any dead men, enemies though they were, who would have gloried in scalping me. The smoke lifted, and I saw my people riding furiously to overtake the big party, which had already turned and was fleeing up the valley. I turned again, and let my horse take his own gait homeward. I found that I was weak and faint.

There were now no berrying parties along the trail. Instead, man after man dashed by me, some in their gorgeous war-dress, all with the light of battle shining in their eyes. I met an old man whose horse had gone lame, and he turned back with me.

I told him all that had happened from the time we killed the elk to the tumbling of the two men from their horses, and asked anxiously if he thought Ap-si would manage to elude the enemy.

"*Ai!* That I do," he replied. "The gods were surely with you from the start. It was allowed that you should discover the enemy, not they you. And then, some watchers on that high butte by the camp saw the chase, and hurrying down, gave the alarm. Those who had horses started in at once to save you and warn the berriers. The rest got in their herds as soon as they could. *Ai!* There will be a beautiful fight up the valley. I hoped to be in it. I wanted so much to be in one more good battle, for I am very old, you see, and may never have another chance."

All the way back he grumbled about his bad luck, and talked to his horse just as if it could understand. "O you wretch! O you stupid!" he whined. "To go lame this day of all days, and deprive me of a pleasant time!"

It was an anxious mother and sister who came running to me as I entered camp, inquiring for Ap-si. I told them what he had done to try to save them, and tears came to their eyes. "Was there ever a better son?" said the mother, proudly. "But he should not have taken the risk. What am I that he should sacrifice his life for me?"

Thus spoke the Blackfoot mother. Never yet was there one, I am sure, who would not gladly die to save her son. And it was the same with the fathers. Intense love for children is a characteristic of the Blackfeet.

It was late in the night when the warriors came trooping homeward, singing songs of triumph, and bearing among them the scalps and weapons of five of the enemy, who had proved to be Sioux. There had been a running fight which lasted for hours, and then the retreating party had vanished in the darkness.

Sunlight was streaming into the lodge through the smoke-hole when I was awakened by a familiar, cheery voice: "Awake, Brother Spotted Robe! I have brought you some of the elk meat."

I wrapped a blanket about me and hurried out, and there was Ap-si astride a mountain of meat rolled in the big elk-hide and lashed on the saddle. "Oh, I am glad!" I exclaimed, running up to him and grasping his hand. "I was so afraid they would kill you! How did you get away from them?"

"It was not difficult," he replied. "I had a good start, you know, and I rode and rode until I saw a small willow-covered island in the river. There I went and hid, and the enemy—five on one side and two on the other of the river—dared not come out of the shelter of the groves to attack me, for they thought I had a gun, a fast-shooting gun. So there I stayed. Night came, the moon shone. Still I waited. I saw no enemy, heard no sound of them. At last the moon went down and it was very dark. I got on my horse and rode down a long way through the water so deep that he made no splashing noise, and then going ashore, I rode hither, stopping by the way to get our meat." Running Crane's women came out and took the meat Ap-si had brought for me. A little later we breakfasted on the fat, juicy ribs of the elk, broiled to a turn over cottonwood coals.

2

The Making of a Warrior

Originally published under the topical title "Memoirs of a
White Indian" in *The Youth's Companion*, December 8, 1910.

Young as he was, my friend Ap-si had all the cares and responsi-
bility of a grown man—a widowed mother and a sister to support, no small task for one with only a bow for a weapon and a few
slow horses to ride. Several years earlier than was customary, therefore, he determined to go through that ordeal without which one
could not become a warrior.

He must go away by himself and fast and pray until, exhausted,
his body became inert, and his shadow—as they said—went forth on
adventure into the shadow world, and there found the shadow of
some animal, or bird, or reptile, or some star, perhaps, that would
promise to help him in everything he did.

"Where is my friend?" I asked one morning, lifting the curtain of
Ap-si's lodge and looking in.

HE WAS AWAKE, AND SMILED WHEN HE SAW US.

"He is lying away yonder, fasting," his mother replied, looking up from her work. "I go soon to take him some water, and you may ride with me."

We started, she, Pai-o-ta (Flying), the daughter, and I, the mother taking with her a small skin holding a pint of water. We rode up Crooked Creek a couple of miles, past the high butte where from daylight to dark sat two or three watchers, scanning the country for any signs of an approaching enemy.

Soon we left the valley and rode up a steep hill to the foot of a sandstone cliff. Here we left our horses, and climbing to a shelf about midway up the cliff, walked out on it a distance of fifty yards, and then we came to Ap-si, in a sort of niche or cave formed by the overhanging rock.

Wrapped in his blanket, he was lying on a buffalo robe, and beside him were his bow and quiver of arrows, his knife, and a red-painted, empty water bowl. He was awake, and smiled when he saw us.

"*Ai!* There you are," he said, "and my good friend, Spotted Robe, too."

"Of course," I answered. "I shall come every day to see you, if I may."

We sat down beside him, and his mother poured the water from the skin into the bowl. "I wish it were more," she said. "I lie awake thinking of you alone here in the night, hungry and thirsty, and I can hardly keep from coming to you with meat and water."

"Brother, had you any vision last night?" Pai-o-ta asked.

"None," he replied. "I slept but little and lay looking out at the stars."

We remained with Ap-si only a few moments, according to the rule, and I did not see him again for five days, and the seventh one of his fast. Then once more I went with the women up to the niche in the cliff.

I was surprised and alarmed at the change in his appearance in this short time. Emaciated and yellow, he lay on the robe, and there was a feverish glitter in his eyes. But for all that, he had a happy, if somewhat dreamy, expression. And as soon as he saw us he weakly raised one of his thin hands in greeting, and said, almost in a whisper:

"I have found that which I sought; take me home."

At once the mother gave him a drink of water, and then fed him a little pemmican, a very little, and then went back to the camp after a *travail* and another horse with which to draw him in. Pai-o-ta and I sat by his side, she occasionally giving him another morsel of food, and he brightened up rapidly.

"Last night as I slept," so he told of his dream, "I, my shadow, left the body and traveled far, crossing a great plain. After a long time I came to the edge of a valley and saw a wide river in it, and I was glad, for I was burning with thirst. Down I ran to it, and kneeling, I drank of the cool water. Then, rising, I sat on a rock, listening to the singing of the big stream. Never had I heard so pleasant a sound; it cheered me, and again I cried out, as I had all the long way across the plain: 'Pity me, you of the shadow world, O wise ones! Help me to survive the dangers of my trail, and to live to great age!'

"I was looking down the river as I spoke. I heard a splash the other way, and turning, there, almost beside me, was a certain water animal, sitting at the edge of the water, looking at me. He was so old that his hair was mostly white. 'O boy,' he said to me, 'I will be your helper; from far I heard your cry and have come to you.'

"And then, friend Spotted Robe, then, my sister, he talked long with me, directing what I should do, how to call him to my aid when in need. But what he said, who he was—that I may not tell you. I wish I could, but you know that no one can speak of what is between him and his secret helper, lest bad luck come to him."

That evening, somewhat recovered from his fast, for the first time in his life Ap-si gave a feast, and all who were invited came—staid old warriors, and even medicine-pipe men, who were supposed to be especially favored by the sun. They ate the rich berry pemmican set before them, and during the smoking of the three pipes which succeeded, congratulated Ap-si on his endurance and the success of his fast.

I was there, too, although I really had no right to sit with such dignitaries. But many privileges were accorded Running Crane's "white son."

As Ap-si filled the last pipe and passed it to the man on his right to light, he said, "Without a shield, one cannot go to war. Who will make one for me?"

"I will," said Red Eagle, the oldest of the medicine-pipe men. "And I." "And I," spoke up the others.

But Red Eagle had been first to answer, and it was agreed that he should do it.

"I am glad that you are to do it." Ap-si said. "I will make you a present of a horse."

To ask that some renowned man make the shield had been the object of the feast, and all who came knew it. After they had gone,

Ap-si asked me if I would assist him in getting the necessary bull's hide, and the eagle tail feathers for the fringe, and I gladly consented. As a buffalo could be killed at any time, we decided to secure the feathers first. Now while it was customary to kill eagles in any way possible for a war-bonnet or ordinary purposes, there was but one way to kill them for the decoration of a shield, which to a Blackfoot was his most cherished possession.

With a couple of buffalo-bull shoulder blades for shovels, Ap-si and I rode to the top of a high, sharp butte a couple of miles from camp, and there, with great labor, we excavated a pit about six feet long, three wide, and three deep, scattering the earth removed so that no trace of it remained.

Then we picked up a lot of willow sticks and laid them crisscross over the pit, and covered them with grass in so natural a manner that anyone would have thought the place solid ground.

Better than anything else, not excepting even the young of antelope or deer, eagles liked the liver of a wolf. As it might require a hunt of several days to kill one, we sewed up a wolf's skin and stuffed it with grass in as lifelike a manner as possible, and securely pegged it to the ground beside the pit. Lastly, we cut a gash in the side of it, and inserted a large piece of buffalo liver, leaving a small portion protruding.

All was in readiness now to catch an eagle when it should come to the bait. Ap-si was to lie in the pit, waiting, and when one went to eating the liver he was to reach up, grasp it by its legs, and, drawing it down into the hole, kneel on its breast until life was extinct. This was a very hazardous thing to do, and required extreme quickness of sight and arms.

That evening was passed by Ap-si praying to the sun for success in his undertaking. The next morning he rose before daylight and burned a couple of pinches of sweet-grass, bending over the smoke and grasping handfuls, with which he rubbed himself. Sweet-grass was a sacred plant: its delicate perfume was thought to be highly prized by the sun; the smoke of it was said to remove all human odor.

Having purified himself, Ap-si now made the customary little speech to his mother and sister. "I am going this morning," he gravely said to them, "to attempt to catch an eagle, and you women must do all you can to aid me. Until I return you must remain in the lodge, continually praying for my success. Also, lest in seizing an eagle he should pierce me with his claws, you must not put any thorny wood on the fire, or eat the berries of a thorny bush. For the same reason you must not use a needle or an awl, or scratch yourselves."

In the meantime I had managed to awake, and after a bath in the river and a breakfast of roasted buffalo tongue, I went over to Ap-si's lodge to tell him that I was ready. He asked me to purify myself also with sweet-grass smoke, and I did so, to please him. Then we mounted the horses we had picketed the night before and rode to the eagle pit, stopping on the way to pick up a human skull we had found, which was to serve as Ap-si's pillow.

There was nothing the Blackfeet dreaded so much as such a skull. But for this very reason it was considered necessary in a youth's eagle-catching; it was a test of his courage, a severe one, too, for him to lie upon it in the dark pit during his hours of watching and waiting. Also there was no possibility of his going to sleep and losing the chance to catch a bird, with such a fearsome object under his head.

When Ap-si had crawled into the pit with his skull, I waited until he was stretched out as comfortably as possible, and then carefully replaced the willows and grass he had removed in order to enter. Then, saying that I hoped he would catch at least four eagles, I mounted my horse, and leading his, rode to another butte a mile or more away, where I sat down in the shade of a lone pine to await the results of our work.

The sun was now up, and I searched the sky anxiously in all directions, hoping to see an eagle, but none was in sight. The great birds were very plentiful on the plains in those days.

Hours passed. I was unused to rising at such an early hour, the day was warm, and more than once, with my back against the tree, I fell asleep and dozed—I know not how long. Every time I awoke I would hastily snatch up my telescope and eagerly look at the place where Ap-si lay, but only to be disappointed; no bird was there. I could even see the dark liver in the side of our stuffed wolfskin; no bird had been there.

It was past noon when an eagle at last came in sight. When I first saw him he was circling round and round, high above the bait; then suddenly he dived straight down and alighted on the ground fifteen or twenty yards to the right of it. I leveled the glass at him. How very big and proud he looked as he sat there preening his feathers, occasionally cocking his head sidewise and looking sharply at the stuffed wolf!

He seemed to be suspicious of it, for he stood there a long time, anxiously watching it. But at last he moved, stalking slowly around the pit. Just then a crow came along, and without any hesitation whatsoever, began greedily to tear off morsels of the protruding liver. That seemed not only to allay the eagle's suspicions but to anger him. With wings half-stretched, he swiftly ran to the bait, driving away the other bird, and himself began to feast.

"O Ap-si!" I cried aloud, in my anxiety. "Now! Now! Seize him!"

Long before I reached the pit Ap-si climbed out of it, and lifting the eagle, held it before him for me to see. It was so large that his body was almost hidden by it.

"O Spotted Robe, isn't it a fine one?" he cried, as I rode up and dismounted beside him. "O sun! O my powerful little underwater animal! You have been good to me this day!"

It was indeed a magnificent bird, a large old male war eagle, his tail-feathers large, smooth, glossy black, with pure white tips. As we rode home with the bird, I think that I was as pleased with the success of the day as he.

Now that he had such a good pit constructed, Ap-si decided to catch more eagles if he could, and for a week or more he went and lay in it. Altogether, he captured four eagles, which was wonderfully good luck. He had now enough tail-feathers for a shield and a war-bonnet, and claws sufficient for a necklace. And then one day we went out hunting, and with my rifle Ap-si killed a buffalo bull, an old, old fellow, whose once sharp, crescent-shaped horns were now mere stubs.

"He has been brave; he has fought many battles and survived them," said Ap-si, as we were removing the skin from its neck and shoulders. "I think it is a sign that a shield made of his hide will bring me safely through more than one fight with the enemy."

There spoke his superstition. To the Blackfeet, as to all Indians, there was a sign, an omen, in everything, no matter how trivial. We took the hide home, and after soaking it in water a few days, rubbed off the hair, leaving the thin, glossy, brownish-black surface intact. Then one afternoon it was delivered to old Red Eagle, and the interesting ceremony of transforming it into a shield took place.

Red Eagle was dressed in his war-clothes, soft buckskin shirt, leggings, and moccasins beautifully embroidered with various colored porcupine quills, fringed with weasel skins, and the shirt painted with the quaintly drawn forms of turtles and lizards—"medicine" creatures. On his head was a war-bonnet of buffalo bulls' horns and weasel skins, and his face and hands were painted a dull red, the sacred color.

By the side of his lodge the bull hide was stretched and pegged to the ground, and kneeling on it, he began to pray, at the same time starting to cut from the skin a circular piece about four feet in diameter.

"O sun, O Old Man," he said, "O all ye above people, listen, and pity us this day. All of us, men, women, children, give us long life, good health, shelter from cold and rain, and abundant food. Help us, ye great and powerful ones, to escape the dangers of the trail, where always the enemy lies in wait to destroy us."

Nearby some women were heating a number of stones in a fire, and near the blaze a small pit had been dug in the ground. The women rolled some of the red-hot stones into it as soon as the old man had cut the circular piece of hide, and with three tried warriors to help him, he quickly placed the hide over the pit, and inserting pegs in slits that had been cut at regular intervals along the edge, fastened it to the ground.

As each man drove a peg he recounted a coup; that is, told in a few words of some fight in which he had been a victor. Tightly as the hide had been fastened down, it began to shrink at once under the influence of the hot rocks, until it pulled the pegs over. As fast as they loosened, the men drove them in again. Red Eagle carefully supervising their work, feeling of the hide to see that it did not get so hot as to burn, and calling for more hot stones as they were needed.

In about an hour the hide had shrunk to about half its original diameter, and was at least an inch thick. No arrow, nor a ball from a Hudson Bay Company flintlock could pierce it.

The four men now fell in line and danced around it, and then it was handed to Ap-si, who proudly carried it home. There he trimmed and smoothed the edge of it, burned two holes in it for the suspending string, and lastly bound the rim with buckskin, to which were fastened at regular intervals thirty-two of the eagle tail-feathers. Lastly, he made a buckskin cover for it, and then hung it to a lodge-pole above his couch. He was ready to go to war.

3

The Bad Luck of Low Horn

Originally published in *The Youth's Companion,* December 25, 1919.

When the first geese of the season came honking up from the south, the Crows left the trading post on Flatwillow Creek, where Ap-si and I were staying, and returned to their hunting ground beyond the Yellowstone. Our trade with them had been satisfactory; they bought almost everything we had, and our warehouse was fairly choked with fifteen hundred fine buffalo robes and almost as many beaver, wolf, and other pelts. The traders' big teams were busy for several weeks hauling them to the main post on the Missouri.

The chief of the Crows, Grey Bull, and some of his leading men went over to the Missouri and visited Big Lake, the Blackfoot chief. There was much feasting and smoking and talking; and finally the two tribes concluded a treaty of peace. During the summer the

HE DID NOT RESIST, DID NOT SPEAK, BUT STOOD WITH HIS HEAD DOWN
AND WITH HIS WHOLE FIGURE, DROOPING AND LISTLESS,
EXPRESSING THE UTMOST DEJECTION.

Blackfeet were not to hunt farther south than the Musselshell River,
and the Crows no farther north than the Yellowstone; war parties
from either tribe were not to cross the territory of the other. That
was the agreement, and both chiefs hoped to be able to hold their
men to it.

The Blackfeet had determined to pass the summer in the vicinity of the Musselshell River and the Snowy Mountains, and they

asked us to keep the Willow Creek post open for their convenience. So it came about that Eli Guardipe and his wife and Dan Fitzpatrick and Ap-si and I remained there. By the time the green grass came the Blackfeet were encamped beside us. There was very little work for me to do; and Ap-si and I proceeded to have a good time hunting and enjoying the dancing and other social activities of the tribe.

One evening when we were sitting in Running Crane's lodge, he told us that on the next evening there was to be a meeting of the Sistsiks—that is, the Little Birds—and that we ought to become members of it. Ap-si spoke right up and answered quickly that we would.

For the enforcement of the laws, there was an organization called the I-kun-uh-kah-tsi—All Friends, or, perhaps more properly, All Comrades. As a whole it was under the orders and direction of the head chief, but it was divided into eleven different societies, each of which was under its own leader. Each society had its own peculiar songs, manner of dancing, and dress. The Sin-o-pahks (Kit Foxes) and some of the others had secret rites and religious ceremonies, but you could not be a Kit Fox until you had graduated from lesser bands.

The Sistsiks were the least of the bands; it was for boys of from fifteen to eighteen years of age. Next after that came the Kuh-kwo-iks, comprising young men who had several times been to war. Then came the Su-yis-ksiks (Mosquitoes), men who were constantly going to war. After you had been a member of that band you could join any one of the others—the Mut-siks (Brave Men), Kun-uts-o-mi-taks (All Crazy Dogs), Stum-ik-iks (Bulls), I-in-ah-kiks (Seizers), and Mas-two-pa-ta-kiks (Carriers of the Raven). Old men only were members of the bands respectively named I-me-taks (Dogs) and I-is-su-yiks (Tails). You did not have to give anything to join the Sis-tsiks, but to become a member of any of the other bands you had to buy out some man's rights and costume. Membership in some of the more prominent bands was worth many horses.

The next evening Ap-si and I put on our war clothes and went over to the appointed place of meeting. Running Crane himself was sitting at the back of the great lodge, with two old priests of the sun, or medicine men. Near the doorway were some of the mothers of the boys, and outside were still others, preparing a little feast for us.

There were at least a hundred of us boys inside, sitting in a circle, and the small, bright fire in the center was as cheerful as were our spirits. Everyone was talking and laughing and admiring his neighbor's fringed and beaded and feathered costume, as well as his own fine outfit. While we ate the broiled dried tongue and dried berries that the women passed us, the old men talked to us.

"We old people look at you boys here with pride, " one of the priests said. "You are all so fine-looking, so strong, we believe that you are going to be brave and in your turn keep all enemies where they belong, and our great hunting ground for ourselves. To do this you are going to risk your lives many, many times; yes, some of you will die in battle. But that is nothing: it is better to die in battle quickly and be remembered as a great and brave chief than it is to live on and on to feeble old age; to become a child-old-man, to suffer old-age aches and pains, which are worse than death."

The other medicine man said, "I know that every one of you here wants to be a chief. Now always remember this: the man who would be a chief needs to be more than brave; he must love his people; he must be kind to the sick and old, a brother to the widows and a father to the fatherless."

Next Running Crane talked about observing the laws of the people: "You Sis-tsiks must never forget that our laws, as well as our bravery, have made us the powerful people that we are. The laws are for us all and must be obeyed by all. If your dearest friend breaks them, you must take your part in punishing him, no matter how badly it hurts you to do so."

So they went on for half an hour or more, until every boy there was filled with ambition to become a great and good chief.

At last the drummers and the old men began the Kai-spa Pes-Ka, or Parted Hair, dance song. Up we all sprang and began to dance in time to the tune and the drumbeats, making the double steps first with one foot and then with the other in perfect time. We tossed our heads in order to make our war-bonnets sway;

brandished our weapons and shields, looked fierce and proud, as if we spurned the very ground. Presently the singing and drum beating ceased, and we rested for a few minutes while the old men again talked to us. In that way the dance continued for several hours.

When the last dance of the evening was finished, Running Crane dismissed us with these words: "You Little Birds must always keep your eyes on the big birds. Watch what they do and help them all you can, for some day you are going to be big birds—Braves or Bulls or Kit Foxes—and it will be your turn to carry the laws."

When the time for making new lodges came—that is, when the buffaloes had shed their heavy winter coats and their hides were more easily tanned into leather—the big camp left the foot of the mountains and moved out to the Musselshell River, two or three miles below its junction with Flatwillow Creek. Eli said that he could spare me for a couple of weeks. Ap-si and I went with the tribe.

When they had been in camp at the foot of the mountains, the Blackfeet had hunted independently of one another, where and when they willed. But now that was changed. The hunt was to be for buffaloes only, and it was important that every family should get enough skins for a new lodge. Through the camp crier the chiefs announced that no one was to hunt by himself and run the risk of frightening away the animals that everyone needed. Scouts were to keep track of the different herds, and the chiefs were to give notice when a hunt was to be made, so that all the hunters could join in it. At daybreak of the morning after we went into camp on the Musselshell, the scouts, who had been out all night, reported a big herd nearby, and the crier soon afterwards gave notice that a run was to be made. At that there was a wild rush for the horses; everyone rounded up his own band and roped his favorite buffalo runner. The members of the Braves society were in charge of the hunt, and they rode here and there, urging men to hurry and watching at the same time that no one should start out until all were ready.

In the course of half an hour we started, with at least three hundred in the party. Following the scouts, we rode down the valley for a mile or more and halted near the upper edge of the valley slope. The buffaloes, the scouts said, were coming to water.

In a few moments we saw an old bull off to our right stop for a moment at the edge of the plain and then, followed by other bulls, move on towards the river. At the same time another string of bulls began wending its way into the valley at our left. Such processions of bulls always led a herd. We had not long to wait now.

"*Ok-yi! Oh-wak-i-mat-ou!* (Come on! Strike them!)" cried the scouts, and we charged up over the remaining few yards of the slope and out onto the plain, to find ourselves almost nose to nose with the bull leaders of many long columns of thirsty cows and frisky calves. Spreading out fanlike, we killed several animals almost before they had time to turn back. A moment later they were fleeing madly away from the river, and we were right in the thick of them. The thunder and rattle of several thousand hoofs were deafening. Guns cracked and arrows whizzed; clouds of spurned dust rose, and the odor of trampled and crushed sage was strong in the air. But there was no bellowing; the frightened animals did not give voice to their terror, and we who pursued were as silent as they.

The chase lasted for several miles. One by one the hunters dropped back, for only the very strongest and swiftest horses could keep up the terrific speed. When my runner wearied and I turned back, the plain we had traversed was black with dead and dying buffaloes. Instinctively, the wounded were limping and hobbling together in little groups for mutual protection. Here and there the huge long-bearded animals stood with lowered head and humped back, so badly wounded that they could not move. Some of them stood tense and stiff and suddenly toppled to the ground with a crash; others slowly sank down and died with a last futile toss of their massive heads. But none were permitted to suffer long; riders were hurrying everywhere to give them the finishing shot. There must have been at least a thousand dead on the plain, and the men, and the women who had followed the hunt, were busy skinning the animals and taking the best of the meat.

As usual in such a big run, there was some quarreling about the ownership of various animals. None of the controversies were so bitter, however, as they would have been between white men in like circumstances. Indians—at least the Blackfeet—rarely had serious quarrels with one another and never let themselves come to blows. Though they argued hotly, they called no names beyond saying that the opponent was a *mo-ka-pi tup-pi* (bad man) or an *i-mi-tus-ky* (dog face). They never under any provocation took the name of their gods in vain.

As a result of these altercations over the dead buffaloes, a man named Low Horn found himself without one animal to butcher. He rode a fairly good horse, shot a good muzzle loader and declared that he had killed five buffaloes; but every animal that he claimed was already in the possession of some other hunter, who succeeded in putting up a good argument that it was his kill. Several men offered him one or more of their animals, but he refused them. I had killed six fine big cows and intended to give three of them to Ap-Si and three to Running Crane; but now I went to Low Horn and said:

"I have no family to feed and clothe, nor do I need a lodge: take the six animals that I have killed,"

"You are a generous boy," he replied, "but I may not take them. My dream forbids it. I have been warned that trouble will come to me if I accept food or skins from anyone. We have still a little dry meat in the lodge."

With that he turned and rode away to camp, with his women following behind on their travois horses. It was no use to argue with him, he would obey the warning of his dream even if he and his family went hungry.

Two days later there was another run and a big killing; and the day after that, at daybreak, a large herd of the buffaloes was discovered in the valley just above camp, and several hundred more were killed. In the first of these runs Low Horn again failed to get a single buffalo, although he declared that he had shot four; he did not find his horse in time to join in the second one. By that time the last of the food in his lodge was gone.

Many of his friends offered him some of their killings, or food for his family, but he still declared that his dream would not let him accept anything.

Before midday a large herd of buffaloes was reported to be grazing on the plain not far to the east of the river, but the Chiefs decided to put off running them until morning, because the horses of many of the hunters were tired from the daybreak chase.

Early in the afternoon the chiefs heard that Low Horn had gone out to hunt by himself, and they sent for Lone Person, the chief of the Mut-siks, or Braves society.

"It is said that Low Horn has gone out hunting, " Big Lake told him. "Get your men together and find where he went: If he has broken the law and chased the buffalo herds, then do you that to him which our laws require."

Lone Person quickly called together a dozen or more of the members of his society, and they rode across the river and out of the valley onto the plain. The big herd of buffaloes was gone; where it had been were some black carcasses, and a man was bending over one of them with his horse standing motionless close by. The Braves rode slowly out there, for they did not like the thing they had to do. Low Horn saw them approaching him, but he did not stop skinning the buffalo, or look up again even when they stood beside him.

"Friend, you know what you have done," Lone Person said: "you must come with us."

"There is nothing to eat in my lodge; my women are starving," said Low Horn as he continued his work.

Lone Person made some signs to his men, and, jumping from their horses, they seized the hunter, took the knife out of his hand and broke it on a stone, picked up his gun and bent the barrel by striking it against the buffalo's head. He did not resist, did not speak, but stood with his head down and with his whole figure, drooping and listless, expressing the utmost dejection. Nor did he object when he was told to mount his horse and ride with the Braves to camp. Two or three of them rode in swiftly ahead of the others and told the

chiefs that they had found the man skinning one of five or six buffaloes that he had killed, and that he had driven away the big herd.

This was a serious breach of the law; if it happened often it
would imperil the food supply, the very existence of the people. Big
Lake decided that an example must be made of Low Horn. Turning
to old Red Paint, the Instructor and priest to the Sis-tsiks:

"Call out your Little Birds and let them do their pecking and
scratching," he said.

Red Paint at once hurried through camp shouting, "*Wo-ke-hai!
Wo-ke-hai Kun-nai puk-si-put, Sis-tsiksi!*" (Listen! Listen! All come,
Little Birds)."

Some boys repeated the cry, and others farther on took it up in
turn, so that in a moment Little Birds came running from all directions to follow the old man. He went straight to Low Horn's lodge,
a fine, large one of sixteen skins. Near the top, at the back, was a
design in red paint somewhat like a Maltese cross, which was the
symbol of the butterfly, bringer of good dreams. In Low Horn's case,
alas! bad dreams had come instead of good.

Ap-si and I were of course in the party of Little Birds. As we
came to the lodge, one of Low Horn's three women was standing
outside watching our approach; she called to the others and they
rushed out and stood watching us, with their eyes wide with terror.

"What are you doing here?" asked one of them, advancing toward
Red Paint, with her arms extended and her fingers spread and rigid.

He did not answer her, but said to us, "Cut that lodge into small
pieces, smash the lodge poles and these travois."

"Oh pity us! Have pity on us, old man!" the women cried, and
begged him, as he loved his own helpless women and children, to
have pity and not to destroy their home.

The Little Birds stood wide-eyed and silent, watching the piti-
ful scene. They hoped that Red Paint would relent, they did not
wish to destroy the home of the poor women, for they had heard all
about Low Horn's bad dream and knew that hunger was in his
lodge.

"Come! Hurry and do what I told you!" said the old man to us.

KNIVES FLASHED AND RIPPED, AND DOWN CAME THE LODGE COVERING IN TATTERED SECTIONS.

And then, as no one made move to obey the order, he cried, "What! Are these my Little Birds? Are these the boys who are looking forward to doing great things—to become members of the Braves and other societies of great warriors? Why, instead of that we shall have to dress you all in women's clothing!"

That taunt was enough: the boys rushed to do his bidding, and anxious to have the unpleasant task over as soon as possible. They swarmed around the lodge, and the women tried to stop them, pushing back one and another and crying miserably: "Oh no, Little Birds, oh, good Little Birds, we are so poor! Surely you will not destroy our only shelter!

But knives flashed and ripped, and down came the lodge covering in tattered sections: the Little Birds threw over the lodge setting, pulled out the poles separately and broke them, as well as the family travois.

Meanwhile Low Horn had been escorted into camp. "You have done me great wrong, " he told the chiefs. "You knew about my dream, knew that my women were starving. I had to get meat for them. You should not have set the Braves on me."

"The law is the law," Big Lake told him. "There are deer here in the river bottoms, and you could have hunted them, it was not necessary for you to go out on the plain and drive away that big herd of buffalo."

Low Horn made no answer and, turning away, started toward his lodge. When he arrived, walking slowly and leading his horse, the Little Birds had just finished their work. The three women were sitting on their couches around the still-smoldering lodge fire, sobbing hysterically. Walking through the litter of his demolished home, Low Horn sat down on his couch, drew his robe over his head and bent forward—a picture of utter dejection. We Little Birds looked on him a moment and then scattered our different ways. Ap-si and I turned and looked back several times at the hungry and destitute family sitting so forlornly amid the wreckage of their home. We knew that even now Low Horn would not, on account of his dream, accept any of the offers of food and shelter that his friends would surely extend to him.

I went with Ap-si to his lodge. In a few moments his mother came in, angry and excited. "I am ashamed of you both!" she said. "I don't care if it is the law; you boys have done a mean thing in helping to destroy the home of those poor people!"

WE WENT OUT AND FOUND LOW HORN STILL SITTING
IN THE RUINS OF HIS LODGE.

"We could not help it; they made us do it," Ap-si told her. "It made us feel bad to see Low Horn and his women sitting there with only the sky for lodge covering."

Just then a woman from a neighboring lodge came in, and from her we learned what had been done to Low Horn out on the plain: that he had not been allowed to take any of the meat he had killed, and that the Braves had broken his knife and ruined his gun.

"Oh, that was enough punishment to give him, more than enough!" Ap-si exclaimed. "Come, my friend, it is not yet night—let us do something to help him; he shall have my gun, and we will drive the timber for him. If we succeed in scaring out any deer, he will get shots at them and maybe kill one for his women."

We went out and found Low Horn still sitting in the ruins of his lodge. One of the women was aimlessly wandering here and there and picking up pieces of ruined lodge skin, only to toss them away. She told us that the other women were out gathering night wood and trying to find a few roots to stay their hunger. When we spoke to Low Horn, he looked up at us blankly and seemed not to understand what was said to him. Ap-si repeated our offer more slowly and in a louder voice.

"Oh, very well," Low Horn answered listlessly. "I'll go with you. Yes, yes, you are good boys; we'll go out and kill a deer."

He would have started out right then without a horse, or even without the rifle that Ap-si offered him; he seemed to be dazed by all his misfortunes. But after we were all mounted and riding away down the valley he brightened perceptibly and said that without doubt his troubles and misfortunes were over now, that without a doubt he should be able to take meat home to his women. Once the bad spell was broken, he said, he should soon be able to kill enough buffaloes for food and for new lodge skin.

We did not spare the horses, for the sun was already low. About three miles from camp we crossed the river, and Low Horn took his station at the upper end of a cottonwood grove. Ap-si and I rode through the grove toward him. I had a glimpse of a fine, big, whitetail deer; but he was a wise old buck and made a little circle around to our rear. We drove no deer out past Low Horn.

We all rode on again for half a mile and came to a still larger grove. Ap-si and I waited until we were sure that Low Horn had time to skirt the timber and to select a good position, and then we rode on through the brush, making all the noise we could.

"We've got to scare a deer out of here for him," Ap-si said to me as we came together in the center of a tangle of willows. "It will soon be too dark to make another drive."

A moment later we heard a shot, but before either of us could even open his mouth to say anything the shot was followed by a loud, hoarse roar that we knew only too well was a maddened grizzly's bellow of pain. For a moment we sat still, listening, Ap-si said that he could hear the sound of something running, and that it seemed to be a horse. At that we rode out of the timber as fast as we could, and then along the grassy bottom to the end of the grove. There we came upon a sight that made our hearts throb fast: two prone and motionless figures side by side on the ground, one the unfortunate Low Horn, the other a large grizzly bear. Springing from our horses, we bent over the man.

"He is dead!" Ap-si whispered.

"He is not," I said, feeling his pulse. "Run and bring my hat full of water."

There was a bad wound on the man's head, a strip of the scalp wider than my hand was torn loose and hung down so that it nearly covered the left ear; the left shoulder was also torn, and I found that his collarbone was broken. I washed the wounds as well as I could and bound them with strips of our shirts.

Little by little consciousness returned to Low Horn, and presently he sat up and looked round vacantly until he saw the bear; then his face suddenly lighted up, and he laughed long and happily.

I thought he had lost his reason, but his words proved that he was sane enough.

"What my dreamed warned me of has happened," he said, "And I can do what I wish. I shall have good luck now. Take me to camp and give my women and me a feast of fat meat."

I have seen few men of Low Horn's vitality; his terrible wounds and loss of blood seemed to have no effect on him. With only the slightest assistance from Ap-si and me, he rose and climbed on my horse; his own had run back.

"Oh, I forgot," he said as we were about to mount the other animal. "Just cut me a strip of that bear's hide from the top of its back: I want it for an offering to the sun."

We arrived in camp long after dark. None there was happier than Low Horn and his women. In the assurance that all would now be well with them, they completely forgot their troubles and poverty; and they now gladly accepted offers of food and shelter. Low Horn was laid up with his wounds for a long time, but many friends hunted for him as a matter of course; by the time he was able to ride again he had set up a new lodge. Then he got on credit a fine new gun from the trading post and soon paid the debt with beaver skins.

4

The Punishment of Afraid Eyes

Originally published under the topical title "Memoirs of a White Indian" in *The Youth's Companion*, December 29, 1910.

Ap-si and I had an enemy—a boy of about our own age named Un-o-pah-chis (Quiver), but nicknamed Co-pah-pin-e (Afraid Eyes), because he could never look anyone fearlessly, honestly in the face. He had eyes like a mink, small, deep-set, shifty, always fairly glittering with the evil thoughts and desires that possessed him. Probably his father and mother loved him, but certainly no one else did, and at his approach little children ran squalling to their lodges, mindful of sundry excruciating pinches, ear-twistings, and even blows that had befallen them when they happened to get within his reach.

Neither Ap-si nor I had done anything by word or deed to incur the enmity of Afraid Eyes, and we could find no reason why he should hate us as he did, except that the failures in life often hate and

'I WILL SAVE YOU IF YOU WILL OWN UP, IF YOU WILL TELL
THE TRUTH HERE BEFORE THESE MEN.'

bitterly envy the more successful ones. Afraid Eyes was a failure; a
poor hunter, a worse shot, no warrior—he had never counted a
coup—and he rode none but the meekest-spirited horses of his
father's band. That Ap-si was everything he was not, was probably
the reason for his hating my friend, but there was absolutely no cause
for his enmity for me, an alien having no interests that could clash

with his own. Yet every few days during many months this friend and that friend had come to see us with tales of threats he had made against us, whom he had chosen to call cowards, and liars, and I know not what all. These friends warned us to look out for him, and said that he would surely injure us in some way if he got the chance; but we merely laughed. How, we asked, could such a puny, insignificant little fellow as Afraid Eyes possibly hurt us?

Winter came, and my friend, the trader, and the great camp moved from the Judith Basin down to an immense timbered bottom of the Missouri River, about thirty miles west of the mouth of the Musselshell. Buffalo seemed to have deserted the basin, but here they were as plentiful as ever, fairly darkening the plains on each side of the big stream. While the river was open they came to it daily to drink from pasturage frequently ten or fifteen miles away, traveling in single file, led by big bulls, over deep-worn trails centuries old. But with the freezing of the streams they came no more, depending on the snow drifts piled in the coulees to quench their thirst.

Thus it was that as the season advanced the hunters were obliged to ride farther and farther away from camp and the river to make their killings, and that on a January day at noon Ap-si and I found ourselves on Big Crooked Creek, ten miles south of the Missouri breaks. In all that way we had seen nothing but a few old bulls, too tough for any use. We wanted a fat cow, both for its rich meat and the soft, dark robe it wore.

The day was piercingly cold, but there was no wind, and the air was full of glittering frost particles that settled and clung to grass blades and sagebrush, and were so dense that the sun gave but a ghostly light. We stopped, recinched our saddles, and considered whether to hunt farther or return to camp.

"Oh, let's go a little way up the creek," said Ap-si, "Just a little way, and then if we find nothing, we will turn back."

We mounted and went on. The frost was so dense that we could not see more than a few hundred yards in any direction, so there was some excitement, some expectancy in riding through the haze and wondering what the next few yards would reveal. Dimly at first, although quite near, and then looming up in huge proportion, owing to the peculiar atmospheric conditions, we did soon sight a small bunch of cows and calves soberly cropping the short grass. Finally giving free rein to our eager, trained horses, we were right on them before they took alarm. Heads down and bushy-tipped tails curved up, they bolted up a narrow coulee; and Ap-si and I each shot a fine young cow before they had run a hundred yards. But we went some distance farther, having no little trouble in stopping our blood-thirsty horses. The buffalo horse was always eager for the chase as a hound is to trail a fox.

Riding back to where the two buffalo lay, we dismounted, and leaving our horses to trail their ropes and graze at will, began skinning the game. It was slow work for me. I could not handle the knife with my thick gloves on, and without them I was obliged to stop every moment or two and warm my numb hands against the animal's carcass. Ap-si, however, made light of the bitter cold. His daily baths in the icy stream had inured him to bear the worst of weather. He soon skinned his animal, cut up for packing what meat he wanted, and then came over and helped me.

At last we were ready to pack up and go, and we looked round for our horses. They were not in sight, and then I remembered that I had seen them graze down the coulee into the creek bottom. Thither we went, certain that they would not be far away; but to our surprise they had absolutely disappeared. We began at once making a big circle round the place where we had started the buffalo, and at last, coming to our trail in the frost-laden grass, we found not only the back tracks of our animals, but those of another.

Three horses going north, and our two no longer dragging their ropes! Someone had stolen them and was leading them away!

Who could have done it? we asked each other, and there seemed to be no answer except that a lone Assiniboin had taken them. No warrior of any other tribe would venture out alone in the dead of winter to steal horses. Well, they were gone, and we were not only angry but very sorrowful as well; we had a deep attachment for the faithful animals that had carried us safely through more than one perilous time. Grimly we set out to walk the long miles to camp. The afternoon was waning fast. We might not be able to reach home, but at least we could make the nearest breaks of the river, not more than ten miles away, and there we could find shelter for the night, and plenty of fuel in the dense pine groves which covered the northern slopes.

We had walked a couple of miles when suddenly a warm, burnt-grass-scented wind began to blow, the frost haze disappeared, and away in the north beyond the river we saw a low, black fog-bank that extended from horizon to horizon, sweeping southward with incredible rapidity.

"Oh, look!" Ap-si cried, pointing to it. "And do you smell the grass smoke? Yonder comes Ai-sto-yim-stan [Cold Maker, god of winter]. That is the way he always does, hiding himself in the black fog, out of which will come whirling winds and stinging snow and awful cold. We must seek shelter, and quickly, too.

"Our only chance," added Ap-si, "is to hurry back to the Crooked Creek coulees, find a big, deep snow-bank, and get into it. Come on!"

Back we went as fast as we could walk, running a little now and then, and looking over our shoulders often to mark the swiftly approaching fog-bank; it was already within ten or fifteen miles of the river.

"If we can only get back to where we killed," I panted, "we can use the hides to put under and over us, and I remember seeing a fine snow-bank close by."

"Ai! Ai! I was thinking that," Ap-si agreed, "but the hides may already be so stiffly frozen that we can't unroll them."

We hurried on faster. The fog had already reached the river. Looking back a few moments later we could see nothing of the dark breaks of the valley; they were blotted out as if they had never been. And then, while we were still a half mile from the creek, the blizzard overtook us in all its fury. We went doggedly on. I could hear Ap-si exclaiming, beseeching his gods for help, and I prayed silently to God to preserve us in this time of awful peril.

At last we descended a steep bank, and knew that we were in the creek bottom, but there was no way of determining whether above or below was the mouth of the coulee in which lay our meat and hides. We turned downstream on the chance that we could find it in that direction, following closely the foot of the slope from the plain and examining every coulee we passed.

The blizzard seemed to increase in fury, and at times buffeted us so hard that we could only stand against one another and gasp, and rub our freezing faces. It was getting dark now. If we did not find the place in the next few moments, then there would be nothing to do but burrow into the nearest snow-bank and take our chances. Could we find one deep enough to cover us, and if so, had we sufficient clothing to prevent the heat of our bodies from melting the snow and wetting us through and through? If not, death was certain.

We struggled on. I was thinking of a faraway New England home; of a cheerful fire blazing on the hearth and my mother sitting before it, wondering, probably, at that moment how it fared with her son. I felt a queer sensation in my throat. I should probably never see that home again.

And then out of the gloom and the whirling snow came a band of buffalo. They were within twenty yards of us before we saw them, and as quickly as numbed fingers could cock our rifles we raised them and fired. One animal pitched over and lay still: another, staggering after its fleeing fellows a few paces, stopped, weaved from side to side, and then sank slowly to the ground.

"*Kyi!* My friend, see now what my prayers have brought us!" Ap-si exclaimed, as we bent over the nearest animal, ripping and flaying with our knives. "Yes, but the sun is good. I will make great sacrifice to him. We shall survive this, my friend. Let bad old Ai-sto-yim-stan do his worst, still we shall survive."

It was not a time to argue, nor did I ever decry my friend's faith in the sun and his other gods; but I thought of my own prayers, and felt they had, indeed, been answered.

As fast as the thick-haired hide parted from the meat under the strokes of our sharp knives, we kept rolling it to prevent its freezing; but it was slow work under such trying conditions, and I, less hardy than my friend, was shivering, trembling, my teeth chattering long before the hide of the second animal was off. Ap-si had to skin the last half of it alone.

"We cannot hunt a snow-bank," said he, "but see how fast it is drifting down here from the plain. We will lie right there on the windward side of the carcass and a drift will soon pile over us."

We hurried to the first carcass, and half-carried, half-dragged the heavy hide over to the second one and spread it out hair side up. Then, placing our rifles on it, we lay down and pulled the other one over us, and there we were, encased in a warm fur bed. But the big cow hide was a far too heavy cover—it must have weighed more than a hundred pounds. We propped it up in the center with our rifles, and supported it above our heads with our arms, and in a very few minutes it froze stiff in that position. There were places along the edges where it did not touch the bottom one, and there the cold air rushed in and kept us shivering. But not for long; the drifting snow soon filled the interstices, and then we began to feel warm. In a half hour or so, we were uncomfortably warm, and each worked a little clear space in the snow to obtain fresh air.

After that we slept, I know not how many hours, but a long, refreshing sleep, broken only by occasional efforts to obtain more air. At last we were wide awake and wondered if the night had passed, and with it the blizzard. Reaching up, I cut a small hole in the roof of our tent bed, stuck my rifle through it, and worked an opening in the six or eight inches of snow that covered it. The night had passed, but the blizzard still raged.

All that day we lay there, and all of the succeeding night. At first we were hungry, but the craving for food soon left us. To pass the time, Ap-si told stories of the adventures of his people, and I in turn tried to give him some idea of the world and the wonders of civilization; but I could never make him believe that the earth was other than a great plateau, covered with mountains and valleys and lakes and plains, with a "jumping-off place" into the unknown clear around the edge.

Clearing the snow from my peep-hole from time to time, we kept fairly accurate account of the passing hours, and at least we saw that the sun was shining, that the sky was clear. It was the morning of our second day there.

We had a hard struggle to leave our quarters, pushing, heaving, and kicking the top hide, which was heavily weighted with snow and frozen to the lower one. But at last we were free, and rising, walked about and exercised our stiffened limbs. The weather was still piercingly cold, but there was no wind. Considerable snow had fallen, but it was all piled up in drifts in the coulees, and walking on the plain was good. We cut some *depouille*—snow-white fat on the hump—from one of the carcasses, and munching it, struck out for home.

We had not walked far; before an hour had passed horsemen began to come in sight out of the river breaks and scatter over the plain by dozens and scores.

"They are searching for us," said Ap-si, and he was right; inside of another hour we were met by some of them and heartily greeted.

"We thought we might find your bodies," one of them, Fish Robe, said to us, "but we never expected to see you alive. How did your horses get away from you? And when? They came into camp this morning. We took their back trail and found where they had stood in the pines during the blizzard."

Ap-si looked at me, and I at him, questioningly, and then he asked Fish Robe if there had been the trail of a third horse.

"No," Fish Robe replied, "there were tracks of only the two, and they were still saddled, still dragging their ropes, but the bridles are missing."

Ap-si had no bridle; he used the lariat as one by making a couple of half-hitches with it round the lower jaw of a horse. But I had a fine one of braided horsehair, and the bit was a Spanish-hand-forged one, heavily inlaid with silver. Before turning my horse loose, I had taken it off and tied it securely to the pommel of the saddle, and in such a manner that it could not have been torn off without the saddle going too.

"We did not lose our horses!" I exclaimed. "They were stolen from us, led off while we were skinning buffalo, and whoever took them came this way."

There were murmurs of surprise from our friends when they heard this, and then a long silence ensued. Said one, finally, "Probably an Assiniboin took them, but was obliged to let them go on account of the storm."

"If so, he would at least have thrown away his own saddle, and taken our white son's fine one, and all the saddle-blankets, " said another.

"True enough, true enough!" they all agreed.

Then in a slow, hushed voice, Fish Robe said: "Afraid Eyes was out hunting that day; he came home long after sunset, long after Ai-sto-yim-stan descended upon us from the north. And yesterday he went about smiling, and rubbing his hands, his mean eyes blazing wickedly, telling everyone, "I always said they were no hunters, noth-ing but crazy, careless fools. No doubt they let their horses get away from them. They are dead, of course."

"He took the horses! He took them!" cried Ap-si. "Oh, if only I could prove that he did!"

"Yes, if we could only know that!" said one, and everybody added an assenting "Ah!"

I mounted behind Fish Robe, and Ap-si behind another of the search party, and we rode home, I to my quarters with the trader and he to his lodge.

"Well! Well!" Kipp exclaimed, when I had told my story. "If you and your friend Ap-si don't get into more scrapes and get out of them again than anyone I ever knew, I'm sure a prevaricator. You are the lucky boy; you ought to go into mining."

It was a week or more later that a little girl came to the trading post one night and said that Last Rider wished to see me. I did not know the young man—there were many I knew only by sight—but I went, wondering what he wanted. Arrived at his lodge, I found

Ap-si there, and a couple of other visitors. These soon went away, and then, after sending the women and children out of the lodge, and speaking scarcely above a whisper, Last Rider said to me:

"I was hunting deer afoot in the breaks across the river today, and coming to the top of a ridge, I saw someone riding toward me. 'He may scare a deer this way,' I said to myself, and I hid in a thick growth of junipers. He came nearer, and I saw that it was Afraid Eyes. I did not wish to speak to *him*, so I sat still and he passed me by unseeing; but I saw that his horse had on your fine bridle."

"You are sure that it was mine?"

"Oh, yes, sure: black-and-white braided horsehair, dark steel jingling bit with shining white trade metal ornaments set in it. Yes, it was yours. I thought I ought to tell you."

"Surely, if he was the one who drove off our horses, he would never dare show the bridle!" Ap-si exclaimed.

"He doesn't; he uses it only when away by himself," said Last Rider. "He goes out riding just to admire it and hear it jingle. I saw him when he returned, and his horse had a rope hitched on its jaw. The bridle was in his bosom; his blanket coat was puffed out and something was hidden there."

"We are glad you have told us this," said Ap-si. "Do not say anything about it to others. We must consider what to do."

And when we were outside by ourselves, he continued, "There is nothing to do but kill him."

We went together to the post, and I reasoned with him, entreated him not to do that; but he would not listen until I pointed out the fact that we had no absolute proof that Afraid Eyes was the guilty one; that we had not seen the bridle in his possession. Then he agreed not to take revenge without first consulting me.

Strangely enough, the next two days brought a climax to the affair, and in a most unlooked-for manner. I was not present at the beginning, but I had a vivid description of it, and saw the dramatic ending.

In the morning Ap-si started out with a party, among whom was our enemy, to hunt on the north side of the river, and when they were partway across the stream the ice broke, letting Afraid Eyes and his horse into the water. The swift current carried the animal out of sight at once and forever, but Afraid Eyes, as he was going under, caught at the lower edge of the hole and managed to draw himself partway out, but not clear; the resistless river gripped his legs and body and would not let him loose. He cried again and again for help, but not one of the party moved. It came out later that the story of his having my bridle was known to all the camp—Last Rider's wife having spread the news—and that was why no one would succor him, especially as Ap-si was present.

Finally, just as he was beginning to slip back, Ap-si dismounted, went over to the hole, and seized his arm. "I will save you if you will own up, if you will tell the truth here before these men," said he.

"Oh, yes, yes, what is it? Oh, quick, save me!" the wretch chattered.

"You drove away our horses the evening of the blizzard."

"Yes."

"You have my friend's bridle."

"Yes."

"Then get it for me, and after that prepare to fight me, for there is not room for us both in the Blackfoot land."

And with that he yanked the trembling Afraid Eyes out on the ice, set him on his feet, and pushed him toward the camp, all following. As they proceeded, the crowd grew, until half the camp assembled to see what it was all about. Arrived at his father's lodge, the dripping, shivering wretch went in, and presently reappeared and handed Ap-si my bridle.

"And now, since you have lost yours in the river, take this gun of mine, and I will borrow one from some friend, and we will fight," Ap-si commanded.

"Oh, no, no! I cannot fight, I will not fight!" Afraid Eyes cried, refusing and pushing back the proferred weapon.

"In that case there is nothing to do but kill you where you

stand," said Ap-si, starting to raise his rifle; but just then Running
Crane stepped up to him and whispered a few words. A smile of
delight crossed his stern face, and he turned and went home without
another word.

Running Crane, raising his voice, said, "I ask the chiefs of this
people to come to a council in my lodge tonight."

That was all, and the crowd dispersed.

They were all assembled there when, by request, I entered, not
long after dark, and they sat in silence, chiefs, and medicine men and
other great ones of the tribe, smoking the big pipe in turn and waiting for Running Crane to speak. He soon began, and related how
nearly Afraid Eyes had done Ap-si and me to death, and finally, how
he had refused to fight, or give any satisfaction whatever for his
conduct.

"Therefore," he concluded, "I propose that we give this Afraid
Eyes his choice of two things—that he either fight this youth he has
so grievously injured, or ever after wear a woman's dress, and laying
aside forever rifle or bow, perform the tasks of women."

Then followed a deep, long silence, and then spoke up Little
Dog, another great chief.

"I propose," said he, "that this Afraid Eyes not be given any
choice in the matter, but be made to wear the woman's dress. That
will be the severest punishment, for it will last as long as he lives."

To this, immediate and enthusiastic assent was given, and then a
messenger was dispatched for Afraid Eyes' father, who soon appeared.
When he was told what was the sentence of the council, he pleaded
for mercy, called on men by name to reconsider it for his own sake,
and finally broke down and wept. But sorry as many were for him,
no one was willing to show mercy to his son, and one by one we rose
and went our ways.

It was many days before I saw Afraid Eyes again, but word was
passed about the village that he had finally donned the dress, and
that he sat in his father's lodge in shame, never venturing out except
at night. When he did, at last, come out of his hiding and go about
his tasks, children reviled him, and girls pointed at him with scorn.

But the camp soon got used to him, even tolerated him as he sat in front of the lodge among the women, and in that way he lived for many years. I often used to watch him, and was thoroughly satisfied that he suffered for his attempted crime.

5

The Night Struggle

Originally published under the topical title "New Stories of Ap-si" in *The Youth's Companion*, March 25, 1915.

In the first season that my friend, Joseph Kipp, had his trading post on the Missouri River, he obtained by trade with the Blackfeet four thousand buffalo robes, and more than that number of beaver, wolf, antelope, and other pelts. His profits were $42,000, but he was not satisfied. During the winter the Crow Indians had hunted along the Musselshell River, between the Yellowstone and the Missouri, and he had not traded with them, for they were at war with the Blackfeet.

So the next summer he built a small post on Flatwillow Creek, about seventy-five miles south of the big post. He put a half-breed named Eli Guardipe in charge of the place. Eli's young wife was the cook; Dan Fitzpatrick, a bluff, brave old hunter and trapper, was Eli's helper, and in a smaller way so was I.

'A LONE WOMAN PROWLIN' ROUND IN THIS KIND OF WEATHER!'
OLD DAN EXCLAIMED. 'WHAT DO YOU MAKE OF THAT?'

"It's time you were doing something, boy," Kipp had said to me. "Now you go out there and do what you can to help Eli; you can keep the books and write his letters. I'll give you a hundred dollars a month, your board, and whatever you need out of the stock.'" Ap-si of course had wanted to go with me. At my request the trader had engaged him, at a small salary, to herd the horses of the little post; Kipp agreed to keep Ap-si's mother and sister in meat and other food during the boy's absence. So there we were at the beginning of winter, two men, two boys, and a woman, alone in the little trading post.

The post consisted of three strong log buildings, which formed three sides of a square; along the fourth side, facing the southeast, ran a high log palisade in which was a heavy gate. In the courtyard thus formed we kept our horses at night; during the day we turned them out to graze. Whenever they strayed too far, Ap-si would ride out and drive them back. We always kept one of the animals at hand. The post stood just outside the timber belt that bordered the creek, and about fifty yards south of the stream. From the earth roof of the houses we could see an immense rolling plain stretching away to the south and east; a mile to the west were the heavily timbered slopes of the mountains.

Sitting Bull and his terrible Sioux were far to the east of us, and an ordinary war party of any other tribe would hardly venture to attack the post. Projecting from the northeast and southwest corners, at the height of a second story, were bastions that commanded the entire length of the walls and stockade; two men in each bastion, firing through the small portholes, would be able to keep a large attacking party from scaling the walls. No one could burn us out, for the freshly cut cottonwood logs of which the post was built were full of water.

As far as game was concerned, it was virtually a virgin country. As the weather became colder and snow fell heavily in the high mountains, the deer and elk came down to the foothills, and then out along the streams upon the plains.

Until December twenty-fourth the weather was warm and mild. A chinook wind that blew almost constantly enveloped the high mountains in black storm clouds, but kept the temperature high. On the evening of the twenty-fourth, however, an icy gale swooped down from the north. A blizzard had begun.

But we were storm-proof. Although we had no hay for the horses, we had hauled three or four wagonloads of young cottonwood trunks into the courtyard for them to gnaw; the bark from the saplings is far more nutritious than oats. During the night the wind died down, but the cold seemed to become more intense, and in the morning we could not see the sun because of the heavy frost in the air.

To me that was a depressing day. I kept thinking of Christmas at home. I made a plum duff, but it was so sticky and soggy that no one could eat it. In the evening, Dan, noticing my forlornness, gave me a hunting knife that I had long wished to own. He had fashioned the blade out of a file, and made the handle of the horn of an elk that he had killed himself.

There followed some of the coldest weather I have ever experienced. Day and night a thick haze of frost hung in the air, hiding the sun and the full moon. We kept the big mud-daubed fireplace in the living room choked with blazing wood, but even then we were none too warm. The log walls swelled and cracked with a noise like pistol shots. We covered the horses with buffalo robes, but still the animals shivered. Whenever we went to the creek for water, we could see deer and elk and antelope standing humped up and miserable. In the deceptive frost fog they looked as large as elephants.

It began to grow dark at three o'clock, by four o'clock, it was night. At about that hour on the third day we heard someone shout outside; Eli went up into the southwest bastion with his rifle. He told us to go to the stockade gate, but not to open it until he gave the word. As the gate was made of hewed plank and battened, we of course could not see what was on the other side.

"Who is there?" Eli called out in English. A voice answered in words that we could not understand. Eli repeated the question in Blackfoot, Cree, Crow, and Sioux, but still could get no understandable answer. After a long pause he said to us, "Well, I guess you can open the gate. He says in the sign language that he is a Cheyenne and alone, and anyway if there are others they are not in sight."

We swung open the gate, and admitted a tall person wrapped from head to foot in a buffalo robe. I locked the gate again; and then, with the stranger following us, we returned to the living room. Meanwhile Eli came down from the bastion. The stranger somewhat timidly walked over to the fireplace and loosened his big robe. To our surprise, we saw a woman—a tall, slender, good-looking woman about twenty-eight or thirty years old. She wore a short dress of fringed buckskin, beautifully embroidered with colored porcupine quill designs, leggings to match, and frost-proof moccasins of buffalo skin. As she let down her robe she gave us an apprehensive glance, and then for the first time seeing Mrs. Guardipe, uttered a little exclamation of apparent relief, and moved away from us to the opposite side of the fireplace.

"Well, well! A lone woman prowlin' round in this kind of weather!" old Dan exclaimed. "What do you make of that"?"

"Take her into the kitchen and feed her," Eli said to his wife, "and find out what you can about her."

We could not account for her being out by herself on the plains in such terrible weather. While we were talking, Mrs. Guardipe came in and told us that the stranger said she had started out with her husband and a party of his friends on a raid against the Crows. But one evening her man had got angry, and had hit her because she did not cook some meat to suit him. Furious at him for striking her, she had stolen away in the night and tried to find her way home; then the storm had come; and after wandering for four days, she had come upon this place.

When the woman had finished eating, Mrs. Guardipe brought her back to the living room, and motioned her to a place before the fire; the woman was reluctant to take it, but when Eli tossed a robe down in front of the hearth and signed her to sit down, she obeyed.

Eli began to question her in the sign language, and we watched the "silent talk" with interest.

"Where are your people camped?"

"On the first big stream beyond the Yellowstone."

That was a long way off—down in Dakota, in fact; the stream she meant was the Little Missouri. She went on to say that the party she was with numbered only seven men, all friends of her husband; that they had been more than a month following up the Missouri and Yellowstone rivers in search of the Crow camp, and that they had just started northward from the Yellowstone when the trouble arose.

"Then why did you not take the short trail back, instead of coming away out here?"

"I thought that they would look for me on our old trail; so I walked more toward the big river. And then I got lost, and knew not which way I was traveling."

"What did you do at night—were you not cold?"

"It was very cold," she admitted. "I rolled up in my robe in the timber and slept a little. As soon as day came I would get up and walk swiftly on."

"She tells a big lie!" Ap-si exclaimed. "She has come out of a lodge this day; look at her hair, nice and smooth, recently combed and braided! She could not have done that in the open; she would have frozen her hands, and the water she used would have frozen solid in her hair, so that she could not comb it."

"The boy is right," said Dan.

The woman looked furtively when he spoke; but of course she could not understand what he said. Eli ceased questioning her. "She will bear watching, all right," he said. "Now it's time to turn in."

Mrs. Guardipe gave the stranger a shakedown of robes and blankets in the kitchen, where she and her husband slept. As the rest of us were crawling into our bunks in the living room, Eli came back with a buffalo tongue, which he proceeded to broil.

"Ap-si, you are a smart boy," he said. "I never would have thought about the woman's hair; it sure has been combed today. I expect that she has been sent in here to find out how many there are of us, and how we are fixed. Well, we'll just keep her here for a while. Tomorrow morning some of us had better ride out on her trail and learn what we can—keeping clear of the timber."

But when morning came that was impossible; a terribly cold north wind had set in again and filled the air with snow, so that the day was almost dark as night; we ate breakfast by candlelight. The woman's trail was obliterated.

She watched us furtively all the while. Often I thought that her big black eyes revealed intense hatred for us. We knew that the Cheyennes were allies of old Sitting Bull.

Night came again; the wind died, and then started up softly from the southwest; the frost in the air disappeared; the moon and stars shone bright. I took two buckets, meaning to go to the creek for water.

"Don't do it," said Dan. "There's no telling what's out there in the timber."

"You say true," Eli agreed. "No one shall go out of the gate this night. Scoop up some snow from the roof, and we'll melt it for drinking water."

I noticed that when I set down the buckets the Cheyenne woman seemed disappointed; but when I lifted them up again and started for the door she was all interest. "Watch her," I said. "She is taking a lot of interest in this going for water."

Ap-si got his rifle and followed me out. We remained on the roof for about ten minutes, but saw nothing, not even a stray game animal. The horses were restless; having eaten the last of the bark, they were hungry and wanted to get out to grass. When we reentered the house the others said that the woman had sat up straight all the time, listening and watching the door.

"You can be sure that she's a spy for a war party," said Dan.

As we were preparing to get into our bunks, the woman said by signs: "The cold is gone. Tomorrow I shall start for the lodges of my people."

"As you say, so shall it be," Eli replied. But to us, he added, "Maybe she will and maybe she won't; we'll see what's doing tomorrow."

We all fell asleep soon after getting into our blankets. But Dan was a light sleeper; a slight noise awakened him; a sudden draft of air struck his bald head, and he roused up to find the door open. He looked first at my bunk, then at Ap-si's, and saw that we were both sound asleep. Then remembering the Cheyenne woman, he sprang from his bed, and got to the door just in time to see her opening the gate of the stockade and letting some Indians into the courtyard. He slammed the door shut and put up the heavy bar that fastened it; he was none too soon, for a moment later the Indians flung themselves against it with a force that made it creak.

"Get your rifles!" he shouted. "The yard is full of Indians!"

Ap-si and I sprang out on the floor, and Eli and his wife came running in from the kitchen; Dan told us in a few words what had happened. Eli went over by the fireplace, where the key to the gate usually hung.

"The key isn't here," he said. "She stole it and let them in. We've just got to do the best we can, boys."

Our living room and kitchen—there was a canvas partition between them—were in the long building that formed the back of the square, and so faced the stockade and the gate. No doors opened from it into the trade room on the west side of the square, or into the storehouse that flanked the courtyard on the east side. All the windows of the three buildings looked out on the courtyard. They had been made by cutting a section from the next to the top log in the wall, and were consequently high from the ground. The openings were covered with a piece of thin, oiled rawhide. Although the hides let a fair amount of light enter the rooms, you could not see anything through them.

At all costs we had to know what was going on outside, and how many there were of the enemy. The courtyard was absolutely quiet except for the occasional stamping of the horses. Of course we could not see through the windows, and the bastions had been built for the defense of the outer walls, and did not command the courtyard. Moreover, we could reach only one of the bastions—that at the northeast corner—for the entrance to the other was from the trade room.

"We must find out what they are doing!" Dan exclaimed. "Take your knives and dig some small peepholes in the chinking."

We fell to work, and in a few moments had cut spaces in the mud chinking large enough to admit a beam of moonlight. We eagerly squinted through them, but we could not see an Indian.

"Well, what do you make of that?" asked Eli. "Do you suppose they are on the roof of this shack waiting to pot us if we go out?"

"No! But just look at the windows of the trade room," Dan said.

Sure enough, they were glowing yellow from a fire within, and even as we looked smoke began to rise from the chimney of the building. There was no lock on the door, and the Indians had coolly taken possession of the place.

"I wonder whether they are all in there, and whether they have cut holes in the chinking to watch us?" said Eli.

"Some of them may be standing flat against the wall right in front here, or as you say, they may be up on the roof," Dan suggested. "Let's cut peepholes every foot along the length of the wall here. If there are any of them against it, we can plug them in the back. If there are none, we'll just open the door a little way and see what happens."

We gouged out the holes in a short time, and convinced ourselves that there were no Indians in front of us. Then as Eli noiselessly took out the bar and opened the door, Dan thrust his hat on the end of the fire poker and held it in the aperture; he had no sooner done so that there were three shots from the wall of the trade room, and three bullets thudded into our building; one of them ripped through the hat. Evidently the Indians had also dug some holes in the chinking and were watching for us to come out. Eli slammed the door shut and put up the bar.

"I see their game," he said. "They are laying for us, well knowing that sooner or later we must go for water, or die from want of it like rats in a hole."

"But what about them?" I asked. "They also must have some, and we can pot them when they start after it."

"You forget that there are two barrels of water in there," he replied. And that was true: the barrels were for salting buffalo tongues, and had been filled with water, so that they would not shrink and fall apart. In our building we had less than two gallons of water—the melting snow that I had brought down from the roof.

As we sat squinting through the peepholes, the Indians began to sing one of their songs of triumph, and we could easily distinguish the high, shrill voice of the woman. "Dog! Dog-face woman!" exclaimed Mrs. Guardipe in Blackfoot. "I tell you now, my husband of little sense, the next time you bring a strange woman to me to feed and shelter, she will go straight back whence she came."

Good-natured Eli made no answer, and apparently his wife grew more angry, for without another word she poked her rifle through a peephole, sighted at one of the yellow-shining windows and fired. Following the report, there was silence in the trade room for a moment, and then the singing began again.

Eli went over to the far corner of the room, up the ladder, and raising the trapdoor, entered the bastion. In a few moments he returned.

"I went up there to try to learn whether there are any of the Indians outside," he said, "but not a one is in sight. I think they are all in the trade room. Now isn't this about the worst thing that ever happened—a handful of Indians trapping an outfit in their own bastioned and fireproof stockade?"

"These Cheyennes have got the place," said Ap-si, "but they haven't got us. We can get out of here whenever we wish by digging a passage in the ground under the back wall; then we can run into the timber and, if they follow us, make a good fight. If they let us alone, we can get in to the big river post safe enough."

"It's not to be thought of," Eli replied. "At least not yet. We must make the best fight we can to hold the place, and we can hold it a long time by digging the passage and bringing in plenty of water."

"I have it!" Dan exclaimed, jumping up and slapping his thigh. "See here! We'll dig the passage under the back wall, put all the cartridges we can spare into a sack, and then I'll go and drop them into the top of the trade room chimney. Maybe those Indians won't scatter! Out they'll come, and you, firing through the holes in the chinking, will keep them going—at least those you don't drop."

Eli ran to the kitchen for a hatchet, and then began to chop the ground in a clear space next to the chimney. It was easy work at first, but he soon reached frozen earth, and then his progress was slow; we relieved him in turn and kept watch of the trade room door. At last, after an hour's toil, we had a hole large enough for us to wriggle through. We collected our spare cartridges, in all something like three hundred rounds; each of us reserved a hundred rounds, which would last us to the end of the trouble, no matter how it ended.

When we had put the cartridges into the sack, Eli remembered that he had a flask of powder for his shotgun, and he put that in, too. Then Ap-si grabbed the sack.

"I can run much faster than you can," he said to Dan, "so I shall go out with it."

"Now, wait!" said Eli. "I have thought of something more that will surely drive those Indians out if the cartridges don't. Take this buffalo robe with you: Dan and I will also go out, and we will boost you up on the roof; after we get back in here, you sneak along quietly, drop the sack down into their fire, and then ram the robe tight into the chimney, and get back here. With the draft of their fire stopped, there will be some smoke in that room."

In another moment Mrs. Guardipe and I were left alone; we anxiously watched the trade room, and pointed our rifles at the door of it. The woman was praying. In a few minutes the two men returned; thrusting out their guns, they, too, watched the door.

Boom! The powder flask first exploded, and then followed the lesser, sharper reports of the cartridges; the door of the trade room was thrown open, and in a cloud of smoke a crowd of Indians appeared, struggling each to be the first out. *Crack! Crack, crackety crack!* went our rifles, and that one volley was the only one that had any effect, for the smoke of the discharge drifted back against the wall and hid the Indians from us. We kept firing, however; Ap-si had returned by this time and now joined in the fusillade.

When we first fired, one of the Cheyennes shouted something, probably a command; then we heard a shriek of pain, and that was all; not a shot was fired in our direction. A sudden swirl of wind cleared away the powder smoke; no Indians were to be seen in the courtyard except one, lying motionless in front of the trade room door, and another not far from him, trying to rise.

"Now then, for the gate!" cried Eli. He sprang up, and unfastening the door, rushed out; we followed him. Ap-si, in front of me, suddenly shouted, "Look out!" and springing against Dan, sent him reeling to his knees; out of the corner of my eye I had a glimpse of the wounded Cheyenne aiming his rifle at the old man. The Indian fired, and Dan—sturdy, brave old Dan—dropped his gun and pitched forward. As I ran to him, Ap-si fired, and the Cheyenne keeled over on his back. At the same time Eli got to the gate, slammed it shut and fastened it with the hasp. When I bent over Dan and touched him, he flinched and partly turned on his side.

"Go easy, boys," he said with a groan of pain, "the rascal has broken my leg."

We lifted him carefully and carried him to his bunk, and a little later Eli dressed the wound and set the bone. But first we had to go up into the bastions to see what had become of the Cheyennes: none were in sight, but later Ap-si, who remained on guard, reported that they were leaving the creek bottom not far below, and that they were heading for the breaks of the Musselshell. There were eleven of them.

Dan, who was laid up for about two months, stoically bore the pain of his wound and long confinement. It was the seventh time he had been wounded by Indians. Superstitious Ap-si often said to me:

"Ask him what medicine he has and whether he will give me some of it. Whatever he has, it is a very powerful medicine, or he would have been killed long ago."

6

Trouble At Flatwillow

Originally published under the topical title "New Stories of Ap-si"
in *The Youth's Companion*, April 8, 1915.

We had built the new post on Flatwillow Creek to get the Crow trade, but the Crows did not come to trade with us. The winter was passing; if they did not come at all, the work of building the place and stocking it with goods would result in heavy loss for Kipp. Eli Guardipe finally thought of a plan to bring the Crows to us. Early one morning he started for the Missouri River post to consult with Kipp about it. Kipp approved, and in a few days Eli returned, bringing the only man on the plains who could go anywhere and everywhere with absolute safety—who was welcome in the lodges of every tribe.

He was an English-French half-breed named Thomas Faval. The Indians called him "Skunk Cap," because he always wore a cap of that animal's fur, with its big bushy tail drooping down behind his left ear. He was to go on a mission to the Crows in our behalf.

"BLACKFOOT, I HATE YOU! GO GET YOUR GUN. I WILL GET
MINE, AND WE WILL FIGHT!"

To their chief, Grey Bull, he was to say that a trading place had been built on Flatwillow especially for him and his people; and he was also to carry to him a message from the chiefs of the Blackfeet, camped on the Missouri, that none of their men would be allowed to go to war before the moon of new grass—April. He also took to Grey Bull a present of twenty pounds of tobacco from Kipp, and a smaller amount and a peace pipe from the Blackfeet.

Skunk Cap dealt in mysteries. The Indians did not dare to kill him lest his spirit should return and do them harm, for his whole personality tended to create awe in their superstitious minds. He was more than six feet tall, and had a stern, commanding presence. His large, deep-set greenish eyes always seemed to see things invisible to others. He wore his hair long, and loosely combed over his shoulder. He dressed in Indian style, and carried at his belt a little buckskin sack filled with various medicines for every kind of ailment. In the Indian sense, however, his great "medicine" was a staff about seven feet long and an inch in diameter, to which were tied at intervals bits of fur, feathers, and bones of animals and birds unknown to the people of the plains. Those things were all from arctic regions, where Skunk Cap had been as a member of a relief expedition that went out in search of Sir John Franklin.

Day and night that staff was never out of his hands or his reach. He told the Indians that the things tied on it represented a great medicine—sacred, mysterious, all-powerful animal gods who, moved by his prayers, would heal the sick and insure success to the warrior and the hunter.

Skunk Cap never had to work like other men; the Indians gave him horses, fine robes, and furs for his services, and he exchanged their gifts at the trading posts for his simple needs. His one pastime was to exercise his dogs; he had a peculiar breed of long, low, bench-legged little fellows that would crawl in and kill beavers in their dens and drag the bodies out to him.

Skunk Cap found the Crows at the junction of the Yellowstone and the Bighorn Rivers, and had little difficulty in persuading them to move over to our place. They had remained so long where they were that the game had left the vicinity of their camp, and they had been preparing to move to fresh ground.

So one day we saw the long cavalcade of Crows approaching us from the south, like a huge and gorgeously spotted snake wriggling across the wintry plain. An hour or two later they had set up around the post more than three hundred lodges.

We gave a feast to the chiefs and head men of the tribe, and they attended it dressed in their finest apparel. With the possible exception of the Blackfeet, the Crows were the proudest, the tallest, and the most elegantly dressed Indians in all America. The shirts and leggings and moccasins of our visitors were made of white, soft buckskin, had long fringes at the seams, and were embroidered with beautiful, brilliant, mystical designs of colored porcupine quills. Some had foxtails attached to the heels of their moccasins. Others wore necklaces of huge grizzly bear claws. Over all they wore buffalo robes for togas, with the hair side in; on the outer side of the robes were painted in brilliant colors pictographs of animals, gods, and slain enemies. Several of the men were more than six feet tall, yet as they walked, their hair, dressed in two long braids and bound with a strip of otter fur, actually touched the ground.

After they had feasted, Eli filled the big pipe and Grey Bull made a little speech. He was a big, fine-looking man—unquestionably one of the bravest, most intelligent, and just chiefs the West ever produced.

"I would have led my people over here some moons ago," he said, "had I not known that the Blackfeet are hunting over there on the Missouri. I know the Blackfeet chiefs. They are good men; they have tried to keep peace, and so have I. But the young men cannot see things as we of gray hairs do, and so they throw our advice and commands to the wind and break the peace that we have made. Sometimes it is my young men that are to blame, and sometimes the young Blackfeet."

The next day, and for many days thereafter, we were busy at the post from morning until night trading our goods for buffalo robes, beaver, wolf, and other pelts. The time soon came when we should have to replenish our stock; we needed especially powder and balls, and rim-fire cartridges. Eli finally told Ap-si and me to ride in to the Missouri River post and ask Kipp to send out a wagonload of these articles, and other loads of such supplies as he could spare. We were to start early the next morning. That evening there was dancing in the camp, and for some time we stood on the roof of the post watching it. The wild song, rising and falling to the beating of the drums, set Ap-si to dancing on the roof. Presently he started for the ladder.

"Come!" he called. "I'm going to put on my war clothes and go over there. I'll show them that the Blackfeet have just as fine clothing and can dance just as well as the Crows."

The Crows greeted us pleasantly, and by signs invited Ap-si to join them in the dance. He sprang into the thick of it; in his fine clothes he was as handsomely dressed as any of them, and he certainly was as good a dancer. Now bending low with his arms extended, now straightening his body and holding his shield aloft, he made the double-spring step with the rest around the fire.

Before Ap-si had completed the circle, a boy of about his own age and size bumped into him, and stopped and spoke angrily as if blaming him for the collision. Ap-si thought that perhaps he was at fault, and with a good-natured smile told the Crow by signs that he had not seen him. The other said nothing, but the angry expression did not leave his face. A few moments later he again collided with Ap-si, and this time he turned on him and fairly shrieked in anger. His words were of course unintelligible to us, but we did understand his signs, which said, "Blackfoot, I hate you! Go get your gun. I will get mine, and we will fight!"

"I take your words; I go to get my gun," Ap-si replied, and turned to leave.

But some of the older Crows seized the two boys, and others ran to get Grey Bull. He came in a few moments with Skunk Cap, listened to what some of the bystanders had to say about the trouble, and then turning to the young Crow talked to him sternly. The youth listened with averted face and made no reply. Then through Skunk Cap as interpreter Grey Bull spoke a few words to Ap-si.

"They tell me that my child"—chiefs called all of their tribe their children—"is to blame for this. Do not mind him; he is no doubt crazy tonight and knows not what he is doing. My camp watchers shall watch him. Leave your gun where it is, for he will not harm you. I hope you will take my words."

On the way home, Ap-si said, "This is not the end of it: that boy wants to kill me. Ever since the Crows came here he has been watching me with hatred in his eyes."

Soon after we got home Skunk Cap came in. "You must look out for that High Bear," he said to Ap-si. "His father was killed in a fight with your people last green-grass time. He has been telling people that he is going to dance with your scalp, and so wipe away his mother's and his sisters' tears."

"Ah, is it so?" Ap-si exclaimed. "Well, maybe it is his scalp that will be used at a dance. There are some of my people also whose tears are still falling."

"Ap-si," said Eli, "there must be no fighting between you and High Bear; if one of you were to kill the other, the two tribes would be at war in no time. You had better stay with your people when you and Ap-pe-kun-ny get in to the Missouri. He can return with the wagon outfit."

"Then it would be said that I am a coward!" Ap-si cried. "No! I must return. If I am not to stay with you, then I will have to bring my mother and sister and set up our lodge right beside these Crows."

"Of course I want you with us," said Eli, "but you must promise that you will do your best to have no trouble with the young Crow."

Ap-si promised. We saddled our horses early the next morning, but before we were out of the stockade Grey Bull sent for us. He handed Ap-si a beautiful otter skin—considered as a great medicine—and told him to give it to his Blackfoot brother, Chief Big Lake, and to say that he should like to have a visit from him. When we arrived at the Missouri River post, my friend, Joseph Kipp, was well pleased to learn of the fine trade we were having with the Crows. He told us to rest a day, and then to start back with three pack-horse loads of ammunition—enough to last the Crows until he could send some teams out with a good supply.

During the evening Ap-si and I went to Big Lake's lodge and gave him the otter skin and the message from Grey Bull. He told us to say to the Crow chief that before long he would himself tie a horse at the doorway of his brother's lodge—meaning that he would visit the Crow and make him a present of a horse.

The next morning we started back with three pack-loads of ammunition. We made such a late start, and had so much trouble with the pack horses and their loads, that night found us not more than fifteen miles from the Missouri. That meant that we should have to camp another night on the trail.

We pushed on as soon as it was daylight, and made fairly good progress that morning. About noon Ap-si stopped his horse and leaned over the bow of his saddle.

"What do you see?" I asked.

He pointed toward some low buttes south of Crooked Creek. "Look there, just under the farthest hill. What do you see?"

"Some antelope running."

"Yes. This is the third time since we started this morning that game has been scared away to the east of us. Some enemy is watching us and traveling just as fast as we do."

"I think that we had better keep on," I said. "If there really are enemies off there, they must be waiting to make a night attack on us. Let's try to reach the timber just before dark; then we can build a fire near the edge of it to make them believe that we have camped. But as soon as the fire is going well, we will ride on—keeping in the heavy timber."

"You forget that the snow is very deep in the timber; the horses couldn't travel through it," Ap-si said.

He was right; I had not thought of that.

"Here is what I think we had better do," Ap-si continued. "We will ride until it is almost dark. Then, after picketing the horses and building a fire, we will make down our bed. But instead of getting into the bed we will lie down away from the fire where we can watch it and the horses. If enemies come, they will shoot into our bed, and we will shoot them."

"But what good will that do? We may kill one or two of them, but the rest will get us—if not in the night, then as soon as day breaks."

"No, they won't. There are only three of them: I saw them. Surely we can get two of them, and then the other will run away."

"But perhaps you did not see all of them."

"Three or more, it makes no difference. There is nothing else for us to do unless we abandon our packs and ride away from here as fast as we can."

During the afternoon we saw game running off to the east four times, but we got no glimpse of any riders. A short time before sundown we arrived at the foot of the butte. Ap-si chose a camping place in a rather narrow, low-banked coulee. We tied the horses fast in a thick clump of willows on the east side of the coulee. Then we built a large fire and close beside it we made the bed. We placed some brush between the blankets to represent our sleeping forms. Then we took a robe and our rifles, and hid in a small, low patch of sagebrush on top of the east bank of the coulee. We could look down at the fire, and see for some distance out on the plain.

The darkness deepened. An extremely cold wind sprang up from the north and we shivered under the robe. I felt a choking sensation in my throat and tears came to my eyes. I was lonely and miserable. I felt that death was near. There was no moon, but the stars were bright, and we marked the time by the Big Dipper; it seemed to me that it had never swung so slowly in its course.

Some time before midnight Ap-si nudged me, and whispered, "Look! There they are out on the plain!"

I saw only a vague, moving shadow darker than the night itself, but the shadow came nearer and nearer until I could make out three men on foot. We could hear a faint rustling of the brush as they skulked through it.

We had agreed that if the enemy came we would not shoot until they fired at our empty bed; but in the excitement of the moment Ap-si forgot that. He raised his rifle, and whispered, "Shoot when I do."

I could not see the sights of my rifle. I held the weapon pointed as nearly as possible at the middle of one of the three dim forms, and fired almost simultaneously with Ap-si. The flash of the powder was blinding; one of the enemy shrieked with pain and called out something as the other two fired at us. Ap-si and I kept shooting as fast as we could; but we had to fire at random, for the burning powder dazzled our eyes. After we had used six or seven cartridges, we stopped, and peering into the darkness, tried to see our foes. There was no sign or sound of them. In a moment or two we heard the thump of hoofs growing fainter and fainter.

"They have gone," said Ap-si, "but our troubles have only just begun. They are Crows; we have wounded or killed one of them, and they are sure to have their revenge."

"How do you know for sure they are Crows?" I asked. "You could not see them plainly."

"The one we shot cried out. I don't understand Crow talk, but I know it when I hear it. They are Crows."

I hoped that Ap-si was mistaken. If he was right there was trouble ahead for us, even if we managed to get home. And not only for us: trade would be ruined, and in revenge for what we had done, the Crows would perhaps attack the post.

We sat there listening a few minutes longer, and then decided that we had better pack up and start at once for the post. It was a very cold night; our fingers were so numb that we could hardly cinch the saddles on the horses and lash on their packs. At last we started out on foot; Ap-si led his saddle horse, and I followed in the rear with mine; the pack animals went ahead of me. What with the fear in our hearts and the cold in our bodies, and our weariness, it was a night that neither of us would ever forget. We did not dare to mount our horses, for without the exercise of walking we should have frozen to death; and to stop and build a fire and warm ourselves—and let the enemy know our whereabouts—was equally out of the question. Luckily, the wind changed to the southwest just before daylight. By sunrise a chinook was burning our almost frozen faces, and we climbed into our saddles.

It was nearly noon when we passed through the Crow camp. We entered it expecting trouble, but no one paid any more attention to us than usual. In a few moments we rode into the stockade, and fairly tumbled from the saddle. When Eli and Fitzpatrick heard our story they looked serious enough. Well they knew the Indian law; a life for a life. The Crows would disregard the fact that they themselves were wholly to blame. The result would be war between them and us and the Blackfeet. Our trade would of course be ruined.

We thought it strange that there was no commotion in the camp, either the party we had fought with were not Crows, or they had not yet returned. Eli sent for Skunk Cap, who was visiting the camp, and told him what had happened.

"It is best that I go back into the camp," Skunk Cap said after a moment, "and stay there until I can hear something about this. Perhaps Ap-si is mistaken; it may not have been a Crow that you boys shot."

The day passed quietly; so did the night; Eli and Dan remained in the bastions until morning, watching the camp.

At noon the next day a Crow hunter hurried into camp and told Grey Bull that the Blackfoot chief, Big Lake, with fifty or sixty men, was coming to pay him a visit. Skunk Cap brought us the news, and then hurried out, saying, "Be ready for anything, and watch the stockade gate."

In an hour the Blackfeet arrived, and Grey Bull welcomed them. He took as many as he could into his lodge, and the rest became guests of minor chiefs; a big feast was cooked for them. About this time a commotion arose in the farther side of the camp; two riders had come in bringing with them on a stretcher their comrade, who they said was dying. Skunk Cap, who was sitting with Grey Bull and Big Lake, quickly explained the attack on us and the shooting two nights before. Grey Bull declared that whoever had attacked us should die. But the crowd of Crows assembled, and shouted, "A Blackfoot has shot High Bear!" "High Bear is dying!" "Kill all the Blackfeet!" "Kill the white men!"

Grey Bull rushed out of his lodge, with the Blackfeet following him.

"If we are to die, we will die bravely!" Big Lake cried to his men.

Grey Bull, springing in front of them and facing the crowd, shouted that if they attacked the Blackfeet they must fight him, too. Skunk Cap shook his long medicine staff at the Crows, then at the Blackfeet, and cried out in each language in turn that his powerful and terrible gods of the ever-winter land would destroy the man who fired a shot—him and all his relatives.

With weapons ready, the men of the two tribes stood facing one another, and for a moment it seemed that the efforts of the peace-makers would be of no avail. Had even an accidental shot been fired, no doubt all the Blackfeet and many of the Crows would have been slain; but the awful threat of Skunk Cap held the Indians in check, and presently the shouting ceased and silence followed. Then a woman whispered something to Skunk Cap; he turned to Grey Bull, and said:

"High Bear is not dead; he has nothing worse than a broken leg, and will soon get well."

Grey Bull repeated that in a loud voice, and then began to scold his people, who soon broke and scattered to their lodges. The danger of an outbreak was past, and the next morning all the Blackfeet went peacefully home.

High Bear's object, of course, had been to kill Ap-si—and incidentally me. Visions of pack loads of ammunition that were to be had for the taking had probably tempted his two unscrupulous companions to go with him. It had been a narrow escape for us.

7

A Medicine Animal Hunt

Originally published in *The Youth's Companion*, March 27, 1919.

When my friend, Joseph Kipp, was trading with the Blackfeet at his big post on the Missouri River, he built a second small trading post on Flatwillow Creek, seventy-five miles to the south, in order to establish trade with the Crow Indians. He put Eli Guardipe in charge of it. Eli's young wife, Dan Fitzpatrick, the old hunter and trapper, Ap-si, the young Blackfoot, and I were Eli's helpers. Skunk Cap, a half-breed medicine man, who had come down to help us get the trade of the Crows, was also there.

One day a trapper with three or four pack animals came riding into the post. He gave us to understand that he was called Long Hair. His real name he never mentioned; in those days it was not wise to ask a man his name, or whence he came, or whither he was bound. The man's name fitted him exactly, for his dark-brown locks were at least two and a half feet long and were braided in the Indian style into two long tapering ropes and fastened at the ends with a lashing of buckskin. His hair was so unusual that we could not help staring at it.

"He must be a great chief!" Ap-si exclaimed. "That is the way Long Knife chiefs of the Big Mud Fort wore their hair." He was referring to the officials of the American Fur Company.

Of course we made the stranger welcome at the post. In those days anyone was welcome anywhere so long as he behaved himself; the host would have felt insulted had he been offered pay for board and a place by the fire.

So we all lent a hand in unpacking the man's horses and in piling the loads in the storeroom. Long Hair had a hundred and thirty beaver pelts which he was planning to sell at our main post on the Missouri. He had been trapping in the mountains to the west of us since early November, thinking that no war parties would be roaming round there in the cold weather. He said that there were almost unbelievably large numbers of elk and deer up on the Judith River and Warm Spring Creek, and that he had discovered a new game animal in the mountains that lie in the fork of the two streams.

The animal, he said, was much like the mountain sheep in color;

A MEDICINE ANIMAL HUNT ⊰▤◆▥⊱
by James Willard Schultz

DRAWINGS BY GEORGE VARIAN

'I HAVE KILLED IT!' AP-SI SHOUTED, AS HE RUSHED FORWARD.

it was nearly as large as an elk and had long, round, sharp-pointed, backward-curving horns and a long tail. It had disappeared before he could shoot. The animal was not alone, for he had heard others crashing through the low pines in their flight and rattling across the shell rock beyond them. He had followed their tracks, but it was so late in the day that he had had to give up the chase in order to make camp before nightfall.

None of us had ever heard of such an animal. Skunk Cap made inquiries of the Crows, who declared that if the beast had very large ears it was undoubtedly Wind Maker, the animal that made the breezes blow hard or soft by fanning the air with them. Long Hair declared that he had noticed the ears particularly, but they could not have been especially large.

Old Dan laughed when I asked him privately what he thought of Long Hair's tale.

"It's just a yarn," he replied. "Long Hair is a man of mighty few ideas, he loves to talk, and he has to invent such tales to make people listen to him."

Skunk Cap and Ap-si, however, believed that the trapper really had seen the animal he described; and Eli admitted that there might be such a beast, for he thought it not unlikely that in the heart of the big mountain ranges there were animals that neither Indian nor white man had ever heard of.

Skunk Cap and Ap-si were convinced that it was a great medicine animal, and they at once prepared to go on the hunt. Eli readily gave me permission to accompany them. Old Dan was probably right, I thought, but even so I should enjoy two weeks of hunting and camping.

As Skunk Cap took his whole outfit—his family, his fine lodge and many pack horses loaded with bedding and camp equipage—we were well prepared for cold weather. Heading north and then west round the point of the Snowy Mountains, we made camp on Warm Spring Creek three days after we had set out.

There at the foot of the Judith range a huge spring of hot water gushed up from some fiery source and ran in a good-sized stream for several miles to its junction with the Judith River. Dense volumes of

steam rose from it in the intensely cold winter air and settled back
on the shores and brush nearby in long, glittering ice crystals. There
were hundreds of ducks and not a few Canada geese scattered along
the streams, except on the upper part, where the water was unbear-
ably hot. They were very tame; I easily approached a bunch of geese
and, firing at the neck of one, had the good fortune to kill two as
they stood huddled together. As soon as camp was made, the women
buried them in a pit under the lodge fire, covering them first with a
little dry earth and then with hot coals; and late that night we had a
feast of the best roast goose I have ever eaten.

Many people think that the Indians in their winter homes were
half frozen and almost blinded by smoke, but that is not so. The
lodge of the plains Indians was the most comfortable portable
dwelling ever devised by man. To make one of the ordinary size, sixteen large cow-buffalo hides, tanned into soft leather, cut to shape,
were sewed together with sinew thread and then stretched over
tough, slender poles of mountain pine. The lodge was about twenty
feet in diameter at the base and tapered to a height of about eighteen
feet. It was impervious to wind and rain. The lower edge of the lodge
skin was pegged about four inches above the ground. There was a
leather lining all round the inside of the lodge except at the doorway,
and that lining was firmly weighted to the ground by the couches
and other household belongings of the family. It extended upward
for five or six feet, and at the top was fastened to a rawhide rope that
ran from pole to pole round the inside of the lodge. There was an air
space between the two skins; the cold air rushing up through it from
the outside and out of the hole at the top created a fine draft for the
fire and at the same time kept the lodge free from smoke.

The lodge was always set up with its back toward the prevailing
wind. If the wind shifted, and blew from the opposite direction, then
the two big "ears" at the top were shifted also, in order to prevent the
smoke from being driven back into the interior; and so the air inside
was always clear and warm. A very small fire would keep the inmates
comfortable even when the temperature outside was thirty or forty
degrees below zero.

A circle of good-sized stones round the fireplace gave out heat

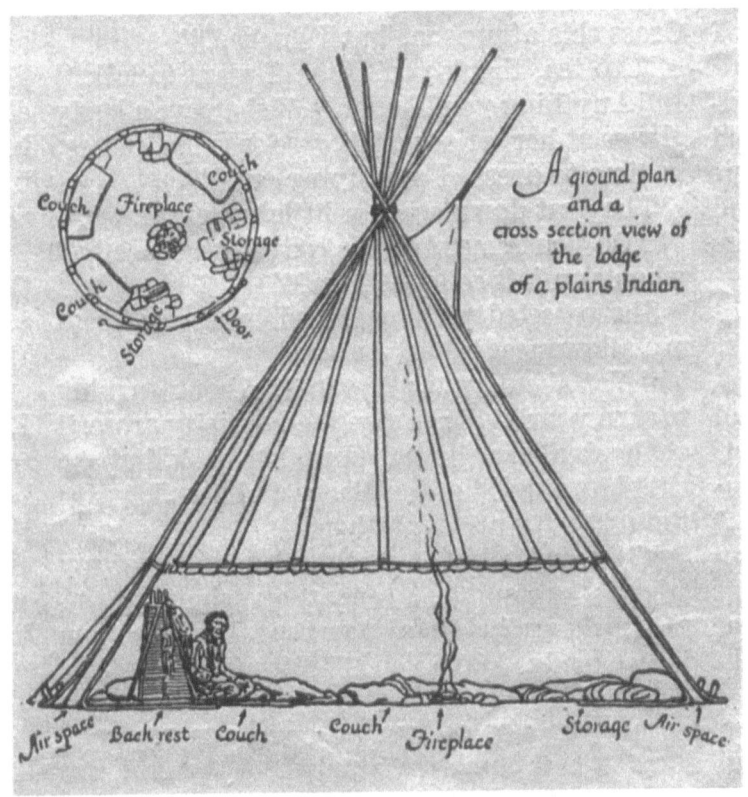

A qround plan and a cross section view of the lodge of a plains Indian.

A GROUND PLAN AND A CROSS SECTION VIEW OF THE LODGE OF A PLAINS INDIAN. [NO ATTRIBUTION FOR ARTIST OR DRAFTSMAN.]

through the night after the fire had died down; but as a matter of fact the soft buffalo-robe couches that the Indians slept in would have kept a person warm at the North Pole. The Blackfeet bathed every day—in winter they cut holes through the ice in order to reach open water—and so they were hardened to cold and could hunt on the blizzard-swept plains without much bodily discomfort.

We had brought our snowshoes with us, but we did not need them until we got into the heavy timber on the mountainsides. There the snow was five or six feet deep and very soft. On the open plain and the partly timbered, grassy foothills, we had seen plenty of elk and deer and antelopes, and not a few buffaloes, but we had not shot any. The sight of so many wild creatures feeding, resting, and playing was something of which none of us ever tired. Ap-si had an extremely emotional temperament, and at such scenes he would frequently break out in a prayer of thanks to the gods for this abundance, as he put it, of food, clothing, and of shelter for the Nit-Si-tup-pi—as the Blackfeet called themselves.

It was almost noon when we passed the upper fringe of the timber belt and came out on the windswept, rocky heights of the mountain. Here the snow was packed hard, and we took off our snowshoes and slung them over our shoulders.

We had no more than cleared the evergreens than a bunch of bighorn sprang from their beds on a slant of bare shell rock and without giving us a second glance bobbed their white-patched rumps round a projecting ledge and out of sight. Skunk Cap's dogs whined and, looking up at him, begged permission to chase them. When he shook his head and said, "No, my little ones, not now," they hung their heads in dejection.

Climbing to the very top of the mountain, we carefully examined every track on the snow and in the loose, dry, fine gravel that showed here and there. Bighorn tracks were plentiful enough, but we found no signs whatever of any larger animal's having been there. We crossed to the next peak to the west, and from that to another one, but nowhere did we find any trace of the mysterious long-tailed, sharp-horned animals.

At last we had to give up the quest for the day, and Skunk Cap led the way straight down the mountain. We put on our snowshoes again to go through the timber, and when we were partway down, the bow of one of my snowshoes snapped. Skunk Cap cut a small withe and was splicing the broken place when Ap-si, who had gone on ahead, suddenly fired a shot.

Come on!" he shouted in great excitement. "I have hit it—the animal we have been looking for!"

Skunk Cap made short work of the splice, and we hurried after

Ap-si. We soon came up with him, and he pointed excitedly to the bloody trail of a big animal.

"I didn't see its head or its tail!" he exclaimed. "Only a part of its body was in sight between two trees, and when I fired the smoke blinded me until it was gone. Its hair was almost white; different from that of any animal I ever saw. It must be one of the kind we have been looking for. I am sure it is great medicine."

Skunk Cap took the lead, and we went on. I thought it strange that the animal could go so fast in the deep snow. A moose or an elk or a deer could have made no headway in it, but this creature had not anywhere sunk more than a foot or eighteen inches below the surface.

We were all excited; it was certainly a strange animal. We had to run it down ourselves, for the dogs with their short legs were useless here for the chase; the little fellows floundered along on our trail, whimpering as they fell farther and farther behind. The plentiful sprinkling of blood led us to hope that our quarry would soon weaken.

"I see him!" Skunk Cap cried suddenly, and when we came up to him he pointed to a clump of young pines in which we could dimly see an animal standing. "It is yours, Ap-si," the old man continued. "Take the shot."

Ap-si was a long time in aiming. When at last he fired, the animal lunged heavily down and in its fall threw up a cloud of snow that almost hid it from view.

"I have killed it!" Ap-si shouted, as he rushed forward. "I have killed the great medicine animal!"

Skunk Cap and I followed close behind him. The beast's antlers, which were larger than those of a deer and had irregular semi-palmated tines, were very different from Long Hair's description. Ap-si dug into the snow, got hold of a leg and yanked the rear end of the animal into view. It was short-tailed like a deer. But its feet! They were enormous—long, wide-sprawling hoofs that looked at least four times too large for the body. I noticed that the light-colored hair was much longer and heavier than that of a deer. Grasping an antler, I pulled the head into view; the nose was blunt and heavy, more like that of a cow than that of a deer.

"It doesn't matter; I have killed a medicine animal anyhow!" Ap-si exclaimed.

"*Ki-kai nit-ah o-muk-tsis-tsin* (You have killed a big hoofs)," Skunk Cap said to Ap-si. "It is a caribou."

Then we both knew that it was no new medicine animal. Ap-si was much disappointed; for one fleeting moment he had believed that his kill was something that had never before been seen by mankind.

We began to skin the beast, and as we worked Skunk cap told us what he knew of its habits and its range. It was very plentiful in the arctic regions, he said, and farther south in the muskegs and hills of the country that drained into Hudson Bay. Its large feet enabled it to travel over the treacherous surface of the muskegs, or swamps, where any other animal, and man even, would perish in the muddy ooze.

Ap-si had heard his people tell of its being plentiful in the country of the Kootenay, on the west side of the Backbone-of-the-World, nearly opposite the headwaters of Old Man's River. I afterwards learned that that was correct; it was true that caribou were plentiful in the extreme northwestern part of Montana and in British Columbia.

Two other caribou, I learned later, had been killed on the plains of the Missouri: one at the junction of that stream and the Musselshell, and one at the foot of the Belt Mountains. Both were lone bulls. Repeated questioning of the Crows, the Blackfeet, and white trappers brought to light no more tales of them; so in all probability the caribou that Ap-si killed that day had reached the extreme southern limit of the range of its species.

Taking the hide and a portion of the not over-fat meat, we returned to camp. The women roasted some of the ribs, and we all agreed that the coarse-grained meat was not so fine in flavor as that of a deer or antelope.

Skunk Cap had had a complete change of mind. He declared that we could hunt until the waters of the rivers ceased to flow, but that we should never find any such animals as Long Hair had told us he had seen.

"Old Man knew what he was about when he made the animals," he said. "Each kind he created for some special purpose. The bighorn, the white goats, the antelope, the deer, the moose, the elk—none of them have long tails. Why? Because they would become heavy with snow and ice in winter, and so be a hindrance in traveling, and in escaping from their enemies."

"Then why did he put a long tail on a horse?" Ap-si inquired.

"He didn't," Skunk Cap replied with conviction. "You know as well as I do that Old Man did not create the horse; it is a white man's animal."

That silenced Ap-si for a time, and then he suddenly exclaimed, "I shall hunt some more for the long-tailed, sharp-horned animal! The stranger has long hair, therefore he must be a chief; and it is well known that white chiefs do not lie."

Reasoning from the experience of his people with the factors of the American Fur Company, he was right enough; to their credit, none of them had ever told the Indians an untruth.

Although I was fully convinced that Skunk Cap was right, I set out with Ap-si early the next morning for the peaks south of the hot spring. Skunk Cap, refusing to join us, rode away to set some traps for beaver.

Ap-si and I walked along the edge of the plain until we reached the base of the third mountain. There we started to climb, and as soon as we got into the timber we put on our snowshoes.

When we were partway up the mountain I thought I saw a black, furry object spring to the side of a pine tree and whisk upward and out of sight. I said nothing but followed my companion until we came to the base of the tree. There in the snow was the trail of an animal that traveled just like a weasel; the tracks were two and two and two, and so on, at intervals of about three feet, with one footprint always slightly ahead of the other. The trail ended at the tree.

A few paces farther on I stopped and looked up into the dark, dense foliage and at once caught the outline of a black, furry object sprawled out on a big limb. I fired and down it came into the snow.

The report of the rifle caused Ap-si to turn so suddenly that his snowshoes locked and he wavered, lost his balance, and fell flat. I had to help him up, but he looked so serious and mortified that I stifled the jest I had on the end of my tongue.

"What did you fire at?" he asked.

In reply I lifted a fine, big fisher from the bottom in the hole in the snow.

"O Spotted Robe! O my brother!" he cried stretching forth his hand. "Give it to me! This animal is great medicine. I need its skin. My dream told me that I must have one."

I shook the snow from the beautiful animal, king of the weasel kind, and stroked the long, glossy fur. "Take it," I said after a second, and the smile of pleasure that lighted up Ap-si's face was well worth the value of the skin to me.

As soon as Ap-si had ripped off the pelt and tucked it into his belt, we went on. It was a relief to get out of the timber on the open summit of the mountain. When we had removed our snowshoes we felt so light of foot that it seemed as if we could have stepped off the mountaintop and walked away on the air.

With his head down and his eyes intent, Ap-si scrambled in and out of deep erosions, across banks of snow and beds of rattling shale, looking for tracks of Long Hair's big medicine animals. He would not let himself be discouraged when he found none.

We went across the next peak, and then on to the next one, but there were no tracks of animals other than bighorn. It was now time for us to turn homeward, and we were ravenously hungry. As we rounded the peak on the side nearest the plain we came face to face with a big, fat ewe bighorn, and Ap-si shot and wounded it. Before either of us could fire another shot it wheeled, made a few jumps, and suddenly vanished. Following its trail, we found that it had jumped off a sheer rock wall. It lay dead on the deep snow of a shelf fifteen feet below. Tossing our snowshoes down beside the bighorn, we made the leap ourselves and in another moment were busy skinning the animal.

As we worked, our hunger grew for some of the fine meat, roasted brown over a bed of cottonwood coals. I had my portion of the carcass ready for packing first, and while waiting for Ap-si I walked out to the edge of the shelf. To my surprise I found that except in one place it had an almost sheer drop of several hundred feet; that one place was at the extreme right, where the cliff merged into a snow-covered talus, which fell away at an angle of at least seventy degrees to the timber four hundred feet below.

"We can't go down there," I said to Ap-si. "We must get back the way we came."

At first that, too, seemed impossible, for the wall offered no hold either for hand or foot; but near the place where we had jumped a root of mountain juniper as large as my wrist hung loose from the rock.

That was our one chance; by standing on my shoulders Ap-si might be able to reach it and to draw himself to the top. Then he could haul me up with our belts. We heaped up some snow at the place, spread the ewe's skin over it, and I took my stand. Ap-si climbed to my shoulders.

"I can't quite reach it," he said.

"Stand on my head and try again," I said, and braced myself for the strain.

The next moment I was relieved of his weight, and he cried, "I have it!" Then, in another second, down he tumbled with the whole length of the root in his hand. He got to his feet, and we stared at each other in silence. There was now no possible way for us to scale the cliff.

Walking out, we looked at the talus, well knowing that we must take our chances on it or freeze before morning.

"Let's hurry and have it over," said Ap-si, "If this is our time to go to the Shadow Land, let us go without fear."

The slide itself was not dangerous; there was not a protruding boulder in its whole length; the risk lay in our being unable to check our momentum, in which case we should almost certainly be dashed to death against the trees at the foot of the slide.

"Let us throw the meat on the slide and see what happens to it," I proposed.

"Oh no! It would take along with it what little loose snow there is on the place, and we need all the snow to bank up ahead of us and check our descent," Ap-si replied. "The snow is deep and soft here, but farther down where the sun hits strong it looks as if the slide were almost solid ice."

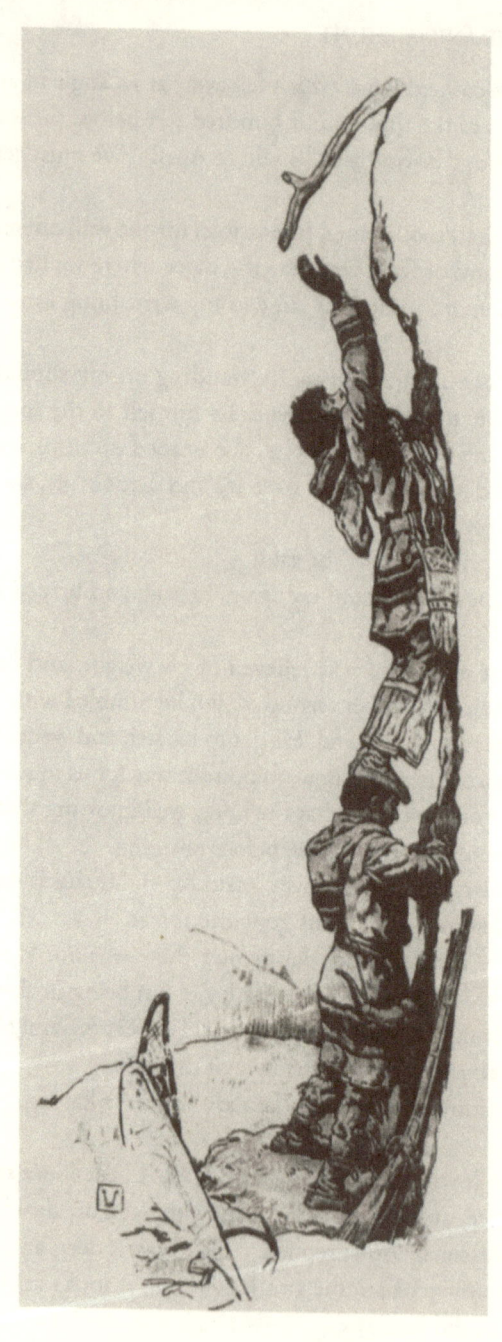

I BRACED MYSELF FOR THE STRAIN.

I had nothing more to say and followed Ap-si's directions. He gently laid the meat on the slide and sat down behind it, with his rifle pointing upward between his legs. I took my place behind him.

"Now hear me," he cautioned me. "Press the point of your rifle stock hard against the snow, and bear down still harder when we get to the icy place. Keep your legs close together and don't let the rifle jar out of your hands. Now, here we go."

We went sliding along easily at first, with loose snow piling up ahead and retarding our descent. Then the bank of snow thinned out and finally disappeared, and we shot forward at tremendous speed. My rifle suddenly flew out of my hands and I whirled round and round and over and over. I seemed to be falling through a wide world of space. Years seemed to have passed since I left the top of the slide; I was almost overcome with nausea. Then suddenly I seemed to have been plunged into a bed of icy feathers; I could hardly believe that I was lying still in deep snow. Struggling to my feet, I brushed the snow from my eyes and saw that I was several yards down in the timber. I had shot safely past a dozen or more trees.

I could see nothing of Ap-si and got no answer when I called. A moment later, however, I found him lying outstretched and apparently lifeless in front of the first tree at the foot of the slide. There was a faint tinge of blood on his lips.

As I raised his head into my lap I was quite sure that I should never hear him speak again, and in that moment I realized how large a place he had in my heart, and what a terrible loss his death would be to me.

You can imagine my joy when, slipping off a mitten, I thrust my hand into his bosom and felt the throb of life beneath it. A moment later Ap-si sighed, opened his eyes, smiled and said feebly:

"I had almost reached the Shadow Land when you called. I have come back. Oh, how it hurts—my breast!"

I raised him up, and he spit some bloody froth—a very evident sign of internal injury. Seeing my anxiety, he laughed bravely.

"It's nothing. I shall soon be all right," he said. "Draw me up with my back to this tree that tried to break my ribs and then build a fire. But first, bring me a cutting of that red-willow bush near you."

'IT IS NOTHING. I SHALL SOON BE ALL RIGHT,' HE SAID.

I handed the cutting to him, and he began to tear off and chew the bark and to swallow the juice. It is an excellent astringent. By the time I had built the fire, his slight hemorrhage had almost ceased.

I poked and pawed round in the snow and finally found our guns. The snowshoes and meat were in plain sight. After breaking down a lot of boughs for Ap-si to sit upon, I roasted some of the ribs; but he was still too sick and faint to do more than taste them. It was long after nightfall before he felt able to go on, and then our progress down through the timber was very slow. At the lower edge of the timber Ap-si said that he could go no farther; so I built another fire and made him as comfortable as possible.

We were discussing whether or not I should go on to the camp for help when we heard a shot in the distance. I answered it immediately, and in a little while Skunk Cap appeared on horseback. He had come in search of us.

The rest was easy. We got Ap-si on the horse and reached the lodge about midnight. Some days later, when he was well enough to travel again, we returned to the fort by easy stages. He did not completely recover from his injury for several months.

Long Hair was gone when we arrived home. We never saw him again, but Ap-si always maintained that the trapper had told the truth: he declared with positiveness that somewhere in the great range someone, some day would find the long-tailed, sharp-horned medicine animals that Long Hair had described.

8

A Hunt With Skunk Cap

Originally published under the topical title "New Stories of Ap-si"
in *The Youth's Companion*, April 22, 1915.

We were ready for a big winter trade at the Flatwillow post. The shelves in the warehouse and the trade room were laden with goods—cartridges, powder and ball, blankets, and gay-colored trinkets and cloths, tobacco, tea, and sugar. The Crows were again coming from the Yellowstone to hunt buffalo, and then to trade with us. As in the preceding winter, there were at the post Eli Guardipe and his wife, Dan Fitzpatrick, Thomas Faval (Skunk Cap), and Ap-si and I.

After the heat of the Montana summer the cool days and frosty nights of October were very pleasant. Ap-si and I wanted to be doing something; we found idleness tedious.

"I am going to hunt beavers for a fortnight," Skunk Cap said to Ap-si and me one evening, "and if our chief is willing, you boys may go with me."

ABOUT TWO MILES OUT ON THE PLAIN THREE MEN WERE
RIDING SOUTH AT TOP SPEED.

Eli gave us permission the next morning. We rode south, and
then west along the foot of the mountains. Skunk Cap led the way,
looking very fierce and mysterious in his fringed and beaded buckskin clothes and his furry headpiece. He carried in his right hand his
long medicine staff, ornamented with bits of fur and feathers from
the creatures he had killed in the far north. Of course he had his

remarkable beaver dogs with him. Ap-si, who regarded Skunk Cap with awe and veneration, was very proud to be in the company of such a powerful medicine man.

About noon we camped at the foot of the mountains, near the bank of a little stream that flowed into the Musselshell River. The lodge that we had brought with us we set up in a grove of cotton-wood trees. Almost from the doorway we could look out on limitless plains stretching away to the east and south. Buffalo seemed to be as plentiful as ever; behind us the mountainsides were alive with elk and deer, and judging from the signs, wolves and bears were also plentiful.

We passed the afternoon in making camp and in building a small corral for the horses. At sunset Ap-si shot within fifty yards of the lodge a big, fat, white-tail buck; we dressed it, and swung the meat to the limb of a tree.

Night closed in; we lay round the cheerful lodge fire on our soft couches of blankets and buffalo robes. When the deer ribs that we had hung on a tripod over the lodge fire were cooked, we attacked them and the tea and yeast-powder bread with keen appetites. It was late when we finally got into our warm beds.

The horses were all in the corral and well guarded by Skunk Cap's dogs; but even without their watchfulness there was little danger that the animals would be stolen, for all the Indian tribes of the country feared the old man and his powerful medicine of the far northland.

The furious barking of the dogs woke us. As there was not a red coal left in the fire, I knew that we had slept for several hours. The dogs rushed up the grove for some distance over the crisp, new-fallen leaves, yelped frantically for a moment, and then came hurrying back. They gathered outside at the edge of the lodge, whimpering and whining in fear. Skunk Cap hissed at them, and they bounded away again, brave for the moment; but they soon returned, to whine and shiver as before.

"Either a bear or some enemy is up there," the old man said in a low voice. "They don't act that way for anything else. Listen!"

We strained our ears to catch the least sound. The interior of the lodge was dark as pitch. Outside there was no moon, and clouds hid the stars. We could hear no sound, not even the faintest stirring of the dry leaves. The dogs, encouraged by their master's hisses, sallied out again and again. But they never went beyond a certain point; there they stopped and barked fiercely. There is nothing so trying as danger that you cannot see or hear. My heart seemed to be throbbing in my throat.

"Maybe it is only a black bear the dogs have treed," Ap-si suggested in a whisper.

"Then they would stay there and bark," said Skunk Cap. "And if it were a grizzly he would move round and chase the dogs. Some enemy is out there, and I am going to let them know whose lodge this is."

He thrust aside the curtain over the doorway, and standing just outside, shouted in the Sioux tongue, "I am Skunk Cap! Go away before you anger my powerful north medicines!"

He repeated this in the Crow, Cree, Blackfoot, and Gros Ventre languages, and then came back to his couch. A moment or two later we heard a distant rustling of the leaves; then all was still again. Skunk Cap waited a few moments, and once more hissed to the dogs; they ran out, barking as wildly as before, but soon lowered their voices to uncertain growls and occasional yelps; we could hear them trotting round in the grove. Whatever it was that had been so near us in the darkness was gone. But there was no more sleep for us that night. Skunk Cap smoked pipeful after pipeful of tobacco and red willow bark. Ap-si and I tossed restlessly on our buffalo robes and longed for day to come; we were impatient to get out and see what had caused the excitement in the night.

In the first faint gray of dawn, we took our rifles and crept from the lodge. We crawled into a thicket on top of a little knoll, and then, standing up, waited for the light to grow stronger. Skunk Cap hissed to the dogs, and away they went, ranging through the grove on both sides of the little stream. They found nothing suspicious and we saw nothing; our fear that an enemy might be lying near to shoot us as we came out of the lodge was groundless.

As soon as full daylight came we set out on a round of inspection, and soon learned why the dogs had barked so furiously in the night. Three men had crossed and recrossed the stream not a hundred yards above the lodge. We followed their tracks easily enough through the thick carpet of leaves, but lost the trail where the men had passed out of the grove to the short, springy grass of the plain.

"You are great medicine," Ap-si said to the old man. "They came to kill and plunder, but when they heard you threaten they fled."

Skunk Cap laughed. "It is good to have medicine that people fear," he said.

After the morning meal we saddled our horses and rode off on a beaver hunt; we took the pack horses along with us, in order to have an eye on them as they grazed.

In half an hour we found a fine beaver pond in a grove of willows and young cottonwoods and quaking aspen. Here the wise little animals had thrown up a dam six feet high across the creek, and flooded several acres of the woodland. The four beaver houses that stood in the pond were about twelve feet in diameter at the base, and rose three or four feet above the water. In the upper part of every lodge was the sleeping and living chamber, lined with soft grasses, and ventilated by a few interstices in the roof. Below that was a feeding and drying room, the floor of which sloped down into the water. The entrance to the lodge was several feet below the surface of the stream, so that even the thick winter ice would not close it.

The timber in the shallow water and along the shore looked as if a lumbering crew had been at work in it. The beavers had cut down many of the trees, and after recutting them into small pieces, had dragged and floated them away. Some of the pieces they had used in building their dam or their lodges; others—the limbs with smooth, new bark growth—they had stored away in piles in the deep water beside their houses, to serve as food during the winter.

I was not eager to hunt the beavers, and merely looked on while Ap-si and Skunk Cap attacked the dam with an axe and stout fir levers. Little by little they cut a channel across the deepest part of the dam, and soon a small torrent was rushing through it. The level of the water in the pond sank rapidly. Several times I saw beavers bob up near their houses.

In about two hours the pond was completely drained except for the natural flow of the little stream through it. The four lodges now stood exposed; the bleached dome of each house contrasted sharply with the dark, shiny mass that had been below the water line.

Several beavers had escaped in the torrent that poured through the dam, but the more timid or inexperienced animals had no doubt remained in their lodges. Skunk Cap, with the dogs close at his heels, led the way to the first hut. The long-bodied, bench-legged little fellows held their tails up rigidly, and whimpered and quivered with impatience.

As usual, the beavers had dug an avenue of escape; a deep, narrow trench, which ran from under the lodge to the creek. Across the ditch, which of course was still full of water, Skunk Cap and Ap-si drove a row of stakes, and then the old hunter told Slit Ear, the leader of the dog pack, to do his work.

The dog dived into the ditch at the edge of the lodge. In a moment two beavers, trying to escape through the trench, were stopped by the line of stakes, and the hunters quickly killed them. Then the water began to bubble and swash at the edge of the lodge, and the tip of Slit Ear's tail came into sight. Skunk Cap leaned over, seized it, and pulled out the dog and a large beaver that the sturdy little fellow had killed.

At the end of the hunt, Skunk Cap and Ap-si washed free from the mud the thirteen animals that they had killed, and then we followed the creek a little way until we came to a warm, sunny spot, where my friends set to work to skin them. Sitting in the warm sunshine, I watched my companions as they busily plied their knives. After a while I got out my telescope and had a look at the mountains that towered above the little valley. In one place I saw a band of elk lying on a grass slope. On a bare summit of rock were some mountain sheep. Then I saw a splash in the creek away up where the head of the pond had been; a beaver was swimming downstream; presently it climbed out on the slimy bank, and sitting on its haunches gazed at the ruined lodges. I did not tell my friends what I was looking at. At last the animal slid back into the stream, ascended the ditch to the first of the lodges and went inside for a moment, and then visited each of the other lodges in turn. Finally it came back into the creek and swam away upstream, no doubt to hide nearby and wait for night, when the survivors of the colony would return.

Our horses, which had been cropping the grass in a long, open park below the dam, grazed slowly toward the lower end of it, and after a while strolled into the timber. I volunteered to go after them and bring them up to our end of the park. Ap-si wiped his knife, stuck it into the sheath at his belt, and said he would go with me. We walked leisurely down through the park, and found some of the horses feeding just within the timber. We passed one after another of the animals until we had accounted for all except our own four—two that we used for pack animals and two that we rode. The horses that we rode were saddled and trailed their ropes. It was not strange that our horses should be grazing apart from Skunk Cap's, because days and sometimes weeks pass before horses of two different kinds become friendly enough to herd together.

We went on down through the grove, easily following the trail of the four animals. When we came into a second grass park, we were surprised not to find them there. We quickened our pace, broke into a run, and were halfway down the park when Ap-si stopped so suddenly that I bumped into him. He stood pointing at a little mound of earth thrown up by a mole; in it was the fresh imprint of a moccasined foot. All round the place the grass was trampled where the horses had milled, and we saw that the animals had gone on at a swift run. "Stolen!" I exclaimed.

"I think so," Ap-si said, "but maybe the enemy didn't catch them. Come on! We'll follow the trail through the timber; at the other side of it we can see out on the plain."

After a hundred yards or more we came to a wide sandy wash. The trail of the horses led across it; the hoofprints indeed showed plain in the sand, but beside them there were no snake-like lines made by dragging ropes; evidently the thieves had caught the horses and were riding them. We stopped, undecided what to do. *Zip! zip! zip!* some bullets flew by us and three shots rang out. We saw three puffs of smoke down in the edge of the timber, about two hundred yards away. We were standing on the edge of the wash; instinctively we dropped down into it, and then ran across to the opposite bank, which was high enough to conceal us from the enemy, even when we stood upright. Looking through a bunch of oat grass, we saw no signs of anyone in the timber. Had the horse thieves fired a farewell shot at us and gone their way? Or were they still there in the grove waiting for another chance to shoot at us?

Ap-si told me to go up the wash as far as the first bend and then to raise my hat above the bank. I did so, and a shot rang out. Ap-si immediately fired at the brush from which the puff of smoke had come. Apparently he did not hit his man. I lifted my hat three or four more times in different places, but the enemy paid no more attention to it. Then Ap-si joined me.

"What do you think?" I asked. "Are they still there in the timber?"

"We have got to find that out, but we can't both go. You stay here to warn Skunk Cap. He will be coming soon, and for all his medicine, it would not do for him to go into that timber. I will go down the wash into the timber bordering the creek, then round through the grove far enough to see whether the enemy really are watching for us."

"But they are three; you would have no chance against so many."

Ap-si laughed. "If they are still there," he said, "they shall not see me unless I want them to." With that he turned and ran down the wash.

I moved back to where the trail crossed the wash, and then kept running from one bank to the other, watching for any signs of the enemy, and for Skunk Cap. Soon I saw the guide on horseback, herding his pack horses toward me. Quirting his horse, he urged it forward at top speed; in his left hand he held aloft both his gun and his medicine staff. He was soon beside me in the wash, and I quickly told him what had happened.

"I knew that you boys did not fire the three shots," he said, "and I came as quickly as I could. Come on!"

I mounted one of the horses and followed him. We heard shooting down in the timber, but it soon ceased. When Skunk Cap and I burst out of the lower end of the grove, we found Ap-si stalking up and down, talking to himself and crying with anger and shame.

"It was my old Crow enemy, High Bear, and two others," he said. "See! There they go!"

About two miles out on the plain three men were riding south on our horses at top speed and leading the fourth horse. It was useless for us to try to overtake them, for none of Skunk Cap's horses were swift.

We dismounted, and waited patiently for Ap-si to become calm. Never had I seen him in such a rage. As soon as he could control his voice, he broke out, "High Bear! My Crow enemy, High Bear! O sun! Why do you let him live? What medicine has he that every time saves him from my careful aim?"

"I suspected last night that it was High Bear who was near us," Skunk Cap said.

"Yes, it was High Bear and two of his friends," Ap-si continued. "When I crawled round near the place from which they had fired at us, I saw our horses, and I knew that Skunk Cap was coming. I had a fine shot at High Bear as he untied a horse, and another as he sprang on his back. As long as I could see him I kept shooting at him, but all for nothing. The gods have forsaken me."

"Shame on you, Ap-si!" said Skunk Cap. "You blame the gods. Well, they just now saved you from the bullets of High Bear and his friends. You would be lying back there dead if they had not protected you. Your medicine is still strong, and some day you will have full vengeance on High Bear. Come, have courage. Laugh!"

Ap-si brightened somewhat. We watched the three Crows ride out of sight on the far plain, and then went back to the beaver pond to finish the work of skinning the animals. Although humiliated by the theft, Ap-si and I did not regret the actual loss of our horses. We could walk back to the post easily enough.

Ten days later, after a good hunt, during which we killed three grizzlies, we returned home, well enough pleased with our outing. But although Ap-si said little, I knew that the quarrel between him and High Bear still smoldered and that it had yet to be settled.

9

High Bear and Real Bear

Originally published under the topical title "New Stories of Ap-si" in *The Youth's Companion*, April 29, 1915.

A few days after we had returned to the post from the hunt with Skunk Cap, the Crows trailed over to Flatwillow Creek and set up their several hundred lodges; they had come for the winter trading. As usual, we gave Grey Bull and the minor chiefs and medicine men a big feast and some valuable presents. While the pipe was passing from hand to hand, Ap-si rose and addressed the old chief.

"I am a poor boy doing all that I can to make life pleasant for my widowed mother and my sister," he said. "I try not to have any enemies except those with whom my people are at war. But one of your young men is my enemy, although I have never sought to do him harm. Three times he has tried to take my life. Only a few days ago he robbed me and my friend, Spotted Robe, of four good horses and two saddles and bridles. I hope you will have pity and help us get them back."

"SOME DAY,' HE SAID VERY SOLEMNLY, 'IT IS TO SAVE MY LIFE.'

Grey Bull did not reply for several moments. He looked inquir-
ingly at Eli, who quickly made the signs: "Yes. He speaks truth."

"Who is this enemy?" he finally asked.

"He is named High Bear," Ap-si replied.

Grey Bull turned to one of the chiefs at his left. "High Bear is a
member of your band. What about him?"

"He and two others have just returned from a raid. They brought
in many horses."

"Well, you have them all rounded up and driven here for these boys to see," Grey Bull commanded; and then he added to Ap-si, "If High Bear and his friends have taken your horses, they must return them, and pay you, too, for the trouble they have caused you."

In the late afternoon the minor chief, Black Bull, and some of his men rounded up the horses, and brought High Bear and his two companions to the fort. Ap-si and I looked over the band of twenty or more horses, but we did not find our animals among them.

"Where are they? What have you done with our four horses?" Ap-si asked.

High Bear's eyes fairly shot fire at us as he replied: "Your horses! I don't know anything about your horses!"

"Do you say that you did not steal four from us the other day and then try to kill us?"

"That is what I say. We three have been to war against the Sioux, and took these horses from them."

Without another word, Ap-si turned and walked back into the fort. His breast was heaving with anger and he clenched his hands; we heard High Bear laugh derisively as he rode away.

"You must be careful, Ap-si," said Eli, when we came into the trade room. "There would be great trouble here if you should kill High Bear. Be patient and give him no chance to attack you. I feel somehow that you will get the best of him before the winter is over."

Skunk Cap and Dan also gave him good advice. We all believed that High Bear had the four horses running by themselves up in one of the mountain parks, for he would surely not have abandoned such valuable animals.

The next day Ap-si and I saddled our horses and rode through the bands of the Crow stock, on the chance of finding our animals among them. That was something of an undertaking, for there were several thousand of them scattered up and down the stream and out on the plain. We did not find our horses. As we rode wearily homeward in the gathering dusk, High Bear swept by us, driving his herd to water; he grinned derisively at us.

That was more than Ap-si, whose patience had already been so sorely tried, could bear. There were several riders in sight, but he did not hesitate: with a frightful expression of rage on his face, he tore the buckskins case from his rifle, and in another instant would have fired it if I had not jumped my horse to his side and snatched the weapon out of his hands.

"Are you crazy?" I asked. "Don't you see those riders out there? I want to live a while longer even if you don't."

"You are right," he answered. "I did not see the others. I saw only his face laughing at us as he passed. Give me back my rifle; I will not try to shoot him."

When we returned to the fort and unsaddled our horses, we were not very cheerful. I did not tell the others how near we had come to starting a big row. At the supper table Eli looked at us thoughtfully more than once; but he did not ask any questions.

Christmas was not many days off. Dan proposed that we should celebrate the occasion by getting up the grandest dinner possible.

"Right you are, old hunter!" Skunk Cap exclaimed. "I'll go out myself and kill a deer and roast its saddle for the piece of the feast."

"That's where you show the English part of you," said Dan. "Now I was born in Rhode Island, where they always have roast turkey for Christmas. We can have birds that are better eating than the finest turkey that ever was. I vote that these boys go up into the mountains and kill a dozen or so grouse for us."

"Good!" said Skunk Cap. "You boys shall have my smoothbore; I still have a pouchful of fine shot for it."

The next morning we rode up to the mountains in quest of the birds. We found a number of ruffed grouse in the quaking aspens and willows on the lower slope of the mountain. I got four of them. Then we rode up through the pine timber in quest of blue grouse, which are twice as large as the ruffed variety. Two-thirds of the way to the summit we came to a succession of rough ledges over which the horses could not scramble, and so we left the animals and went on afoot. It was not easy to walk in the deep snow, but fortunately we soon flushed a large covey of the big grouse. They flew into the thick foliage of the pines and sat immovable. They were so much the color of their surroundings that at first we could not see them. At last we made them out, however, and at our shots they came tumbling down one after another out of the trees. Soon we had killed nineteen.

"That is an unlucky number," said Ap-si. "Let us make it twenty."

We went on up the mountain where in a few minutes we came upon the trail of a grizzly bear. With rare exceptions, bears retire in November to the places they have selected for their winter quarters. As we believed that this belated grizzly was hurrying to some cleft or cave nearby, we dropped the grouse and hurried away in the tracks of the animal.

After turning the shoulder of the mountain, we had proof enough that the bear was really hunting winter quarters. He had pawed away the drifted snow and leaves under a partly uprooted pine, and a little farther along had explored a small cave; but apparently neither spot had been to his liking. We hurried on in the hope of trailing him to his den. His tracks led up the mountain along increasingly steep slopes and across piles of big boulders. The higher we went, the deeper was the snow. In places we were up to our waists in it and made slow progress, but we had no thought of giving up. About three o'clock our trailing came to an abrupt end. Just ahead of us the bear's tracks vanished into the darkness of a triangular hole about four feet wide and as many high. As we stopped and stared at it, a swirl of wind drifted down into our faces, and Ap-si whispered, "I smell him."

I thought that I, too, caught the rank odor of the grizzly bear. "Well, how is it?" I asked. "Do you intend to go to the mouth of that place and dare him to come out?"

"I am not yet wholly crazy," Ap-si replied. "There is nothing up on that slope to shelter us, no tree to climb. He would come out quickly and if we did not shoot just right, he would tear one of us— and maybe both—to pieces. Come on, let's go home."

"We will come back tomorrow with Skunk Cap's dogs, " I said. "We can sit up there on top of the cliff, and when they make him come out we can fill him full of holes."

It was late when, after picking up the grouse, we reached our horses. They pranced round and were so bad-tempered that we had some difficulty in getting into our seats.

All day long we had watched our back trail as closely as we had watched the trail ahead, for thoughts of High Bear were ever in our minds.

We started down the mountain. I was leading, and presently turned my horse to the right.

"Hold on, you have left the trail!" Ap-si called out.

"Yes," I replied, "but we don't have to follow our old trail. I'm thinking that our enemy may be waiting for us somewhere along it."

"I thought the same," Ap-si admitted, "only I didn't like to say so."

I kept on down into the narrow valley of the creek. Thick brush and wide piles of driftwood choked the bottom of the gorge. The horses stumbled and floundered, and we lost much time. When we were nearly out, we came to a narrow, walled canyon so choked with boulders that we did not dare to enter it. I led the way up on the ridge and along the top of the cliff. At last, just where the timber ended, we came to our trail of the morning. There was still enough light for us to see that a third horse had followed ours up it.

"A-ha! The gods surely warned us of this!" Ap-si muttered, as he leaned over his saddle and examined the trail. "Someone followed us and has not returned. Well, we will just hide here and wait for him." We felt sure it was High Bear that had gone up on our trail, and that he was somewhere along it waiting for us to return. It was almost dark; he would soon be coming back. We tied our horses in a thicket of pines, and then returning to the trail, got behind two large trees. Night came on rapidly. At last we heard the crack of a stick far up the trail, and then the thud of a horse's feet as it approached at a fast walk. I heard the click of Ap-si's rifle lock, and I cocked my weapon, too. And then—first one and then the other of our horses whinnied loudly. The horse up the trail answered them, and at the same time went crashing through the brush toward the plain on our right; its rider, suspecting danger, was going around us.

A moment later he burst out of the timber and rode furiously down the slope toward camp, but in the darkness he was so far away that we could not see who he was, and we had no desire to fire at the wrong person. We waited for about ten minutes, and then rode down to the fort by a circuitous route.

"It must have been High Bear," Ap-si kept saying. "I think he will kill me in the end; his medicine is very strong."

At the supper table we told our adventures. Eli became very serious when he heard about the rider in the dusk. "I think you boys had better not go out by yourselves any more," he said. "You wait until spring comes and the trade is over, Ap-si, and then you give Mr. High Bear what he needs, even if you have to follow him to the Yellowstone to do it."

When I told about finding the bear's den, Skunk Cap rubbed his hands together and smacked his lips.

"Ha! We'll get old sticky-mouth tomorrow," he exclaimed. "Think of the fine cakes we can have with plenty of his lard to fry them in! The dogs shall rout him out for us."

But the next morning a furious storm was raging. It lasted three nights, and when it stopped there was a foot or more of snow on the plains; that meant that in the high mountains the snow would be three or four feet deep. It was very light snow, too, and Skunk Cap decided that we should have to wait for it to settle and harden before we went after the bear. He set about making three pairs of snowshoes for us.

Christmas Eve came. The holiday, of course, meant nothing to the great camp of sun worshipers, but Ap-si had taken a fancy to it, because he thought the giving of presents a beautiful custom. For more than a month he had been planning a surprise for his mother and sister, for whom we had partitioned off sleeping quarters in our living room.

We sat up late, and when the women were asleep Ap-si stole in and laid by the side of each couch a fine new blanket and a dress pattern of our heavy blue English cloth, and also a little package for each of them from me. I had had the day in mind away back in summer, when the steamboats were running, and had sent to St. Louis for some things for the occasion.

After all the others were sound asleep, I stole around noiselessly and put in conspicuous places what I had for each one of those dear friends of mine. The packages that Ap-si had taken into his mother's room contained each a workbasket filled with all sorts of tools, and needles, and threads, and strings of fine-cut beads, and bracelets and necklaces of the best gold plate. I had a similar package for Mrs. Guardipe. I had knives for Dan and Skunk Cap, a sealskin cap for Eli, and for Ap-si a silver-mounted revolver.

It was good to see the pleasure that the women took in their presents. They were inordinately proud of the gold-plated jewelry, which they put on at once. Ap-si could not let his revolver alone for a moment, but he handled it and gloated over it between mouthfuls at breakfast.

"I feel somehow that the gods put it into your mind to do this," he said very solemnly, "because some day it is to save my life."

The women had worked hard to make some presents for me; they gave me enough moccasins and fur mittens to last me several winters. Mrs. Guardipe gave me a gorgeous bead belt that she had been making in her spare time for several months. I had it sewed on my buffalo overcoat, and when I wore it later on a short trip east it aroused much interest on the city streets.

Our Christmas dinner was a grand affair. The grouse, roasted in Dutch ovens, could not have been better cooked. Dan made us wonderful "plum duff" or boiled dough, raisins, and sugar, shortened with buffalo marrow grease; and in addition we had baked beans, dried camas roots boiled, dried applesauce, and coffee. As our daily fare consisted of meat and beans and bread, you can imagine how much we enjoyed our Christmas feast.

The morning after Christmas we started out to get the bear. The winds had swept the snow from the plains, and the walking was good; but when we came to the heavy mountain timber the snow lay deep enough. There we put on our snowshoes.

It was afternoon before we came in sight of the bear's den. Snow had nearly filled the entrance.

"It couldn't be better if I had laid it out," said Skunk Cap. "Old Wind Maker has done us a good turn by piling the snow in there. The dogs will have just room enough between it and the roof to go in and tease the old fellow. When he gets mad and starts after them, they can run out while he is pawing a bigger opening for himself."

After looking the place over carefully the old man decided on his plan of attack. He sent Ap-si and me, with four dogs, to the top of the cliff, directly above the entrance to the den. We had to go nearly a quarter of a mile off to the left before we could find a place where we could climb up. Skunk Cap waited patiently until we reached the position, and then, leading the remaining dog, he walked up to the entrance of the cave. The dog sniffed the air and tugged and strained on the leading thong. After a moment Skunk Cap dragged him away, and following our trail, joined us on the cliff.

"Now we will send the dogs back down there and the fun will begin," he said.

He released the leader. Away the dog went on our back trail, with the others following in single file; they were all whining and uttering muffled little barks. We saw them disappear into the entrance to the cave, and a moment later heard their muffled barking. Minute after minute passed; at last, one by one, the dogs came out panting, and began to sniff around the foot of the cliff.

"Here, you!" Skunk Cap roared. "Go back in there! Sick him! Sick him!"

Thus encouraged, they went in again; but soon they came out yelping, and then turned and barked furiously at the entrance. One, a pup of eight or ten months, was missing; blood dripped from a gash in the shoulder of another.

"He's got my little Howler pup!" Skunk Cap exclaimed. "He won't come out, and they'll all die trying to make him show himself."

But the dogs would not go back into the cave, nor would they come up to us when Skunk Cap called to them. Instead they stood around the mouth of the den, whining uneasily. We looked at one another and down at them; the hunt had taken a most unexpected turn; it seemed to me that the only thing for us to do was to call off the dogs and go home.

"No, we can't go home without that bear's hide," Ap-si declared.

"We must get him," Skunk Cap agreed. "Come on. I will take the big risk; you boys stand on either side of the entrance and try to keep him from reaching me."

When we were near the cave, Skunk Cap stopped and explained just what we were to do: Ap-si was to take his stand against the cliff about fifty yards to the right of the cave, and I about the same distance to the left. Skunk Cap himself would go up to the entrance, fire a shot into the depths of the cave and then run; if the bear came out, we were to do our best to kill him quickly.

The dogs had been watching us as we approached; they were whining, and trembling, and shifting their feet. Encouraged by our presence, they suddenly bolted, with shrill yelps, back into the cave. Before we could move, they came flying out with the bear almost at their heels. They ran straight toward us; and the bear, throwing up clouds of the soft fluffy snow, followed them with immense leaps. We all fired, and then turned and ran. Ap-si's snowshoes locked together, and out of the corner of my eye I saw him go tumbling down the steep slope. Skunk Cap, too, saw him, and cried to me, "Stop! Stop! Shoot!"

We fired almost together, and the bear, bawling with pain, paused to bite at a foreleg where a bullet had struck. That gave me a chance to get in two good shots with my rifle while Skunk Cap was reloading his old-fashioned gun. At each shot the bear stopped to bite at the fresh wound. Then Ap-si, struggling to his knees, opened fire. The old man's rifle boomed again; the blood spurted from the bear's brisket and his speed slackened noticeably; he kept on, however, straight toward Ap-si, who made a desperate effort to untangle his snowshoes and to get up.

Failing to get them apart, he bravely gave his whole attention to shooting at the big, bloody creature now drawing so near to him. Despair and a sort of stupefied wonder were in my heart as I kept on shooting. How could an animal keep on with such a load of lead as we had fired into him? He was not more than three paces from my friend now. I aimed again, but when I pulled the trigger the hammer clicked dully. I reached into my pocket for more cartridges, but not with any hope that I could ever use them. At that moment, following a third shot from Skunk Cap's old powder-and-ball weapon, the bear sank head first into the snow and lay still.

"He is dead," Ap-si calmly announced. "Come and help me up."

Skunk Cap and I looked at him with astonishment. The old man muttered, "Not capable of fear, that boy!"

The dogs ran back and bit the big carcass of the grizzly and growled their triumph just as if they had killed the beast. He was a fine, dark-furred animal, and must have weighed five hundred pounds. We were a long time in taking off the hide and removing the thick layers of fat.

"I take it that the killing of this bear," said Ap-si that evening at table, "is a sign that I am to live longer than my enemy, High Bear. Yes, I am going to count coup on him."

10

The Warning of the Gods

Originally published under the topical title "New Stories of Ap-si,"
in *The Youth's Companion*, May 13, 1915.

We seldom received any mail in winter at the post on Flatwillow Creek. It accumulated in Fort Benton for weeks and months, until some trader or trapper who happened to be coming our way brought it out to us.

That winter I had hard work waiting for mail to come, for I was anxious to get a certain package that I had ordered to be sent from St. Louis.

It was after New Year's Day when the mail sack, containing a few letters and many papers and periodicals, arrived by way of the Missouri River Post. Eagerly I thrust my arm deep down into it, and fumbled for a certain small, cylindrical package. I found it at the bottom of the sack, and hastily drawing it out, thrust it into the bosom of my shirt without being noticed. As soon as I could I hid it under the pillow in my bunk, where I left it until I could determine how to use it.

**THE SOFT DEER-HAIR BRUSH, SLIDING NOISELESSLY OVER THE
LEATHER, LEFT A TRAIL OF FAINT, WAVERING FIRE.**

The package contained a small, heavy glass vial of phosphorous
dissolved in chloroform. I was always planning unusual pranks to play
upon my friends, and I had gleefully thought how thoroughly I could
surprise them by a judicious use of the phosphorous paint, which
glows so weirdly in the darkness. I intended to go stealthily out into
the camp, when the people were all asleep, and paint various symbols

and animals on the lodges of some of my friends. I also planned to paint "repent your sins" on the footboard of old Dan's bunk.

I did not sleep well that night; my brain was too busy thinking of effective ways to use the paint; and during one of my wakeful periods I hit upon what I thought was a very bright plan. I would use the phosphorous to scare the young Crow, High Bear, so thoroughly that he would make no more attempts to kill Ap-si and me.

I slept all the next afternoon, and so, when the others went to bed, I was wakeful enough. I built a good fire in the chimney place, lighted three or four buffalo tallow candles, and tried to interest myself in the magazines that had come in the mail. Old Dan snored peacefully. Ap-si was restless; once he sat straight up on his couch and extending an arm and forefinger, exclaimed:

"*Mo-kap Is-sap-wi-kan, ki-taks i-nit-ah!*" (Bad Crow, you I will kill!)

Shortly after midnight I stole away from the fort with the phosphorous and a brush that I had made of deer hair in my pocket; I carried a gun. I had wrapped a robe round me in the Indian fashion to allay the suspicions of the numberless dogs at the Indian camp. They were very savage, and even in the daytime we white people were not safe in camp unless we wore a toga of some kind.

My moccasined feet made no noise on the hard, frozen ground as I went straight toward the lodge of High Bear's family. I knew that High Bear's couch was just halfway from the entrance to the rear part of the lodge, on the right-hand side as you entered.

On the wall of the lodge, at a point directly over my sleeping enemy, I began to paint a picture. The soft deer hair brush, sliding noiselessly over the leather, left a trail of faint, wavering fire. When I had finished the picture, I was more than pleased. Every Indian in camp would think it was the work of a ghost.

There was no doubt about the identity of the animal I drew; the five remarkably long claws and the wide, rounded ears proclaimed it to be a grizzly bear. I had pictured it in the conventional Indian manner; by painting its heart, and the line leading from it to the mouth, I showed that it had life. The man standing nearby with the arrowless bow had shot the bear. The arrow, piercing its lungs, had given it a mortal wound; blood was flowing copiously from the animal's mouth. The meaning of the picture was clear: High Bear is to die at the hands of an enemy.

I painted as fast as I could; in a few moments the work was done, and thrusting the little vial and the brush in my coat pocket, I turned back toward the fort. Just beyond the last of the lodges I stopped to rouse the camp. First I imitated the cry of a coyote until all the dogs in the vicinity were barking and rushing toward me. Then I fired three rifle shots in quick succession, and ran home as fast as I could. As I entered the small gate and fastened it, I could hear men shouting and children squalling in the camp. I slipped into my bunk without awakening my companions. The thick walls of the log building deadened the sounds from the camp. They came to me like the faraway murmur of a noisy brook. After a while they died away, until not even the howling of a dog broke the stillness of the night, and I fell asleep.

Skunk Cap had set up his lodge at the outer edge of the camp, where he did a thriving business, ministering to the sick with his spiritual and physical medicines of mystery. He always took his meals with us. The morning after my adventure he came in early, almost bursting with excitement.

"I tell you, my friends," he cried, "I am an old man, and thought I had seen everything; but last night there happened something so strange that, if all the Crow people had not also seen it, I could well believe it was only a crazy dream of mine! But I did see it: a picture painted on High Bear's lodge—a picture warning him that he is to die at the hands of an enemy. And it was a picture painted with fire—fire that was glowing and trembling like the air of the plains on a hot summer day, and yet fire that was cold, fire that did not burn the leather lodge skin! I know that it was cold, for I put my hand on it."

"Skunk Cap, wake up!" Dan said. "You are still dreaming; your brain is all fogged with the big sleep you've had."

Skunk Cap impatiently waved his hand. "It was just as I tell you!" he cried. "Someone fired three shots; that is, we heard three shots, though probably they were not real shots, just as the fire was not real fire. At any rate, the people rushed out of their lodges, thinking that the enemy was attacking the camp. And there must have been something; the dogs must have seen something, for they were all running toward the fort, barking loudly. But it is well known that they can see things hidden from the eyes of people: ghosts and others of the shadow world. Well, the people found no enemy, but they did find the fire picture; they crowded round it and stared at it. As I said, it foretold High Bear's death. There was the picture of a bear being shot by a man with a bow. The animal was up off the ground, and so it was High Bear. It had been shot in the lungs, a death shot, because blood was running from its mouth.

"High Bear himself stood there looking at the picture, but he said nothing. When his mother saw it, she cried out to me to help—to make medicine; but for once I did not know what to do. The picture was right over the place where High Bear sleeps. I went and put my hand on the fire, though the people tried to stop me, crying out that the bad medicine would harm me; but the fire did not burn my hand. Then, as we stood there, the fire began to grow dim, and soon it had faded entirely from our sight.

" 'I cannot help you now,' I said to High Bear's mother. 'This is something strange. I must go home and think about it.'

"I went home, but I could not sleep. All night I sat thinking about this strange thing. I went into the camp again just now. There is still a crowd at the lodge; they stand and look at the place where the picture burned; they talk and talk about it, but no one can explain how it came to shine there, and to die away."

"And what of High Bear and the others of the lodge?" Eli asked.

"They took their bedding and things and went to a neighbor's lodge. The women are going to cut out the leather that the picture was on, and sew in a new piece."

"My medicine has told me all the time," said Ap-si, who had been listening open-mouthed, "that this enemy of mine is soon to die. He must have done something worse than we know of. I don't see how anyone could get worse punishment than this, to be warned that you are to be killed. High Bear's heart is heavy with fear; it serves him right."

It is hard to describe just how I felt. I half wished that I had not painted the picture; it was not pleasant to know that I had caused so much distress to High Bear's poor old mother. But I hoped that all would turn out for the best, and that High Bear would be so thoroughly frightened that he would make no further attempts to kill Ap-si.

At the breakfast table I was the only one that made no comments on the strange occurrence. More than once I caught Dan's shrewd eyes on me. Later he found me alone in the trade room. I tried to avoid him, and started for the door with the water bucket, but he caught me by the sleeve and whirled me around.

"Come now," he said, "out with it! What's your point in all this mischief? What kind of stuff did you use to make the fire pictures?"

I told him everything. He laughed over the story until he nearly choked.

"I knew right away 'twas you did it. Man, man! What wouldn't I give to have been there and seen the faces of those Indians when they stood staring at the picture! High Bear's eyes must have stuck out a foot!"

Dan agreed with me that the motive for my prank was justifiable. "Mr. High Bear is so scared," he said, "that he won't even dare go out and hunt buffalo, to say nothing of trailing after you boys. He isn't going to give that fire picture warning the least chance to come true."

And that, it seemed, was the case. The wonder and gossip about the strange warning passed. But High Bear did not forget. Skunk Cap brought us daily news of him; he stayed close to his lodge, made many sacrifices to the gods, and rarely spoke to anyone.

The trade was now at its height; the Indians were bringing us from thirty to fifty buffalo robes a day, and many skins of wolf, beaver, and deer; so we were all kept busy in the fort from morning to night. It was not until a day in early February that Ap-si and I found time for another hunt.

There had been some chinooks; and the buffalo, drinking from the pools of melted snow, had become poor in flesh. It is a curious fact that they retained their fat only as long as they had to take their necessary drink in the form of cold, dry snow. Antelope meat was the most palatable at that season, and we started out to get some of it. As we mounted our horses, Eli came into the stockade, and in passing, advised us to keep in the open plain and to look out for High Bear.

"Ha! There is nothing to be feared from him!" Ap-si exclaimed. "Since he saw that fire warning he has never been out of camp."

Old Dan kept my secret, and as time passed, we agreed that my prank could not have been more successful. Ap-si and I went about in the camp nearly every evening, and joined in the dances and feasts of the young men, who really liked us. High Bear kept away from us entirely, and if we happened to meet him, he always drew his robe close up over his face and pretended not to see us. So we gave little heed to Eli's warning, except to cross the creek directly behind the fort, so that none of the early risers in the camp should notice our departure.

Smoke was rising from only two or three lodges, and we could see no one moving about. We were sure that we would have a long start ahead of the other hunters, and consequently a better chance to make an early killing.

For two or three miles out from the creek we came on no game of any kind; but as we rode on northward we saw more and more bunches of buffalo grazing to our left in the broken country of the foothills. They were mostly old bulls, which the hunters seldom killed at that season unless they wanted a piece of the tough neck hide to use in making a shield. About ten miles out we saw the first big herd of cows and young animals; with them were a number of antelope.

Fortunately, the wind was from the north; by leaving our horses and crawling for half a mile in a shallow coulee, we thought we could get within easy range of the antelope.

Parts of the coulee were deep enough to let us walk erect. In other places we had to stoop, or even crawl on our hands and knees. In the course of an hour, Ap-si, who was ahead, motioned to me that we had gone far enough.

I crept up to his side, and then, with our rifles cocked and ready, we peered over the bank. The antelope were not fifty yards from us. An old buck saw us immediately, made one long bound, and stopping short, snorted at us; the rest raised their heads in alarm. At that moment I fired and killed the buck. I heard no report from Ap-si's rifle; but as the antelope were bunched and were running away at tremendous speed, I was so busy shooting at them that I had no time to see what the trouble with Ap-si was. Before they were out of range, I managed to kill two more of them. Then I turned to Ap-si.

"It is broken," he said sadly, handing me his rifle.

I took the gun and examined it; the mainspring of the lock had been snapped, and the hammer flopped loosely back and forth on its pivot. "Oh, never mind," I said. "There are at least fifteen of them at the post."

"Good!" he said. "You have killed enough meat anyhow. I will go for the horses; when I come back, I'll help you skin your kills."

He laid down his rifle, which was now useless, and started off at a brisk walk. As the coulee stretched between us and the horses in the shape of a bow, he set out across the plain, on a bee line toward the animals. I went over to the nearest antelope that I had killed, and with my sheath knife began to remove the animal's pelt. Ten minutes later the sound of a distant shot caused me to spring up from my work. I saw a lone horseman riding swiftly toward Ap-si, and the Crow battle song came faintly to my ears.

As I looked, the horseman fired again, and Ap-si threw up his hands and fell to the ground. I snatched up my rifle and ran toward them.

The horseman fired again. I knew at once that the rider was High Bear, and in all my life I never craved anything so much as I did to be right then within range of him. I ran on, faster probably, than I had ever run before. I could see the rider reloading his weapon as he approached his victim.

"He is going to shoot again!" I gasped. "Going to make sure of his work and take the scalp!"

I wondered whether he would then come on to meet me, or whether he would make off with our horses and lie in wait for me in some more advantageous place. And then—I could hardly believe my eyes!—a puff of smoke burst from the grass where my friend lay, and I saw the horseman reel back in his saddle and then pitch forward to the ground. At the same moment Ap-si sprang to his feet, waved a hand at me, and with a triumphant shout ran toward the fallen enemy. I had forgotten that he carried a revolver in his belt— the revolver I had given him at Christmas.

When I reached my friend, he was sitting down, holding the rope of the horse he had captured, and humming—of all things!—a light cradle, or sleeping, song. Now and then he picked up a small stone and tossed it at the body in front of him. Yes, it was High Bear. He lay there on his back, with his arms outstretched. His ashy-gray face looked strangely calm and peaceful; the hatred and meanness had faded from it forever.

"He is certainly dead," I remarked. "Oh my friend, I thought at first that he had killed you!"

"Yes, I know. And you were running here to fight him yourself, and to save me if you could. I shall never forget that, my brother.

And see; this is what killed him, the short gun that you gave me. Who can doubt the gods? They made the fire painting. It worked on this Crow's heart until he felt that his only way to escape what they foretold was to follow and kill me as soon as possible. They put it into your heart to give me this little gun. And when he came riding swiftly and shooting, there was only one thing for me to do. I made him think I was unarmed; at his second shot I fell as if dead; and then when he was near enough I took good aim and shot him."

I looked uneasily over the plain. "Most likely some Crow hunters will soon be coming in sight."

Ap-si sprang to his feet. "You are right. Wait here for me until I get our horses."

He mounted the captured animal and soon brought our own. Then, with a last look at our dead enemy, we rode to the antelope, where Ap-si got his rifle. Without taking any of the meat, we made for the foothills as fast as we could go. In the nearest patch of brush, deep down in a grassy coulee, we unsaddled the Crow horse and turned it loose; the hungry animal would feed there for some time before starting back to its mates.

Turning homeward, we kept in the rough country until we struck the creek above the post. There we hid our horses in an almost impenetra'' 'hicket of willows, and by good luck managed to get into the fort unobserved. About midnight Ap-si went out and brought in the animals.

Skunk Cap and Eli heard with wonder the news of the death of High Bear. "*Ai! Ai!* It was to be!" Skunk Cap exclaimed.

To our great surprise, the hunters never found High Bear's body. When he was missed at camp that evening, everyone said at once that the fate the gods had predicted had come to him. His relatives mourned for him, of course; but to the rest of the camp his passing was of no moment; he had not been well liked and he was soon forgotten. If the Crows suspected that Ap-si and I were responsible for his disappearance, we never knew it.

11

Skunk Cap's Medicine

Originally published in *The Youth's Companion*, September 25, 1919.

There was great rejoicing in both the Crow and Blackfoot lodges over the killing of a white buffalo. The two tribes had joined in the hunt and had amicably adjusted a quarrel between a Crow and a Blackfoot, both of whom claimed the prize. The men of both tribes vied with one another in giving splendid feasts and dances, to which we of the trading post, which was nearby, were always invited. One evening a young messenger came in and said that Last Bear requested us to feast with him.

Skunk Cap, the half-breed medicine man, Ap-si, my young Blackfoot friend, and I went over to the lodge. A large number of guests were already assembled, but there seemed always to be room for a few more. The host gave us a cheery *"Ok-yi!"* in greeting.

"Sit you here at my right hand, man of great medicines," he said

'MY DAUGHTER IS LIKE HER,' SAID THE CROW. 'SHE CAN BEAT
ANY GIRL OF OUR TRIBE. I THINK IT WOULD BE GOOD FOR
THEM TO PLAY AGAINST EACH OTHER.'

to Skunk Cap, and to Ap-si and me he said, "Some-day-to-be-great-
chiefs, sit you there as you can find room."

We found seats next to the women near the doorway, but we
were glad to have even that place in the lodge; it was a great honor
for youths of our age to be asked to feast with those noted medicine
men and warriors.

Last Bear, our host, was a Blackfoot of great prominence,
although he was so badly crippled that he could not ride a horse.
When camp was moved he sat in a travois, built extra large and
strong, and drawn by a gentle and powerful mare. In other days he
had been a great warrior, and it was in a battle with the Sioux that he

had been crippled; a rifle ball that ploughed into the small of his back had partly paralyzed his legs. But for all his misfortune he was perhaps the most sunny-natured and happy man, red or white, that I ever knew. He owned several hundred horses, which relatives herded for him, and he traded some of the increase for necessities and luxuries for his family. His fast buffalo runners he loaned out for one-half of the killings, and so his lodge was always well supplied with meat and robes, although there were many to feed and clothe: three women and five children, all girls of from three years up to eighteen. I once tried to condole with him over his misfortune, but he would not be pitied.

"Listen! It is the way you look at things that makes for content, or for misery," he said. "Whenever I find myself beginning to mourn because I can no longer ride and hunt, and go to war, right there I stop and say to myself, 'Look round and see all that you have!' I look and see my women and children, all of whom love me as I love them. I see my brothers and sisters, all kind and loving. I see my band of horses, so many that I can always sell some to the traders. And then I look up at those three scalps always swinging from the lodgepoles over my head, scalps of the three Sioux I killed just before the bullet struck me here. In sending those enemies to the other world I did a good deed; except for me they might have lived to kill many of my people. And so it is that my heart is always glad."

When we entered the lodge Last Bear was passing his big stone pipe, while the women roasted dried buffalo tongues over the coals. They were fine-looking women, all clad in dresses of soft buckskin or trade cloth, as were the girls, too; every one of the family—even the little three-year-old—had her hair neatly braided. Presently the women placed before each guest a dish containing half a tongue and a little heap of dried bull berries, an acid fruit that went well with the rich oiliness of the meat.

Of course none of us was hungry, but good form demanded that we must each taste the food. So, taking out our sheath knives, we very leisurely cut off a small mouthful now and then, or took a pinch of the berries. It was customary for guests, if they wished, to take home the uneaten portions of food given them, and because dried tongues were a delicacy many prepared to do so after taking a single taste.

Few of the Crows could understand Blackfoot, and none of the Blackfeet could speak Crow; but the sign language afforded a ready means of conversation. During the feasting a Crow told very skillfully with his hands the story of a raid that he and some friends had made against people who lived in houses on top of cliffs in the far south— probably pueblo dwellers of Arizona or New Mexico. It was an extremely interesting story of suffering from hunger and thirst in great deserts, of a battle with the enemy, and of the taking of many horses; by the time he had finished, the last pipe of the feast was going the rounds. He had no sooner concluded it than one of the Crows, a man named Little Owl, pointed at a shinny stick that Last Bear's eldest daughter was rubbing with red paint and said to the host:

"Your daughter has a fine ball stick there, and she looks as if she can use it well."

"She can," Last Bear replied. "She can beat any girl of our tribe playing the ball-and-stick game."

"My daughter is like her," said the Crow. "She can beat any girl of our tribe. I think it would be good for them to play against each other."

"Ah! Ah!" all the guests exclaimed, and one of them added, "I will give a horse as a prize to the winner."

"And I will give one," said Last Bear.

"I will do the same!" Little Owl exclaimed.

I looked at the girl; her eyes were big and bright with excitement.

"Little Mink, you will play against the Crow girl?" Last Bear asked her.

"Yes! Yes! Let the game be tomorrow!" she cried, speaking up quickly then hiding her face in her robe when she saw that all were looking at her.

"Not tomorrow," said her father decisively.

"Oh, no, not tomorrow!" Little Owl agreed, and added, "In the middle of the third day from now, let us say, provided the weather is good." That date was agreed up on just as the pipe was finished.

"*Kyi!* It is burned out," Last Bear announced, ostentatiously

knocking the inverted bowl against the rail of his couch, and at that
the guests rose and began to file out of the lodge. Ap-si and I were
the first to leave, but from the inside Skunk Cap called us back; the
host had detained him, and we returned to hear what it was about.

"I think that three days' time is none too long," Last Bear was
saying. "We have to pray and make strong medicine about this. If
my daughter should lose the game, the Crows would ever after boast
that their women are superior to ours. Now, you have great sacred
power, and I want you to use it; tell me quick what you can do for
the girl so that she shall win."

Skunk Cap did not answer at once; he looked solemnly at the
fire, evidently deep in thought, while Last Bear, Little Mink, and the
rest of the family waited breathlessly for him to speak.

"This is a matter for some thought," he said at last. "I must dream
about it tonight, and perhaps tomorrow night also. Meanwhile all of
you here rest easy; as you say, my medicine is strong. I shall find
something that will help."

As we walked back to the fort, I felt that I would give much to
know whether Skunk Cap really believed that he had power through
the medium of his prayers and medicines to make the sick well, to
bring success to war parties, and hunters, and girl shinny players.

While we were eating breakfast the next morning, Last Bear sent
one of his women to ask Skunk Cap whether he had dreamed anything good.

"You tell him that I was shown a part of what to do," said the old
man solemnly, "but I have to make certain preparations and dream
again tonight. Tell him not to worry; Little Mink shall win the game
if I can find certain things that I am to look for today."

Meanwhile the news of the coming game had spread throughout
both camps. The Indians were eager players of many games, and this
stick-and-ball game was one of their favorites. Naturally, there was
considerable wagering as to the winner, and of course each tribe
favored its own player. Several persons, believing that the greater the
prize the harder their favorite would try to win, pledged themselves to
make a present of a horse or a robe to the victor. Before night, thirty
horses had been promised to the victor; we in the fort contributed to

the outfit a dress length of red trade cloth, a four-point white blanket, and an assortment of beads, needles, and thread.

In the afternoon Skunk Cap took his medicine staff and went out in search of a certain root that his dream had told him to get, and, returning with it, he spent the evening alone, scraping and mashing and brewing the stuff; no one was admitted to his lodge. We heard much talk about Skunk Cap's medicine among those who came in for a little late trading; they all agreed that, even if Last Bear's girl were the poorer player, she would win anyhow through Skunk Cap's help.

After the visitors were all gone I asked Eli Guardipe, the half-breed who had charge of the post, the question that I had been pondering all day:

"Does Skunk Cap really believe in his dreams and medicines and prayers to this and that?"

"Of course he does," Eli replied.

"Though of course they can do no good," I remarked, "they can do no harm to the patient, or whoever seeks the benefit of them."

"Don't be sure that they do no good," Eli said. "I have seen some of these medicine men do wonderful things."

"That's true enough!" Dan Fitzpatrick put in. "We whites don't know everything; some of these old Indian medicine priests and doctors do wonderful things sometimes. More than once I've known them to cure people that I thought would never get well."

"When I was a small boy there was a medicine man in this Blackfoot tribe who could bring thunder and lightning and wind," said Eli.

I laughed; but he stopped me with a gesture of the hand.

"Oh, I'm not joking; I mean it!" he exclaimed. "Anyone will tell you that he did it. My father once took me to the old man's lodge when he was going to bring thunder and lightning. He was a very old man, Seizing Bear by name, white-headed, wrinkled, and bent; yet there was still a lot of strength in his muscles, and he was quick in actions and speech.

"Well, there we were gathered that evening round the old man's lodge fire, and I remember that I trembled as I thought of what was to be done; thunder and lightning are fearful things when far off, to say nothing of when they are booming and blazing close overhead.

"First, old Seizing Bear unrolled his medicine pipe, while he and his woman sang a song for each wrapping; and when the pipe was at last in plain view he lifted it, made a long prayer to the thunder bird, and then danced once round the circle. Returning to his seat, he told his woman to cover the fire. She began heaping ashes on the bright coals and bits of blazing wood, and little by little the light went out until you could not see the person next to you. I snuggled closer and closer to my father and seized one of his hands. It was a still night, with not a breath of wind; looking up through the smoke-hole of the lodge, I could see the stars.

"The old man began to pray: 'Oh, you, my secret helper,' he begged, 'pray for me; ask the gods to favor me this night. Oh, sun, ruler of all the world, and you, World Maker, have pity on me. Come, oh, all-powerful Wind Maker, blow strongly and bring the clouds. Come, oh, you bird of dreadful power, make deafening thunder for us and shoot your fearful fire.'

"He now began to sing his wordless songs, louder and louder, deeper and deeper; once he stopped and cried out, 'The wind! I hear it far off. It is coming. Listen, all you who are gathered here. Listen and you will hear it, too. You do hear it. It is coming, coming, coming closer. Oh, blow hard, you winds, and bring the clouds.'

"He was right. We could hear the wind moaning far off, moaning and booming just as you have heard it many a time, the front of a big wind coming swift across the plain. It struck presently; the lodgepoles creaked, the lodge skin sagged, and the ears of the smokehole fluttered. The old man cried: 'Here is the wind, you hear it!'

"Alternatively Seizing Bear prayed and sang, and he called to us to witness that the elements were hastening to obey him. I could no longer see the stars above. Now the old man was fairly shrieking his entreaties to the gods, and to the thunder bird, finally telling us to watch and be ready.

" 'It comes!' he cried. 'There, you can hear it far off! You do hear it coming nearer and nearer. It is close; it is here; here right over us. Listen! Look! Now you hear it. Poom! Poom!'

"He spoke the truth! Right over our heads there was thunder that shook the lodge, lightning that blinded us, and then silence. No one moved or spoke; there was no more wind; the stars shone in a clear sky; I felt that in a moment more I must in my terror cry out to my father.

"And then I heard the old medicine man say to his woman, 'Uncover the coals; make a blaze; it is all over.' His voice was weak and trembling.

"In a moment or two the flame sprang up, and all was as plain within the lodge. Seizing Bear was sitting, humped over, and his face was wet with perspiration. He feebly raised his hand and gave us the sign to go. It was a long time before I could sleep from thinking of the terrible power that old man possessed. I felt more that I had had bad dreams than that I had actually seen and heard the lightning and thunder and wind answering the call of the medicine man.

"Ah! Friend Spotted Robe, I see you doubt. I do not blame you. I should like to doubt, too, but what I saw I saw; what I heard I heard. You know that I would not tell you an untruth."

"What is it all about?" asked Ap-si, who could not understand English.

"I was telling Spotted Robe about the old medicine man, Seizing Bear, who used to bring thunder and lightning to his lodge," Eli explained in Blackfoot.

"He did that," Ap-si declared, "He died before my time, but I have heard many people tell about it who were in his lodge several times when he made the medicine that brought them."

I went to bed that night in a confused state of mind. Here was the Indian in a new light to me. "How could a man make the elements obey him?" I asked myself over and over. He could not; but there was my friend, Eli, who declared that he had seen it done, and I knew that he would not intentionally tell an untruth.

Early the next morning Last Bear's woman came again to ask Skunk Cap whether his dream had been right and whether he was now ready to begin his work for the girl.

"Not quite yet," he replied, "but I expect to be ready to do something this evening. Go home now and tell your man to purify himself and the girl with sweet-grass smoke, and then to make a fine present to the sun."

I kept pretty close to Skunk Cap all that day. He spent a part of the time pottering with stuff in his medicine pouches, muttering to himself the while; when after supper he left the fort I followed at his heels. Hearing my steps he turned.

"Oh, it is you!" he exclaimed. "Well, come if you want to. I know that you are a friend and will not do anything to break my medicine."

Last Bear was so anxious to know what was to be done that the moment we entered his lodge he began to fidget. According to Blackfoot etiquette it was not his place to introduce the subject, but his impatient nature could stand no further delay, and as soon as we were seated he cried:

"Ah? Ah? Let us hear now what you dreamed! What has your secret helper told you to do for us?"

"I may not tell you my dreams; they are between the gods and me," Skunk Cap replied. "I was told to prepare certain medicines for you and your daughter to drink; here is the mixture in this little cask. You are each to drink a cup of it now, another when you go to bed, one when you arise in the morning, and another just before the game is to be played. Also, in the morning I shall come and paint you both as my dream directed."

"But I am not to play!" the cripple exclaimed, with a sad smile, "Why, then, should I also drink the medicine and be painted?"

"Because you are the girl's father," Skunk Cap replied. "By doing so your courage, your will that she shall win, goes out to her as her need requires. Also, in a way, I got it that some great good fortune is to come to you, provided you do nothing to turn back the good will of certain ancient ones."

There was more talk between the two—eager questionings and vague answers—and then Skunk Cap and I went back to the fort.

The place selected for the game was the open, level plain south of the fort. As the sun neared the zenith the people of both camps began to gather there on foot and horseback until every lodge in the valley was silent. We of the fort went, too, walking behind Last Bear, who rode comfortably in his travois. One of his women led the mare, and beside him walked his daughter, swinging her red-painted, crooked-end shinny stick in one hand and holding the ball of buckskin stuffed with antelope hair in the other. Skunk Cap had already painted the father and the daughter according to his dream. Their hands were red, their faces yellow, with a red sun on the right cheek. The girl walked with a free, easy stride and held her head up proudly. She was fairly tall and her figure finely proportioned. Her beautifully shaped arms and small hands looked as if they had a lot of strength.

Some old men of both tribes had laid out the course for the game, about three hundred yards long. The goal at either end was marked by two buffalo robes thirty or forty feet apart. The player who drove between the two that marked her opponent's side would be the winner. In the centre of the course the old men had gouged a small hole in the frozen ground, and there the play was to begin.

When we took our places in the great crowd lining the course, the Crow girl was walking out to the hole with her father. She was slightly heavier than Little Mink, and I heard some of the Indians near me remark that that was in her favor.

Some young men of both camps now appeared with the horses and finery that had been donated for the winner's prize. There were thirty-eight of the animals and a large heap of feminine stuff. A great laugh went up when someone remarked that the girl who won the outfit would surely have suitors enough.

The old men who had charge of the affair now stationed the Seizer band of each tribe up and down the course to keep it clear, and then gave their instructions to the two girls; they were not to touch the ball with their hands or to strike one another. The Crow girl was to have the east goal, the Blackfoot the west goal.

The ball was now put into the hole, and the girls took their places on either side of it with their shinny sticks crossed at the crooks. An old man stood tensely beside them with hands up.

"Now!" he cried, dropping his hands, and the battle was on.

Shoulder pressing against shoulder, the girls raked at the ball with their sticks, and the clash of wood upon wood was almost as rapid as the rattle of castanets. The Crow girl finally hooked it out and hit it a sharp rap that sent it bounding toward the other's goal. Such a shout as went up from the crowd I thought I had never heard. Above all the voices rose Last Bear's thunderous, commanding orders:

"Run fast, Little Mink! Drive it back!"

Little Mink did run fast—as swiftly and as gracefully as a deer, I thought; she got first to the ball and gave it a lifting blow that sent it high over the Crow girl's head and far back toward the east goal. Then there was another race, a scuffle of shoulder against shoulder and a rattling of sticks. This time the Crow girl got the advantage and kept it until the struggling pair were within a few yards of the west goal, and it looked as if our favorite were going to lose.

Shrieking with excitement, the crowd surged this way and that; the spectators actually became frantic. Last Bear was worst of all. He kept alternately shouting to his woman, who was astride the travois horse, to ride on and keep him opposite the players, and to his daughter to have courage, to play hard, and not to bring shame upon him. Because the horse made an easy pathway for us through the crowd up and down the course, Skunk Cap and Ap-si and I kept close behind it.

THEN FOR A LONG TIME THE TWO SCUFFLED AND
KNOCKED IT ONE WAY AND ANOTHER.

Just as we thought that everything was lost to us, Little Mink again got the advantage, and in three successive hits she drove the ball more than halfway to the other goal. Then for a long time the two scuffled and knocked it one way and another, a few feet to the east, a few feet back to the west. The crowd became silent as they anxiously waited for one or the other to gain the advantage.

Suddenly a great cheer went up from the Blackfeet; Little Mink had hit the ball a strong, free blow and was following it ahead of her opponent. Again and again she reached the ball first and drove it on. At last the two were scuffling for it almost at the line of the east goal. The crowd surged madly that way.

"I can't see them!" Last Bear shouted to his woman. "Ride on! Ride on!"

"I can't!" she shouted back, at the same time vigorously quirting the mare as the animal refused to move.

"Then I'll get out and run!" he cried, beside himself with excitement.

Gripping the edge of the travois, he sprang out and struck the ground standing. His eyes nearly started from his head as he looked down at his legs and saw that they were supporting his body. All of us standing there cried out in amazement, but loudest, weirdest, doubting yet believing, was the cripple's cry:

"I stand! Oh, do I stand?"

He made a step, another one, feebly and with a limp; he gained courage and went on amid shouts of wonder from those who saw. Then from the dense crowd ahead rose another shout, loudest, maddest of all, and a tall, gaunt Blackfoot, turning, came running toward us, crying:

"Little Mink! She wins! She wins!"

And at that Last Bear fell prone in a faint.

It was true; Little Mink had won the game. We got her father back in the travois as he came out of his faint, but he would not stay there; out he crawled and, hanging to the edge, limped along behind it. From that time on Last Bear was able to walk, and even to ride.

"You have done this for me," he said to Skunk Cap, as we gathered in his lodge.

"I tried for it," Skunk Cap answered modestly. "I prayed hard, made strong medicine, but I could not be sure that all would turn out so well."

ALL OF US STANDING THERE CRIED OUT IN AMAZEMENT, BUT LOUDEST,
WEIRDEST, DOUBTING YET BELIEVING, WAS THE CRIPPLE'S CRY.

"Thirty of my horses are yours," said Last Bear. "Choose them
from the herd yourself."

Again I said to myself that I would give much to read Skunk
Cap's mind. I was never able to determine whether he really thought
that it was through his medicine power that the cripple walked and
that the girl won the game. The Indians, and even Eli, believed that
it was. For my own part, I believed that Last Bear had really been
cured of his paralysis for a long time by the healing processes of
nature, but that he had never before been keyed up to making the
attempt to walk, and so had not known that he was able to do so.

"Aha! Now will you believe that the old medicine man really
brought the thunder and lightning?" Eli asked me that evening.

"Hocus-pocus!" I replied. "Hocus-pocus!"

12

A Message to the Mandans

Originally published under the topical title "Memoirs of a
White Indian" in *The Youth's Companion*, January 26, 1911.

The first up-river steamboat of the season tied up for the night in
front of the trading post and the big camp one evening late in
April.

One of the most interesting things we learned was that during
the winter the Mandans had killed a fine albino buffalo, a full-grown
cow, and that the hide had been beautifully tanned into a robe for
Four Bears, the head chief of that tribe. Of course we told this bit of
news to the several Blackfeet chiefs who had come aboard with us,
and it not only interested, it excited them, and they soon went
ashore to talk it over with their people.

Albino buffalo were exceedingly rare, and the Blackfeet regarded
them as the special property of the sun. When a hunter was so for-
tunate as to kill one, none of the meat was taken; but the tongue was

'WHERE ARE THE SIOUX ENCAMPED?'

dried, the hide beautifully tanned, and then, at the great annual reli-gious festival, called by the old-time plainsmen the Medicine Lodge, these were given to the sun, with many prayers for continued favor. With other offerings, they were tied to the top of the great lodge, where in time they were destroyed by the elements.

Later in the evening, when I went to Running Crane's lodge, I found a big council in progress regarding the advisability of pur-chasing the white robe from the Mandans. All were in favor of it, and as each speaker gave his assent he stated the number of horses he would contribute for the purpose. One hundred and thirteen were quickly pledged.

"Well, now that is agreed upon," said Big Lake, "who will go down and make the offer to the Earth-House-People?"

"I will!" cried Ap-si, who was sitting at my side, near the doorway.

"And I will go with him," said I.

Running Crane laughed. "This is not a matter for boys to under-take," said he, "especially for you two who are always getting into trouble."

"But we always get out of it," Ap-si spoke up. "My medicine is good; I have been to war; I have counted coups already; I am not crazy."

"Well, we will think about it. We will talk it over," Running Crane said.

The chiefs had another talk in the morning, and a little later we were told that we could take their message. "Now understand this," Big Lake charged us. "We can give as many as a hundred and fifty horses for the robe; but of course we don't want to pay any more than we can help. You are first to offer fifty head, then, if necessary, seventy-five, a hundred, and up to the limit."

He and Running Crane then handed us a fine pipe and several pounds of tobacco, to be given to the Mandan chiefs, and told us what to say to them in presenting the peace offering. Running Crane added, "You had better cross the river here and ride far out on the plain. In that way you will be less likely to see any enemies, and you will not have to swim the Elk River" (the Yellowstone).

"We are not going to ride," I said. "We are going down in a little boat the trader has given me, and shall return on a fire-boat."

This had been my plan from the start. I had long wanted to make a trip down the river in a small boat, and now the opportunity had come.

It was really a solemn moment when we pushed the little skiff out from shore. Tears streaming from her eyes, Ap-si's devoted mother besought the sun to watch over him and bring him home to her well and successful. The chiefs shouted some last instructions to us; my friend Kipp waved his hat. In a moment or two we rounded a sharp bend and were alone on the river.

Ap-si knew nothing about a boat, and I did not care to row. Nor was there any need to do so, for we had plenty of time, and the current ran all of four miles an hour. I sat in the stern and used a paddle just enough to enable me to steer clear of the many "sawyers" in the stream. Following the channel, there were more than four hundred miles between us and the Mandan village.

Every twenty or thirty miles we passed the cabins of "wood-hawks," as the men were called who cut and sold cord-wood fuel to the steamboats; but we avoided them as much as possible, for Ap-si's sake.

In the afternoon of our first day out, as the time drew near for making camp, we had a serious mishap. Ap-si proposed that we kill some meat. He was hungry, he said, for some nice fat ribs, roasted crisp and brown. Just then an old whitetail buck stepped out of the timber not far ahead of us, and trotting across the wide stretch of sand, plunged knee-deep into the water and began to drink. The boat was exactly in line between him and the low sun, and I knew from experience that he could not see us on account of the blinding glare on the water.

I had no trouble in "sunning the deer," as this method of approaching them is called. I could paddle well and noiselessly, and no doubt we should have got within a few yards had not Ap-si chosen to shoot long before I expected him to. As it was, he missed. The deer wheeled and started back, but at the second shot fell half in and half out of the water, and lay motionless. The skiff grounded in the shallow water about a foot from the deer, and as Ap-si stepped out of it, his rifle in his right hand, he bent over and placed his left hand on the animal's rump to feel if it was fat.

You have seen a jack-in-a-box spring up when the lid was released; that is what the buck did at the touch of the hand, only he did it with all the energy of his four- or five-year-old, two-hundred-pound body, spurred to action by fear. He sprang up, kicked backward, and bolted across the sand into the timber, reaching cover at the same time that Ap-si, completing a most spectacular and unexpected sail in the air, fell, back first, into the river several feet behind the boat, and with a tremendous splash, sank out of sight, closely followed by his rifle, which made an even higher and longer parabola.

The water was deep and swift out there, and when Ap-si came to the surface he was some distance downstream. I started to push out, thinking he might have a broken arm or leg, but he sputtered, "*Mat-si-ki!*" (Nothing wrong!) and made the shore with a few strokes.

But there was something very wrong. Ap-si's fine rifle, the one his good mother had saved so many buffalo robes to purchase for him, was at the bottom of the river.

"'Tis nothing," said Ap-si, stripping off his wet clothing and showing a livid mark on his thigh, where the deer's hoof had struck. "I'll soon have it."

Time and again he dived from the stern of the boat and groped along the muddy bottom. Then we rigged a drag with a line and some fish-hooks, and hauled that along the bottom, with equally useless results. The sun set, and we went ashore, cooked and ate a hasty meal of bacon and flapjacks, then in the darkness pulled across the river and lay down for the night. If any prowling war party had seen the light of our fire, they certainly would not find us there by it. Ap-si felt very blue over his loss, and so did I. To travel through that wild country with only one gun was far from pleasant.

In the morning we made one last try for the weapon, spending a couple of hours in diving and dragging for it. Finally we made up our minds that it was buried deep in the silt of the muddy stream. The Missouri is the most uncertain of rivers, and the most treacherous. Never anywhere flowing smoothly, it ever boils and sucks and swirls, and is full of resistless undertows.

Two days more of delightful paddling and drifting brought us to the Round Butte, a noted landmark of the upper Missouri. It is a sharp-crested, steep hill several hundred feet in height, rising sheer from the south bank of the river.

The sun was an hour high when we landed at the foot of the butte and ascended its rocky slope. On the summit we found, as we had been told we should, a small circular wall of piled stones, within which scouts of various war parties were wont to lie and look over the country. A few shreds of dried meat scattered inside gave evidence that someone had recently been there, and we looked hard in every direction for any signs of an enemy. We saw nothing suspicious. We had a clear view of the river eastward for ten or fifteen miles, and westward for four or five miles. Nothing was to be seen on either of the shores except some deer and buffalo here and there.

We had not attempted to kill any meat since the loss of Ap-si's gun. Hurrying down to the boat, we pushed out. An elk, a yearling cow in fine condition, stood nipping the tender willows along the shore, and Ap-si did the shooting with my rifle. He hurriedly skinned the carcass and cut out a portion of the meat, while I fried some of the liver and made coffee and cakes. It was quite dark when, following our custom, we reembarked and dropped downstream to the opposite shore for our night's rest.

The boat grounded noiselessly on a sandy point; we pulled it up high and dry, spread our bedding close to the bow, and were soon asleep.

Both Ap-si and I were light sleepers. At the muffled crunching of the sand and gravel under padded feet we awoke, nudged one another, and listened. That was all we could do, for the night was not only cloudy, but foggy. Crunch! Crunch! Crunch! Came the footsteps from below, and crunch! Crunch! Crunch! Other footsteps directly out from the timber, still others from a point above us, all closer and closer, with slow but certain regularity.

"What are they, think you?" I asked Ap-si, in a whisper.

"Not hoofed animals. Wait!" he replied.

And then the next instant we knew. From below came the familiar peculiar, breath-expelling, sputtering snort of a bear, and immediately behind and above us it was answered by other snorts, deep, forceful, too loud to be made by anything but grizzlies. A part of the elk we had killed lay on the bow of the boat, and they had caught the scent of it.

For once I had not the slightest idea what to do. In another instant I should certainly have made a break of some kind; but Ap-si's firm hand on my shoulder dragged me down, and with another motion he covered our heads with the robe we had for top cover. "Lie still," he whispered, "and then they won't touch us."

Would they not, indeed! They came closer, walking slowly, frequently snorting. There was a scraping of big claws against the boat, the thud of the side of elk ribs as it was dragged from the bow, the crunching of bones, followed by an angry roar as the other bears came close to the one that had taken the meat. A fierce struggle soon ensued, and one of the fighters planted a huge foot right between us, and with a spurning kick, tossed the covering robe and blanket clear of us. Panic-stricken, we both sprang up, yelling. I blindly thrust out my rifle, and as the muzzle struck against one of them, I pulled the trigger.

The flash of the discharge revealed for an instant three big grizzlies, and one of them gave a fearful growl, or bull-like roar, rather, of pain and anger.

"Run!" cried Ap-si. And I did, straight up the beach in the dark, doubly dark after the blinding flash from my shot. I ran only a few yards when I struck a piece of driftwood and pitched headlong over it into the sand, my rifle flying out of my hand, I knew not where. As I started to rise I heard something crashing away through the brush and timber, and back whence I had come the gurgling and gasping and blowing that every animal makes when shot through the lungs and choking with blood. But that ceased before I got to my feet, and I stood, undecided what to do.

All was quiet. After listening for a moment, I got down on my hands and knees and began to grope for my rifle. I soon found it, and at the same time, from away down the beach, Ap-si called to me.

"Here I am!" I answered.

"Well, you have the rifle. Come you to me."

I set out rather "trembly," feeling my way, walking very slowly listening for any suspicious sound. I intended to make a wide detour round the boat, made it too wide, and brought up against the thick willows at the outer edge of the grove.

"Call often!" I shouted, and Ap-si complied. In a few moments I was beside him.

"Well, they ran away into the timber," he said, "but it is strange that they did so. Nearly always these sticky-mouths [*pahk-si kwo-i*] attack people when they are so close to them."

"One didn't run," I said. "I heard it coughing blood."

"Is it so! Surely the sun was good to us. I consider that he has shown us great favor!" Ap-si exclaimed. And then, pleadingly, "*Hai-yu!* Chief of the sky and earth. Continue to favor us. Allow us to pass safely through all danger by the way, and deliver the words we are carrying to the people of the earth houses."

We had not the courage to grope our way back to the boat and our bedding. The bear I had shot might not be dead, or those that had run away might return, so we sat shivering in the cold mist that rose from the river. As soon as it was light enough to see we got up and cautiously approached the boat. Something that looked as big as a mountain in the shifting clouds or fog lay close beside it. A few more steps, and we saw that it was a bear, a fine, big, dark-furred grizzly. The elk ribs were gone.

We took off the hide as quickly as possible, threw it into the boat, and paddled down to a small island, where we remained all day, fleshing the big skin and sleeping by turns. Straight bread, though, was poor living. Toward evening we reembarked, and soon drifted down to a herd of buffalo, out of which we got a fine yearling bull. Then we did have a feast.

I had come to Montana by way of the river, and had some recollection of various places along it. My friend Kipp, too, had given me a rough sketch of it, so when, two or three days after killing the bear, we passed over a big, swift rapid, I knew that we were close to the mouth of Milk River and the country of the Assiniboin and Yanktonais Sioux. Somewhere in the course of the next fifty to a hundred miles there was certain to be a big camp of them, and we had to pass it unseen.

They themselves were bad enough, but still worse were old Sitting Bull's hostile Brulés, Tetons, and Hunkpapas, who much frequented the camp of their ostensibly peaceful kin.

We went ashore, crossed a narrow bottom, and climbed a low hill, from which we had a view of the country for some miles ahead. Game appeared to be scarce, but there were no signs of men save the smoke of an approaching steamer. We passed it an hour later, and noticed that the pilot-house was encased in steel plates. As we drifted slowly by, and close to it, the captain and a number of passengers crowded to the rail of the upper deck to see us.

"Where are the Sioux encamped?" I shouted.

"They're all gathered at the mouth of Milk River!" the captain answered. "You'd better look out for 'em!"

"You and your red pardner goin' to fight em', sonny?" a big, long-haired, buckskin-clad individual asked, and then inanely laughed.

"No," I answered. "We forgot to put on our fringed buckskin clothes, and can't go to war without them!"

At that the crowd jeered, and he scowled.

"What said he—and the other man?" Ap-si asked.

I told him, and then he scowled. "I have fought them," he exclaimed, "and that is more than Long Hair ever did, I'm sure! Yes, and I'll fight them again!"

About four o'clock we went ashore on an island and had our evening meal, roasting, too, a lot of ribs for subsequent cold meals. According to my chart, we were only a few miles above Milk River and the big Sioux camp, and dangerous as it was, there was nothing to do but travel nights until we should pass the hostile country. We pushed out into the stream again at dusk. Generally, we could hear the roar of the current around the sawyers, but the water flowed silently past some that pointed downstream with a long slant. Twice in the first hour or so I ran afoul of them, and the skiff came near capsizing. The strain on my nerves was wearing. I wondered if I could stand it until morning.

Again the boat struck a sawyer, one with a projecting limb, and swung sidewise on it, dipped, and began to fill. Just in time Ap-si sprang up and broke the branch, and we righted and floated on.

Before long we heard the barking and howling of apparently hundreds of dogs. Then, gliding round a bend, we saw the Sioux camp, cluster after cluster of lodges strung along a big bottom and glowing yellow from the evening fires within them. People were singing, drumming, talking, and laughing. Children shouted and squalled. Horses neighed and squealed. Close to the water forty or fifty young men were performing a scalp dance by the light of a big open fire. Noiselessly we floated down past them and by the long string of lodges, a mile-long camp, and then Ap-si said to me, "Run the boat ashore over there on the north side. I want to go back and have a look at this camp."

I demurred and he pleaded. He wanted to see where the good horses were tied, with a view of returning with a party later and raiding the camp. I gave in and landed at the lower end of a small, narrow grove.

"No matter what happens, what you hear," he said, as he stepped out of the boat, "stay right here until the Seven Persons [the Great Dipper] mark the middle of the night. Then, if I do not appear, go on and deliver the message, for you will know that I am no more."

"Hold on! Wait! You shan't go up there!" I cried. But he had already vanished in the darkness, and all was still. I saw that I had made a mistake; that I should have kept on paddling; but I had not thought that he would do anything more than take a quick survey of the camp. His last words, however, implied that he had something desperate in mind. Before long, what with my nervousness and the strain of the long day, the added worry of trying to steer the skiff in the dark, I became so restless that I could not sit still. I got out of the skiff and paced up and down the sand before it, and every moment seemed an hour.

The noise of the big camp gradually died down, until I finally could hear nothing but the barking of the dogs. Then suddenly a loud tumult of yells, calls, and gunshots broke out, and I was sure that Ap-si was concerned in it. For ten or fifteen minutes I stood listening. At last I heard a twig snap back in the timber. A moment later, as silent as a cat, Ap-si crossed the sand, and in a voice scarce above a whisper, called my name.

"Yes," I answered.

He came up to me. "See what I have captured," he whispered.

I could not see, but I felt. "Why, it is a many-shooting gun!"

"Yes," he said, "just that. I wandered round in the camp, blanket over my face like all the other young men, and no one noticed me. At last I saw one of the dancers going home, and I followed, jerked the gun from him and knocked him down with the barrel of it. But I did not knock hard enough. He yelled, and people came running,

I ran, too, straight back toward the plain, they following. Then I doubled on them, and here I am. Come on, let's push off."

"Ap-si, you shouldn't have done it," I said, after we were several miles down the river. "They had not harmed you. You had no right to take the gun."

He laughed grimly. "They have killed three of my relatives," he replied, "and stolen our horses. I have not even begun to be revenged."

From there on, until we approached the Mandan village, we traveled entirely by night, hiding by day on an island, and covering the skiff with willows. And not a night passed but we had one or more narrow escapes from being wrecked by the sawyers. At last we came to the Mandans, tied our skiff at the watering-place, and ascending the steep bank, entered their village.

By signs we told the first man we met who we were, and he led us to the lodge of their aged chief, who made us welcome, and at once ordered his wives to place food before us. In a few moments a young half-breed, who could talk English, came in, and through me, and then him, Ap-si, with great dignity and impressiveness for one so young, delivered the Blackfeet message and presents.

"My son," the old man answered, promptly, "you have come two days too late. We have given the robe to our gods, and it lies now in the sacred house, from which it cannot be taken, ever."

Later I saw the sacred house, a barrel-like structure ten or twelve feet high, made of poles and split wood and bound with rawhide. It stood directly in front of a big, empty lodge, which the half-breed told us was the council-house. I would have given much to see the white robe and the other sacred offerings in the gods' barrel-house, but they could be displayed only once a year, during the great religious festival which had just been concluded.

But all is well that ends well. We had a week's pleasant visit with the kindly Mandans, and then, loaded with presents to ourselves and for our chiefs, we boarded the *Far West*, and ten days later were at home.

13

A Day's Hunt

Originally published under the topical title "Memoirs of a White Indian" in *The Youth's Companion*, February 16, 1911.

One evening, soon after our visit to the Mandan's, Ap-si's mother sliced some meat, and then quickly brushed the palm of her left hand with the palm of her right one, which in the sign language was telling us that the meat was all gone.

"Well, there is plenty more out on the plains, "said Ap-si.

The big camp had been so long there in the bottom that the game had been pretty well killed off or frightened away from the vicinity. So to make sure of a successful hunt, we rose several hours before daylight, saddled our horses, and rode away south on the trail running up through the pine-clad breaks of the river to the plain. Once on top, the horses were given free rein, and they broke into a lope, which rapidly increased the distance between us and the river. A thin slice of moon and the stars were all the light we had, but that was sufficient for us to keep our southerly course. It was a fine, warm

HE DID NOT ATTEMPT TO BITE . . . AS I PASSED HIM UP TO AP-SI.

June night, and the air was heavy with the odor of sweet-grass, flowers, and fresh-growing sage. Ap-si asked if I noticed it.

"It is all so pleasant," he said, "that I am full up with happiness. It is all I can do to keep from singing a joy song."

We were near Big Crooked Creek when day began to break, and we rode to the summit of one of the steep, flat-topped buttes just south of it for a view of the country. We tied the horses in a clump of gnarled and stunted pines, and sat down. The eastern horizon grew brighter, flushed to a fiery red, and the first rays of the sun wiped out the shadows in the valley at our feet.

Down in the bottom opposite us, at the mouth of a coulee, stood a lone buffalo bull, the only animal in sight near us; but farther south and to the east and west we could see many bands of buffalo and antelope feeding on the short, rich grass. While we were planning to approach the nearest of the buffalo herds, a rumbling noise attracted our attention.

"It is a band of buffalo," said I.

"It is not," said Ap-si. "Horses' feet are making that sound. Perhaps the enemy."

We drew still farther back in the shelter of the pines, quite sure that we could not have been seen climbing the butte in the dusk of early morning, and that if an enemy were approaching, he could not see us now unless he should chance to climb as we had done, to get a view of the country.

In a few moments a band of forty or fifty wild horses swept into sight in the valley of the creek to the northwest, and came tearing down the bottom at great speed. A big, proud bay stallion led them, and he was a beast to stir one's heart as he passed, his heavy long mane and tail streaming straight back, his shapely feet hitting the turf with the springy lightness that a fox might have envied.

Occasionally he turned his head to look back; it was plain that he was holding himself in to suit the pace of those behind. There were no laggards; the herd followed compactly, the old mares on the outside, the colts, yearlings, and two-year-olds in the center. Evidently they had been badly scared.

Soon they passed the butte and disappeared round a bend of the creek. They had not been an unusual sight—wild horses were then fairly plentiful on the plains between the Missouri and the Yellowstone—but the beauty and grace and strength of their leader were something not to be forgotten. "Oh! Oh! If he were only mine!" Ap-si fairly groaned.

But that was out of the question. Our horses had not sufficient wind and speed to overtake him, and if they had, and we succeeded in roping him, he would without doubt put up such a fight that we would have been glad to escape with our lives.

We remained seated in the pines, waiting to discover what had alarmed the horses. The old buffalo bull had paid little heed to them; he had only raised his head for a moment and looked at them. Then he lowered it again and stood motionless and humped up, a most melancholy object.

Patches of his thick winter coat, faded to a lusterless, dingy yellow, still clung to the new growth of dark hair, which, coming so late in the spring, was a sure sign of old age and waning vigor. His once beautifully curved, sharp black horns were now mere rounded stubs. His beard, even, seemed to be ragged and unkempt. Evidently a younger generation had driven him from the herds of which he had long been master.

The horses had barely disappeared round the bend when a big gray wolf—attracted no doubt by the sound of their passing—came to the rim of the valley just back of the bull, and looked inquisitively up and down. More surely than Ap-si, even, he had recognized the thudding of horses' hoofs on the hard ground, and his mouth watered; better than a buffalo calf, better than antelope or deer or elk was the meat of a colt, and he wanted some.

But the herd had passed and he was disappointed. He stared at the bull, turned, and walked away a short distance, turned again, and came back to the rim, sat down on his haunches, and pointing his nose to the sky, gave three long, loud, and melancholy howls. From far to the southwest came the answer of one of his kind; a moment later another long-drawn, wailing cry from the southeast.

"He is calling his brothers. I think he means to feast upon the old bull," said Ap-si.

The wolf turned and looked back whence the cries had come. In a few minutes one of those that had answered him appeared, leisurely trotting, and the two met. They touched noises and wagged their tails, and then looked expectantly off to the southeast. The other one that had heard the call soon came, and with him another, apparently his mate; and then there was more nose-sniffing and tail-wagging, and once two of them playfully leaped into the air and snapped at each other.

By this time they were all mixed up, and we could not distinguish the one that had given the call; but he that was probably the one suddenly led off over the rim of the plain and down the slope of the valley, and the rest followed. Walking leisurely, they made a complete circle round the old bull at a distance of fifty or sixty yards, but he paid not the slightest attention to them. Having completed the round, they stopped and sat back on their haunches and stared at him for some time, occasionally turning their heads to look up and down the valley, and frequently they raised their long, pointed black noses to sniff the passing breeze, trying to catch the scent of anything inimical to their plan. Luckily the wind was blowing from them to us.

Then they made their rush. Two of them made a feint of attacking in front, leaping this way and that past the bull's head with amazing rapidity, while the others endeavored to get to his heels. Instinctively he realized their plan; perhaps he had been attacked before. He sought to protect his hind legs, and to do that he tried to face all ways at once. Old as he was, and huge—he no doubt weighed more than a ton—between anger and fear, he developed a surprising agility. To run from them was impossible; the battle had to be fought out there on the spot. He lunged now at this one, again at that one, wheeling all the time; in fact, spinning round and round like a huge, erratic top. We could hear his snorts of rage. "It is not fair. I am going to save him!" I exclaimed, raising my rifle; but Ap-si stayed my aim.

"It is his time to die," said he.

"But he wants to live as much as we do."

"Yes, he does, but it is not for us to interfere. World Maker created the buffalo for food for men and wolves. Should you save this old and worn-out bull from them, they would only travel on and pull down the next one—and it, perhaps, a young cow that *we* may need some day."

There was good sound sense in that argument, and I lowered my rifle. The bull was whirling round quickly, kicking vigorously and deftly, once planting a hind foot in the side of an animal with such force as to send it whirling away through the air.

But in a few minutes the bull showed signs of weakening, and no wonder; the tremendous strain of his defense was too much for his old and stiffened joints. He kicked less frequently; the wolves dashed in closer and closer. In passing, one of them snapped its jaws on a hind leg, and just above the gambrel joint, where the great tendon—the hamstring—is most exposed. Lightning-like as it was, that one snap severed the cord, and the bull lurched backward and sidewise, and nearly fell. As he struggled to right himself, all four of the enemy made a rush for the other hind leg, and the rear part of his body dropped to the ground inertly. For a moment he held his fore parts erect, his great shaggy head elevated at a most unwonted angle, and what a pitiable sight he was! But the strain was too great; little by little his fore legs gave way, altogether and suddenly at the last, and his whole body was prone on the ground.

The wolves were watching, waiting for this, and made a simultaneous dash for his flank—not for his throat, as is erroneously said to be their method of finishing a victim. It was their intention to take their meal from that part of him, from the living flesh.

But that I could not stand. I broke from cover and ran down the hill. The wolves stared at me a moment, and then, pausing frequently trotted away up the coulee. I could have shot one or two of them, but forbore, as their summer coat was valueless. I scrambled up the bank and put the old bull out of misery with a bullet through his brain.

Ap-si followed me down with the horses, and as I mounted mine and we rode on, he remarked that the whites were queer people.

"You are hard to understand," said he. "To see you drive those wolves away and end their work with a bullet, one would think that you have the heart of a woman."

Born and reared in the elemental life, it was natural for him to look at suffering and cruelty with indifference.

Topping the rim of the valley, we saw the four wolves idling along out on the plain. As soon as they saw us, they turned and circled back toward the creek and the feast they knew was awaiting them. "Let us hunt now and get our morning meal," said Ap-si. "I am hungry."

There was nothing in sight between us and a low ridge a mile farther out on the plain, but just beyond that we had seen a lot of game. We loped our horses to the foot of it, then dismounted, and leading them, cautiously approached the summit.

Peeping over the crest, we saw four or five wee wolf pups, not far down the slope, playing together and awkwardly tumbling over one another. Their mother lay on top of a mound of yellow earth recently thrown up, which we knew had come from the hole she had dug in the hillside for them. Slight as was the exposure of our heads, she saw us as soon as we did her, and almost instantly the pups turned tail and disappeared into their den. No doubt her low growl of a certain intonation had warned them of danger. As they went out of sight, she sprang to her feet, and running off three or four hundred yards along the ridge, stopped and turned to watch us.

"I want one of those pups for a pet," I said to Ap-si. "Will you help me get it?"

"Ask me about it after I have had something to eat," he replied. "What I want is one of those buffalo out there."

There were a hundred or more of them, mainly cows and calves, feeding about on the plain not far beyond the foot of the slope; still farther there were other bands of them. There was no coulee, no rise of ground to screen us, and I did not see how we were to get near enough; but Ap-si, always full of hunting expedients, found a way.

Well aware that buffalo, and for that matter, all game, pay no attention to a horse unless there is a rider on it, he stepped close up to his animal, just back of the shoulder, and guiding it with his bridle of rawhide thong, gently prodded it on in such a manner that it was always moving obliquely in front of him. I did likewise with my horse, stooping so that my head would not show above his back; and thus we went down the slope. It was slow work because there was difficulty in keeping the horses in just the right position. Frequently we stopped and allowed them to put their heads down and crop a mouthful of grass, just as a free horse would naturally do.

At first the buffalo kept raising their heads and staring at us, but before we reached the foot of the ridge, they ceased to pay any attention; there was nothing alarming in a couple of stray grazing horses. A slow stalk of a farther two hundred yards enabled us to get so close to the nearest of the herd that we could hear them rip the grass.

Then Ap-si gave the signal, we sprang into the saddle, and at once the horses threw off their listlessness. One glance at us was enough to cause the buffalo to rush together, the funny little calves bobbing under their mothers to the center of the herd, and then they were off with a mighty rattling and pounding of hoofs.

We soon overtook them, and riding up alongside a fat, two-year-old bull, I gave him a shot in the ribs. Next a fine big dry cow drew my fire, and lastly I shot another young bull. That was all the meat I had use for, and I dropped out of the race. Ap-si kept on, rapidly firing his rifle and leaving a string of dead and dying animals behind him.

I followed and finished the cripples. Among them was a cow whose calf had dropped out of the herd with her. When the little fellow saw me, he ran to the nearest bush of sage, and kneeling down, but still erect on his hind legs, thrust his head into it, and thus imagined that he had securely hid himself.

As the trading post wagon was to come out for the meat I killed, I determined to take the little fellow alive and make a pet of him; he could be taken in by the teamster. Dismounting, I walked over and laid my hand on his back. He flinched at the touch of it, and thrust his head still farther into the bush. Then I gently stroked him, finally raised him, and put my finger into his mouth, and he suckled it greedily. With that I had him. Turning back toward my horse, he followed and crowded against me to get at the finger again.

In a few minutes Ap-si came riding back, and said that he had killed eleven of the band. I picketed my calf, collected some dead sagebrush for a fire, while Ap-si cut out a couple of buffalo tongues, and we soon had a good meal of them, broiled. Then we began skinning our animals and cutting the meat for handling; but before we had cared for more than two of them, a large party of hunters from the camp came riding over the ridge, followed by some of their women and the post wagon, and we had plenty of help. Ap-si gave all but two of his animals to some widows and old men who always followed the hunters; my three I turned over to the teamster and his assistant, also the little calf, and then we were free to go after the wolves.

As we approached the den, both the father and the mother of the little ones were standing farther along the ridge, and there they remained, watching us, no doubt, with anxious hearts. We found that there were three holes in the hillside instead of one, and had we not seen the pups disappear right at the north foot of the larger mount, we should not have known which to dig into. Wolves and coyotes and foxes always have several holes where they rear their young, no doubt for their better protection from any marauder; often the different ones are connected by small cross-passages.

Luckily for us, there were no rocks in the soil. With our skinning knives for picks, and a shoulder blade from a nearby buffalo skeleton for a shovel, we began enlarging the hole. The ground was hard and dry, and the dust of it nearly choked us; our shovel was a mere toy; the hot sun made perspiration fairly drip from us as we gouged and slashed the walls of the den and threw out the debris. Every few moments we would stop to listen, thinking that if we had dug down anywhere near the pups, we could hear them breathe. We learned something about that before we were done.

The hole went down at an angle of forty-five degrees for about

five feet, and then turned sharply to the right much less precipi-
tously. We were two hours getting to the bend. I was doing the digging at the time. A foot or more back from the end of the
enlargement I noticed a tuft of hair in the dust close to the left wall,
and was finally impelled to give it a pull. It remained in place, and
somewhat surprised, I gave it a harder tweak; still it remained fast,
and pulling still harder, lo! I dragged a dust-covered pup from a
niche in the passage that had been just large enough for him to crawl
into.

He did not attempt to bite, nor did he show great fear of me as I
passed him up to Ap-si, who promptly thrust him into a sack that
happened to be tied on my saddle. He was very fuzzy-haired, light
gray in color, and his head seemed enormously large for his small
body.

Thus encouraged, we dug all the harder, and a couple of feet farther on found another pup, also cached in a niche. We should have
passed him, too, had not the tip of his tail betrayed his hiding place.
I found later that wolves always dig these side niches in their dens for
their young to hide in; any large animal—a bear, for instance - in
enlarging the passage, is sure to cover them with the falling earth
ahead of him, and thus oftentimes, no doubt, the helpless pups
escape notice.

"We have one each, now let's go home," Ap-si proposed. "You
know what World Maker said when he caught all the rabbits on
earth for a feast, and then let some of them go. 'One must never take
all of anything,' said he, 'and thus there will always be some left for
others who hunger.' "

We mounted our horses and went home, well satisfied with the
day's experiences. The wolf pups thrived on diluted condensed milk,
and waxed fat, and soon got old enough to eat meat. They became
very tame, and I had many a good time romping and playing with
them. They were never chained up, ran with the dogs, and knew the
call of the dinner bell as well as we did. When they were a year old I
presented them to the St. Louis Zoo.

The buffalo calf did not do well on the canned milk, and was
like to die, when we found a different supply for it, a mother, in fact,

in an old gentle mare that had lost her colt. At first she refused to have anything to do with it, and we were obliged to tie her fast; but she finally became as attached to it as if it were her own colt.

When it was a year old we gave it to Michel Pablo and Charles Allard. It was one of the few they had to start the great herd they recently sold to the Canadian government.

14

Because of Ap-si's Song

Originally published under the topical title "More Memoirs of a White Indian" in *The Youth's Companion*, February 15, 1912.

One August morning, when we rode out from the big camp on the Musselshell, Ap-si sang, "I care for nothing! I care for nothing! *Ahk-si-ki-wa! Ahk-si-ki-wa! Ahk-si-ki-wa!*"

"Ap-si, do not sing that song!" exclaimed his mother, who was riding with her daughter, Paiota, close behind us. "For three days, while your father was preparing to go on that last raid against the enemy, he sang it, and he never returned. It is an unlucky song for this family. I forbid you to sing it!"

That morning we were after antelope; we wanted to get six skins for a soft, light and white dress for Paiota. The embroidery pattern for it had been decided on: two suns of red, yellow, and blue porcupine quills on the breast, and a butterfly—symbol of good dreams and good luck—on the back. Long fringe was to be sewed into all

"DO NOT MIND ME," AP-SI SAID. "I AM GETTING OUT.
SHOOT! SHOOT AS FAST AS YOU CAN!"

the seams, and two hundred elk teeth were to be strung in rows on the shoulders and sleeves. While Ap-si and I hunted, Paiota and her mother were to pick cherries, if some could be found.

After riding along the valley for five or six miles, we turned east up a long coulee to the edge of the plain. Ap-si, who rode in the lead, had on his hunting cap—the skin and horns of an antelope's head stuffed in a lifelike manner with dry grass. As we neared the plain, he motioned us to stop. Reining in his horse, he made it take the last of the ascent slowly, a step or two at a time, while he rose up in his stirrups as much as possible, in order to get a quick and comprehensive view ahead. Suddenly he ducked, slid from the horse, and beckoned us to join him. In a moment we were off our animals and beside him.

"Step on a little farther," he said, "and you will see them, a big band of antelope. Be careful to show no more than the top of your head above the ground."

Sure enough, there were a hundred or more antelope about a mile out on the brown plain, all lying down except a few old bucks. These occasionally cropped a mouthful of grass while they stood on the outskirts of the herd, looking in all directions and sniffing the wind for any signs of danger.

Between them and us the plain was level, but not far beyond their resting place a low ridge was parallel with the river for several miles, and away to the south we could see that it was cut by a deep, long coulee that ran far out from the valley.

"*Kyi!* You two turn back to that berry patch," said Ap-si to his mother and sister, "and we will go on up the valley, then into the coulee, and back behind the ridge until we are opposite the antelope. If they stay where they are, we shall be able to kill all we need from the top of the ridge."

That meant that we should make a circuit of six or seven miles. As we parted from the women at the edge of the cherry-brush patch by the river, Ap-si said to his mother;

"We shall be gone a long time, but no matter; stay here until we come. Or if you hear us shoot, ride out to where we shall be at work taking the skins and meat."

We left them busily stripping the bushes of the ripe fruit, and we rode as fast as we could along a buffalo trail. When we came to the mouth of the coulee, Ap-si rode up the side of it, had another look out on the plain, and reported that the game was still lying down. As the coulee was narrow and rough and winding, we were a long time in working our way in it across the plain and through the low ridge.

Once behind the high ground, we rode out of the coulee and northward along the foot of the ridge until we thought that we must be opposite the game; then we dismounted, tied the horses to some sagebrush, and walked slowly to the summit. Ap-si advanced inch by inch until he could look over it. "They are still lying down," he said, as he drew back, "but we are not opposite them by two long gun-shots. Come on."

After going a quarter of a mile farther north along the slope, we again turned up to the summit of the ridge. Down at its foot, from one to two hundred yards away, the antelope were lying, all unaware of our approach. There was a clump of sage in front of me. I crept to it and looked at them through the leafy stalks.

A few feet to my left, Ap-si quickly rose until his horned cap plainly showed above the summit, and then as quickly dodged down again. He did this four times, and its effect on the antelope was amusing. The old sentinel bucks saw what they thought was the head of a stranger of their own kind, and they resented his presence; he had no right to come and join their family of does and young. At the first sight of Ap-si's cap, their hair bristled like that of an angry dog. At the second sight of it they moved a step or two toward our hiding place, and stood sharply stamping the ground with their forefeet. All the others sprang from their beds in alarm and crowded together behind them, with their hair, too, on end.

The third time Ap-si's cap bobbed up, the old bucks moved forward several yards; the fourth time they came charging toward us to drive off the supposed intruder, and were followed closely by the whole band.

That was what we had ridden all the morning to bring about. We aimed always at one or another of the big bucks. Our first shots nearly paralyzed the band with fright. They turned and ran quartering across the ridge and up wind, while one after another fell to the ground, until the six we needed were down; then we ceased shooting, and hurried to put the wounded out of their misery.

"We have been a long time getting them" Ap-si said. "Mother and Paiota must have been watching us. No doubt they will soon be coming out to help with the work here."

We kept looking for them while we skinned and cut up one animal after another, but they did not come. "They must be gathering a lot of cherries," said Ap-si. "Well, we cannot have too many. It is a long time from now to the next fruit season."

We carried all the meat to one place, laid it out on the clean grass, and tied a handkerchief to a bush of sage in the center of the game, to keep the coyotes and wolves away from it. Then taking the hides and what meat we could handily tie to the saddles, we started for the river.

By the time we came to the cherry patch, the afternoon was half gone. We saw nothing of the woman or the girl, or of their horses. Concluding that they had grown tired of waiting for us and had gone home, we were about to start for home ourselves, when we discovered their rawhide saddle-pouches half-filled with fruit lying in the place where their horses had been tied. The little hand-pouches lay there, too, evidently thrown down in haste, for the cherries that they had contained were spilled on the ground.

"What has happened?" Ap-si exclaimed. "Why did they leave their pickings and hurry away from here?"

We found no signs of anything that could have frightened them, but we did find the trail of the horses, going up the valley, not toward camp, but straight away from it. That was the more alarming and mysterious, as the horses had plainly been going at topmost speed.

It was easy to follow the prints of the horses' feet in the broad, dusty game-trail, which soon led us to the river, and across it into

the next body of timber. But here we found something unexpected.
Since they had passed, a large herd of buffalo had swept up through
the bottom, and their big hoofs had obliterated the tracks of the
horses. Whence had come the buffalo? We had not seen them. And
what had caused them to run so madly up the valley? They had
been frightened into flight after the women had passed the place.
Ap-si rode through the grove this way and that, searching the
ground for some explanation, and crying loudly to his gods for
help.

"O sun," he cried, "help me to find and get them safely home,
and I will sacrifice to you my own body."

By that he meant that he would undergo severe torture at the
next medicine lodge, or annual religious festival—short of death
itself, the greatest sacrifice that a Blackfoot could make to his
gods.

It was I, riding out to the edge of the bottom, who found the
reason for the flight of the women: the tracks of several horses on top
of the split hoofprints of the buffalo. The women were being pursued. Calling Ap-si, I showed the tracks to him.

"I cannot believe," he said, "that these riders were hunters from
our camp. Come on!"

A mile farther on there was an abrupt bend of the river to the
west, and here the buffalo, leaving the valley and going straight
south, had followed a wide, deep depression of the plain that
extended far toward the Bull Buttes. The horse tracks continued on
up the valley. We took it for granted that the women were in the
lead, and we hoped that they would be able to keep their distance.
They certainly rode good horses. Night was coming on; they might
escape their pursuers in the darkness.

Two miles farther on we entered a large, heavily timbered grove,
and as we were dashing through the center of it, Paiota suddenly
sprang out of a clump of willows near the trail and called to us to
stop. Her eyes were big with fear, and when Ap-si sprang from his
horse and embraced her, she began to tremble, and was so hysterical
that it was hard to understand what she was saying.

"They are a war party—eight riders—we saw them coming—had good start—they scared some buffalo on the other side of the river—that followed us—then buffalo turned off—my horse too slow—mother made me get off and hide here—she went on leading it."

"Well, you stay here in this brush until we come for you," Ap-si said. He remounted his horse. "But if we don't come by morning, then go on down to the camp, and mind you keep in the thick timber as much of the way as you can."

"Yes, brother," she replied, and then, as we started, she called after us: "They ride Blackfoot horses—Sings High's old pinto is one—none fast!"

That meant that we had some chance of overtaking them. They had no doubt raided the outside herds of the camp, and in their haste had got none but slow old travois and pack animals that were easy to catch.

Perspiration was washing brown furrows in Ap-si's red-painted cheeks, and the look in his eyes was wild; he was half out of his mind from anxiety. We had not lost more than a couple of minutes with Paiota, and we tried to make that up. We crossed the river from one bottom to another several times, and soon, on the farther side of a ford, discovered that we were not far behind the raiders; for the gravel on the shore was still wet with the water that had dripped from their horses.

"Take courage! Take courage!" Ap-si called out, as he pointed.

"I do take courage," I replied, although I was far from feeling courageous. It was no small thing for us two boys to chase eight men, but we had to go on and do our best to save Ap-si's mother, even if we died for it.

The sun was near setting when we rode up a wide coulee, and came out on the plain; then we saw the eight riders about a half a mile away. Ap-si's mother was perhaps a quarter of a mile ahead of them, and still leading Paiota's horse. She was gradually circling, with the intention, of course, of heading back toward camp; but she was losing ground, for her pursuers were cutting across the circle. We cut, too.

Our horses, which were dripping with perspiration and covered with lather, were gasping for breath; they could not keep up the run much longer, but neither could the mounts of those ahead of us. They also had been going at a killing pace, and moreover, ours were the better animals. It was plain that we were slowly gaining on them.

Every few moments the fleeing woman turned in her saddle to look back. I wondered if she noticed Ap-si and me, if she knew who were, or thought us two more of the enemy. And then I saw her suddenly pull back on her bridle rope, bring her horse to a standstill, and spring from its back. Before I could guess what she was going to do, she had climbed on the other one she had been leading, and was off again.

She had now a fairly fresh horse under her, but she had lost ground by changing, and had allowed herself to get within gunshot of the enemy. First one and then another fired in her direction. Probably they did not wish to kill her, but risked doing so in the hope of shooting her horse.

Up to this time their attention had been centered on the woman. But now Ap-si fired, and I also sent a shot after them, but aimed high above their heads. The pounding of their horses' hoofs probably drowned the report of our rifles, but one or the other of the bullets struck the ground beside them and threw up a puff of dust. They turned and saw us.

They did not slacken their pace or turn to fire at us; but they drew close together as they continued to urge on their horses, no doubt to discuss what had better be done. We fired more shots, but none took effect. Our foes scattered again, stopped, dismounted to get steady aim, and began firing at us.

And now Ap-si's mother, having made out who we were, did exactly what any Blackfoot mother would do in like circumstances; she tried to save her son by sacrificing herself. Pulling in her horse, she began to circle back, in order to entice the party into following her again. Standing up in his saddle, Ap-si made signs to her to go on. We had stopped, too, now, and I was already on the ground, with my rifle carefully aimed at the enemy.

My bullet struck a horse, and down it went. Although that was no loss, since they had captured the horse that Ap-si's mother had abandoned, my bullet had a good effect. They found it too risky to crouch there as marks for our long-range weapons; so remounting, seven came charging at us, and the eighth man continued the chase after the woman. She waited, however, until she saw us riding away as fast as we could from such superior numbers, and then she made haste to outride her pursuer.

Every moment or two a bullet dropped close to us. But we were shooting, too, the enemy were getting no nearer, and night was now beginning to fall. If we could only reach the timber back in the valley, everything might yet be well with us; for in the night, in thick woods, the pursued have every advantage.

I looked at Ap-si's mother as I threw in another cartridge; on her fresher horse, she was easily gaining on the man in pursuit of her. And then *thud!* I knew what the sickening sound meant even before I turned to look, or heard the almost simultaneous scream of pain that Ap-si's horse gave as it reeled and fell.

"This is the end," I said to myself. I stopped my horse, sprang to the ground, and started to help my friend out from under his dying animal. The enemy were not more than four hundred yards away, and were coming as fast as they could ride.

"Do not mind me," Ap-si said. "I am getting out. Shoot! Shoot as fast as you can at them!"

I knelt down, aimed and fired at the nearest rider, fired again; and then I was astonished to see them all wheel sharply to the east.

"Look!" Look!" cried Ap-si, as he struggled to his feet.

Turning, I saw forty or fifty riders coming swiftly from the river, more than a mile away from us, but only a few hundred yards from Ap-si's mother. Best of all, there came to our ears faintly on the still evening air the heartening sound of the Blackfeet war-song. We saw the woman meet them, saw her pursuer go down, and we shouted with joy, and sent a last few shots after our flying foes. Our rescuers headed after them.

We took the saddle from the dead animal, and started toward

Ap'si's mother, who was hurrying to us. She sprang from her horse, and crying with joy, threw her arms about her boy and kissed him rapturously.

"Well! Well! It is all right, my mother," said he, very softly, as he stroked and patted her shoulder.

"Yes, but we might all have been killed," said she, "and it all came of your singing that dreadful '*Ahk-si-ki-wa*' song. Take this as a warning; never sing it again."

For the life of me, I could not help laughing. She scolded me for making fun of the gods and their mysterious powers, but ended by kissing me, too, and calling me her white son.

We looked out on the plain. Pursuers and pursued had vanished in the gathering night. Ap-si mounted the horse that his mother had brought him, and we started homeward; we picked up Paiota at her hiding place in the brush. She had seen the Blackfoot party coming, and had begged them to hurry and save us. She, too, scolded Ap-si for singing the unlucky song. But in a few moments all her fears and sufferings of the day were forgotten, and she began to urge us to hurry and recover the berry-pouches as soon as possible. We did pick them up, and lunched on their contents.

On arriving in camp, we learned that a returning hunter had seen the war party riding away up the valley on the stolen horses, and had given the alarm. The raiders proved to be Cheyennes. The seven managed to escape in the dark night, but our people thought that the one man killed offset the loss of their horses. It was considered a great "coup" to kill a Cheyenne, for the Cheyennes were a brave people.

The next day we brought in the antelope meat and hides. There was a long argument as to whether it would be lucky for Paiota to wear a dress made from the skins of antelope killed on the day of such dangerous experiences. Finally, the matter was taken to Red Eagle, the sun priest, or medicine man, who decided that the garment would be exceptionally lucky because the Blackfeet had got the best of the day's happenings. So the dress was made, and very hand-some Paiota looked in it.

"After all," said the good mother, as she sewed in the last quills of the butterfly symbol, "this giver of good dreams will break any bad luck there may have been in the getting of these skins."

15

Rivois's Tale of Hardship

Originally published under the topical title "More Memoirs of a
White Indian" in *The Youth's Companion*, February 15, 1912.

In November Old Stum-ikso-to-kaw-pi (Bull Turns-round) had a
dream that made the hunters frequent the mountains more than
the plains, in quest of meat. His secret helper—his "medicine"—had
told him that he must procure the skin of a wolverine, and sacrifice
it to the sun; thus would he gain great favor with the god. It was out
of the question for him to go into the mountains for one, for he was
old and fat and short-winded. Even sitting on a horse tired him. So
he offered to give horses to anyone who would bring him the desired
skin

"*Kyi!* Here's a chance for us to earn some horses easily, and have
some fun, too!" Ap-si said to me. "Let's go away up in the big pine
timber on the Belt Mountains and trap one of those animals for
him."

'THEY WERE NOT AFRAID, FOR HAD WE NOT A TREATY WITH THE CROWS?'

Well, we got the skin, but this is not so much the story of that skin as of how we met Rivois, and heard the astonishing tale of his misfortune, which I am going to repeat to you.

We spent the day in preparing for the trip, and started the next morning with three horses, one of which was loaded with our outfit.

At noon on the second day we reached our destination, a heavy body of timber high up on the divide between the Judith River and Arrow Creek. We found a fine camping place beside a small spring, and near a grassy park, where there was ample feed for the horses. Here we put up a pole lodge, and thatched it with many layers of balsam boughs. Inside we put up an old piece of lodge lining that Ap-si's mother had given us. By sundown we were sitting on our couch of buffalo robes, eating broiled venison steaks. Rising early the next morning, we started up the mountain to reconnoiter. There had been one cold autumnal storm. On the plains the snow had disappeared, but here it still lingered in shady places; higher up, the ground and rocks were covered with it.

Taking a diagonal course up the mountain, we came out on the extreme eastern end of its long and broken summit. We now worked westward, looking sharply for game, and soon discovered three big rams lying on a shale slope that extended from the summit down into the timber. We had been traveling very cautiously, just peering over the top of every rise before exposing ourselves. Yet one of the rams caught sight of Ap-si's black hair or my fox-skin turban; he rose to his feet, and standing motionless, stared in our direction. As the animals were at least five hundred yards away, too far for a shot, I told Ap-si to stand where he was, while I tried to get nearer to them.

I backed down out of sight, climbed up a draw to the broken crest of the mountain, and crossed it in the shelter of some boulders. Then I slipped noiselessly along the south slope, until I thought that I had gone far enough. Then I climbed to the summit once more, and looked over to the other side. At that moment I heard the report of a gun, followed by a great clattering of loose shale.

"Ap-si has sneaked up on them and got the shot," I said to myself, as I sprang up on the crest; and then involuntarily I sprang back. On the slope below lay a dead ram, and climbing up toward it from the timber was an Indian.

But was it an Indian? There was something in the glimpse I had of him that caused me to stop and cautiously peer over the crest again.

The man was now bending, knife in hand, over the dead ram. He had on buckskin leggings and a white, hooded blanket coat, such as most of the plains Indians wore in winter. The hood concealed his face, but I had almost concluded that he was an Indian, and perhaps an enemy, when all doubt as to what to do disappeared. Ap-si, with his gun thrown over his shoulder, came into view, walking unconcernedly toward the stranger.

At that I stepped out and began to descend the slope. The man heard me, seized his gun, and looked up. He was a white man. "How!" said I, involuntarily raising my hand and making the peace sign.

"How! How!" he replied, doing the same, and then turning to look sharply at Ap-si.

"How! Ut-sé-na-kwan!" (Gros Ventre Man!) Ap-si exclaimed; and then I knew who the stranger was, for I had often heard of him.

"You are Mr. Rivois," I said.

"Yes. And you?"

"I am Ap-pe-kun-ny," I replied.

"Oh, yes, the boy from the states, who lives with our trader friend down on the Judith. Who would think, now, that we should meet here on this mountaintop?"

We scraped a place free from the snow, sat down, and exchanged news. Rivois said that he had left Fort Benton a month before on a bear-trapping expedition, and that his wife—a Blackfoot—his daughter, and her husband were with him. They were camped under the west end of the mountain, about two miles from our lodge.

I told him then why we were there, and he laughed.

"Bull Turns-Round, the stingy old fish, will be likely to die of fright before he gets that skin," he said. Wolverines are scarce in this part of the country. If it were up in the main range of the Rockies, now, anywhere from Sun River northward, there would be no trouble in finding them. But I don't want to discourage you. Once in a while a wolverine prowls round here."

We rose to go, for we were becoming chilly. When we parted, the old man said he would move his camp up beside us the following day.

Thus it was that I met Charles Rivois, one of the notable characters of the primitive Northwest. His parents—French Creoles—moved from New Orleans to St. Charles, Missouri, in 1798 or '99, and there he was born on July 4, 1803. St. Louis and St. Charles were then in their infancy, and on the extreme border of civilization; westward was the great wilderness, the unknown land extending to the Pacific. Lewis and Clark had not yet started on their adventurous expedition to that far-distant ocean.

It was no wonder that Rivois, the boy, seeing the fur-laden dugouts and *bateaux* of the trappers, and the pack-trains of the overland traders trailing in and out of the little settlement, was fired with the desire to join the adventurers. The talk that he heard was all of the castor (beaver), the buffalo, and the Indians.

In 1820, when he was seventeen, he made his first trip into the Black Hills—the sacred spirit-land of the Sioux—with a small company of trappers. Later he counted Manuel Lisa, Brent and Jim Bridger among his friends, and went on several expeditions with them into the far Southwest and West. In 1829 he entered the employ of the American Fur Company. Pierre Chouteau, one of the founders of the great organization, appointed him post hunter at Fort Union, at the mouth of the Yellowstone. He did not remain regularly with the company, however, but went out with the Indians or on lone trapping expeditions with his family whenever the whim seized him.

Sure enough, on the following day, we found Rivois's big lodge set up close to ours, some children playing round, and women busy tanning buckskins, evidently for some clothes for their men. We felt a little more easy in mind. It was not the season for war parties to be abroad; still, one might come along, and in that case four men were better than two, if it came to a fight.

That evening we were invited over to Rivois's lodge to supper, and met his son-in-law, an English half-breed named Harris, whose father had been a subfactor for the Hudson Bay Company. After supper I asked Rivois for a story. We had been talking about the Crow Indians and the chances of a war party of them stealing our horses, and Rivois recalled a terrible experience that he had with some of the tribe.

"In 1833 the American Fur Company had a little post way up on the Yellowstone River, about a hundred and thirty or forty miles from Fort Union," he began. "I was stationed at Fort Union, and one day Mr. Mackenzie, the factor, sent for me. 'Rivois,' said he, 'I want you to take ten cargoes of powder and ball and vermilion and brass wire to the upper post. Robes are getting prime, and the Crows up there will be needing more ammunition than we have now at the place."

" 'Very well, sir,' said I.

" 'You may take four men with you,' said he, 'and you can choose them.'

"I gave the word to Charles Chouquette, to Baptiste Rondin, Antoine Chabernan (Buckshot), and because we had been boys together in St. Charles, to Louis Niquette, a new employee of the company. The next morning we saddled ten pack animals and others to ride, lashed on the cargoes and a teakettle, and started. We crossed the Missouri on the big ferry-boat that had just been built.

"The packs were heavy and we traveled slowly, not more than twenty miles a day. It was early in November, and ice skimmed over the water-holes at night. All went well with us and we were happy, singing all day the songs of the *voyageur*. At night we cooked fat ribs and tongues of the buffalo, brewed tea, told stories, laughed, and at last, rolled in our robes, slept soundly. We were in the country of the Crows, and they had made a treaty with the factor, Mackenzie, and swore solemnly by their gods that they would kill no more of the company's men.

"It was daylight on the fifth day of our journey that, on awaking, I saw many Crow warriors standing near the foot of our beds. I glanced the other way; Crows were there also. Crows surrounded us—several hundred of them—on all sides. I roused my comrades, and they sat up, rubbing their eyes. Yet, like me, they were not afraid, for had we not a treaty with the Crows?

"But I saw no smile on any Indian face; instead, only scowls. Their leader spoke, and Buckshot, understanding their language, interpreted. 'Get up, white men,' he said, 'and hand us your guns, your pistols, your knives.'

"We obeyed. What could five men do against two hundred? They swarmed round us, and jostled and pushed one another in the attempt to reach our weapons. They seized our robes, our cargoes, our teakettle and little sack of tea, and then our clothing. They made us strip off everything, and there we stood, shivering in the cold morning air. 'Now then,' said their leader, 'return whence you came, and never set foot in the Crow country again.'

" 'Allow us, at least, to go on to the little post and get clothing,' Buckshot said.

" 'No, return whence you came, or die on the trail,' said this cruel savage. And with that the others, taking their quirts, lariats and bows, set upon us, whipping, lashing, beating our freezing bodies, and driving us back whence we had come. Oh, it was terrible what we suffered. The pain could have been borne, but furious rage over our bitter humiliation and our utter helplessness consumed us. They drove us for perhaps three hundred yards, and then, laughing, jeering, left us to go our way.

"Ah, but we were cold and sore! Once out of their sight we ran, in order to get warm. But not far; our feet were tender; the rough gravel of the plain hurt them; we were obliged to walk. We left the trail and took to the river bottoms, cutting across the bends, and again traveling long distances down the soft and sandy shore.

"As the sun rose higher and higher we became more uncomfortable. Water, of course, we had in plenty, but hunger beset us. There was nothing to eat all that day except the dry, tasteless berries of the rose-bush, and they seemed to afford no nourishment.

"Night came. We had dreaded it, and now it was upon us, and there would be no moon, even. We tried to start a fire by rubbing dry sticks together, by using one as a drill twirled between the hands, but the wood didn't even get hot. At last we burrowed into the sand on the shore, and for a time we slept. Then the sand lost its heat; we began to tremble from the cold. One by one we rose and rubbed our numb limbs. It was past midnight when the bit of a moon appeared. Dim as was the light, we stumbled along down the river, now following the shore, again following a game trail through the timber. My old playmate's courage broke; he wept. It was terrible to hear him.

" 'Louis! Louis! Cheer up, my friend; all will be well,' I kept saying to him, but still he wept; and Buckshot, a big, black-eyed, black-haired, bull-muscle man, tried to put spirit in him by calling him 'baby.' Oh, it was terrible, that long, long night!

"The next afternoon we found the bull-berries, a half-dozen trees loaded with fruit, all their acid gone, and now sweet from the effect of many frosts. The sight cheered us. We sprang for them, and began to strip the clusters with both hands. How good they tasted!

"The little trees grew in a patch of rose brush cut by game trails. We had all gathered round one tree, stripped it, and started for the next one, when up out of the brush rose a huge grizzly bear. Snorting, it charged on us. We fled, one this way, one that, running, leaping with all our poor strength. I heard a loud cry, and looking back, saw Louis spring off the high bank into the river. The bear stopped at the edge of it and looked curiously down.

"We all saw him, and running on, circled to strike the shore lower down. Buckshot, who was leading, plunged into the water and swam out with powerful strokes, for Louis was giving up—struggling feebly, at times disappearing altogether. Buckshot got him to shore, and we rolled him round, emptied the water out of him, chafed him, and brought him to life, but he was too weak to walk. Buckshot picked him up, and we went on, leaving the huge bear in possession of the berry patch. After a while Louis became able to walk, but we traveled slowly; the soles of our feet were beginning to bleed.

"Looking back at it now, I don't see how we ever succeeded in reaching the Missouri, half-frozen, hungry, footsore as we were. But reach it we did in the late afternoon of the fourth day. Louis had gone crazy for the time being, and we led him, pushed him, whipped him along between us all the last day. We came to the shore of the river; it is very wide there in front of the fort and, moreover, there was a strong west wind. Nevertheless, we shouted as loud as we could, ran up and down the shore, and waved our hands. The answer we got was a shot; the sentry thought us a war party deriding him. The bullet struck the bank above us.

"At that, both Chouquette and Rondin broke down and wept, and I was ready to cry myself. Our nerve was gone. But not so with Buckshot. We took to the brush, but he remained standing on the shore, signaling, signaling, making the Indian sign for help.

"The sentry's shot roused the fort, and Mackenzie himself, taking up his telescope, climbed into the bastion and had a look at us.

" 'Why, it's a white man,' he said, 'and naked! He looks like Buckshot. Take the ferry, some of you, and go after him.'

"And so we came to the fort, being met at the landing by the storekeeper and a crowd of comrades with robes and blankets to cover our nakedness. Ah, how good it was to sit by a fire once more, to eat hot things! And how we slept that night, and far into the next day! We were soon up and busy again. Even Louis recovered quickly from his madness.

"Ah, well, boys," Rivois concluded, "it's time we were all abed."

He had told that tale in the Blackfeet tongue, so that all could understand. On the way to our lodge, Ap-si remarked:

"And he said that there on the shore of the river he was near to crying, too. That was just his way of excusing the others for crying. No hardship, no pain, could make Ut-se'-na-kwan cry. He is too brave for that."

16

The Passing of Back-in-Sight

Originally published under the topical title "Memoirs of a
White Indian" in *The Youth's Companion*, January 12, 1911.

February passed, and the people began to watch the skies, for it
was the moon-of-the-coming-of-the-web-feet. And lo! one warm
evening a big wedge of Canada geese passed over the camp, honking
loudly. Everybody rushed out of the lodges and stood watching
them, their faces brightening at the sight, their voices expressing
their pleasure and satisfaction. "Summer has come!" "I shall see green
grass once more!" "Berry season is close!" "We shall now go to war!"
were some of the exclamations of those standing near me.

"And you, my son, what shall you do?" my friend Running
Crane asked.

"I shall go trout-fishing," I replied.

My answer did not please him, nor was my "partner," Ap-si, at all
enthusiastic when I asked him to go up on Rock Creek with me.

'COME BACK! COME BACK!'

However, he finally promised to accompany me, saying that while I cast my flies for the unclean things he would do some beaver-trapping.

The Blackfeet have a curious aversion to all things living in the waters—turtles, fish, mollusks—believing them to be the food of the "under water people," dreaded inhabitants of rivers and lakes who are ever on the lookout to seize human beings unaware and drag them down to the black depths.

As the weather continued to be pleasant, a few days later we lashed some bedding, provisions, a pot and frying-pan, and beaver traps on a pack animal, saddled our riding horses, and struck out for the foot of the eastern end of the Little Rocky Mountains, thirty or more miles north of camp.

The sun was setting when we arrived at our destination. Near the banks of the creek we found an old war-house snugly hidden in a grove of pines, but Ap-si objected to using it.

"We know not who built it," he protested. "Most likely some

enemy, Crees, Crows, or Sioux, and it would be bad luck for us to camp in it. There they prayed to their gods, made sacrifices to them, and their medicine still lingers in the place."

"Well, there isn't time before dark to build a shelter," I said, "and it looks like rain. Let's use this one tonight, and tomorrow, if you still wish to, we'll put up a lodge of our own."

He agreed to that, but with many grumblings and prophecies of disaster. We hurriedly put on a fresh thatching of fir boughs, collected some firewood, and having picketed the horses, made ourselves comfortable for the night. Before going to bed I got out my tackle case and put a few flies and leaders to soak, to be ready for some early fishing.

Ap-si woke me with a cry, "Look out, he's going to shoot!" He had had a nightmare, but the dream was a very real thing to him. As he sprang out of his robes and started to build a fire, he solemnly told me that we were going to get into trouble of some kind; that everything plainly indicated its coming. In the first place our sleeping in the enemy's war-house, in the next his dream, and lastly that the rising sun was painted—as the Blackfeet term what we call sundogs—a sure sign that an enemy was approaching us.

I sat up and tried to argue him out of his depression. "Now, listen," I said. "everyone in the country who looks at the sun this morning sees that it is painted. The white men in the mining towns along the big mountains, those in Fort Benton, and those scattered along the big river cutting wood for the steamboats—all see it. The Crows over on the Yellowstone, Sioux far to the east, the Crees away to the north of us also see it. Now do you think that it is warning all these different people that an enemy is approaching them?"

"Probably where they are they don't see the painting," Ap-si replied. "And if they do, it may not be a sign to them as it is to us Blackfeet, given us by the gods away back in the beginning of the world. And then, there is my dream, another warning."

"Yes. Anyone who eats as much buffalo meat as you did last night is sure to have bad dreams. I have bad ones when I eat too much. So does everyone, but the dreams mean nothing."

A pitying smile flitted across his face; he hesitated a moment, and then said:

"As it is with white men's eyes, so it is with their shadows.

[Meaning their souls.] They have not the power to see the many things that we do on every side. Their shadows cannot leave their bodies when they sleep, and go forth on strange adventures; cannot receive warnings of what is to happen, as ours do. I don't know why I say these things to you, except that I love you very much, and wish that you could obtain this power which all white men seem to lack."

That was one of the few times I ever argued with my friend about matters of belief, and it was the last time. Young as I was, I had sense enough to see that no profit could come to either of us by doing so and that if continued, it might someday lead to a break in our relations.

After a leisurely breakfast, we started up the creek, Ap-si with his traps and I with my fishing-rod and tackle, each carrying a rifle. A ten-minute walk brought us to a string of three ponds which the beavers had made by damming the creek, and in each of them were two or more of their houses, mounds of various-sized sticks rising three or four feet above the water.

The dams were new, and from the number of fresh slides and cuttings, and tracks along them and the shores of the ponds, we judged that there were twenty-five or thirty animals in the colony.

At the sight Ap-si forgot his gloomy forebodings, dropped everything, and began to tear out a sluiceway in the lower dam that would lower the water in the pond a foot or more. That would cause great uneasiness among the beavers. At dark they would hasten to repair the damage, and one or more of them would perhaps get caught in the deadly traps set in the break.

While Ap-si tugged and dug and pried I jointed my rod, seated the reel, ran out the line, and rigged a cast of flies. "Don't step near the shore where the beavers will smell your tracks," Ap-si cautioned me. "Stand way back and fish, and if you catch anything I will wade round and lift it out for you."

I had some difficulty finding a place from which to make a cast until I came to a spot where a cluster of trees had been cut down. Standing at the edge of this, close to the trunk of a big cottonwood, and forcing the line out sidewise, I dropped the flies as near as possible to one of the houses, where the water was six or seven feet deep.

The instant they struck, a dozen or more large and hungry trout shot up

at them from the depths with such haste and energy that they all leaped
clear from the water, and over, missing the lines by several inches.

None but a fly-fisherman, and one who has not cast a fly for a
long time, can appreciate the pleasurable thrill of excitement I felt at
the sight of so many big fellows darting up out of the water.

"Ap-si! *Sum-is!*" (See them!) I cried, drawing back the line to
make another cast.

Just as I did so, from some distance up the creek there came to
our ears a piercing, melancholy cry, as of someone in distress. My
line fell limply to the ground, and I listened, rod suspended.

Ap-si had turned from his task to watch my cast. He gave me one
meaning look, as much as to say, "I told you so. Here is the trouble
I prophesied," and then he turned and stared upstream, open-
mouthed. Again, and after an interval, still again that cry of anguish,
of despair, was repeated, and then although we stood listening for
along time, we heard it no more.

Ap-si had snatched up his rifle, and now came across the dam
and round to me, stepping cautiously, frequently stopping to look
round and listen. I laid down my rod, moved back a few paces,
picked up my rifle, and awaited him.

"What was it?" I asked, in the sign language, by holding my right
hand up, palm toward him, and working it rapidly two or there
times, like the inverted pendulum of a clock. For answer he flung his
hand forward and then out to the right, signifying, "I don't know."
He came closer, and we whispered.

"It sounded like the cry of a man in great pain," I said.

"It was more like a woman's cry," he answered. "But I think it
was a ghost."

I shook my head negatively, but knew better than to smile at his
belief. And with the awful cry still ringing in my ears, it was not a
time to laugh.

"Remember that we have slept in the enemy's war-house; that my
dream foretold trouble; that the sun was painted. I am sure something is going to happen to us," Ap-si continued.

I could not assert that nothing would happen. I was, to put it
mildly, very uneasy. "What shall we do—pick up our things and get
out of here?" I asked.

"No, not yet. If it was a ghost, there would be no use trying to hide from it. If it wasn't one, we ought to find out what did make the cries. Let's go up that way."

We started, rifles ready and cocked, and walked very cautiously and slowly, a few steps at a time, with frequent long stops to look and listen. We scrutinized every foot of ground we covered, and thus, in the course of an hour or two, traversed a greater distance than one's voice could be heard. But we saw no one, saw no tracks except those of deer and elk, a buffalo, one big bear's trail, and the very fresh tracks of a mountain lion. Finally we turned and made a big circle through the mountainside timber, and returned to the beaver dams to fish and set the traps. .

But all our pleasure in it was gone. We both would have liked then and there to leave for home; but pride, and chiefly the fear of being laughed at, prevented even mention of it.

Ap-si set two traps, I made one cast and caught two large trout, enough for two meals for myself, and we went back to the war-house. Ap-si would not enter it again, and insisted on packing the outfit and moving down the creek to the last of the pines. There we made a small brush shelter to screen the blaze of our fire, and as soon as we finished cooking and eating supper we put out the blaze, took our bedding, and lay down a hundred yards away. If anyone had seen the fire and should be sneaking toward it they would not find us, and we would at least have a good chance to get away on foot.

"It might have been an owl that made the cries," Ap-si suggested, after we had lain down for the night.

"I believe it was some poor lost woman," I answered.

Neither of us slept much. We were only boys, one very superstitious, both of us abroad where we had no business to be, in a country infested by war parties from many tribes. We were glad when daylight came and we could use our eyes as well as our ears.

After an early breakfast, and watering and repicketing the horses, we walked up to the beaver ponds, but I did not carry my fishing-rod. As we neared the place a band of mule-deer broke from a fir thicket, stopped and stared at us for a moment, and then went bounding, in the stiff, awkward jumps peculiar to them, away up the mountainside. The sight of them encouraged me; they would not have been there if anyone were about, and I mentioned the fact. But my companion gloomily remarked that ghosts could make themselves invisible to animals, as well as to men.

Each of the traps held a beaver, drowned in deep water, as Ap-si had cunningly contrived they should be.

This, at least, was encouraging. We took the two animals back into the timber and skinned them, and then Ap-si started to reset the traps; but he never did it. Again that fearful mournful cry broke the stillness of the mountainside. My friend turned gray, and I must have turned pale.

"Come on! Come on!" said he. "We must find out about this."

"Yes, we'll find out. I am sure it is a person," I said, "and not far from here."

We skulked along the way we had taken the day before, but went more quickly this time. After a lapse of ten minutes or so, the cry was repeated, and we decided that the top of a sparsely timbered, small, rocky butte beside the creek was the spot from which it came. We worked our way more cautiously, keeping in the dense alder and willow growth to the foot of it, then from pine to pine and boulder to boulder up the side.

At last we were near the top, not more than thirty yards from it. We looked up cautiously over the edge of a big rock, and saw a man standing on the extreme summit. He was a man of apparently fifty years, tall, slender, gray-haired, dressed in cowskin shirt and leggings, and wearing and old white blanket. He held an old muzzle-loader across his body, and was looking intently, now one way, then another, as if expecting someone. And as we watched him, he wailed out again the cry we had heard. It seemed to be a word, perhaps a name, he was calling, but the language was strange to us.

"He is a crazy man," Ap-si whispered.

"Yes. Let's shout, and then step out where he can see us," I proposed.

We did so, but he seemed not to be surprised, nor did he raise his gun as he watched us advance.

"*How! How! Nap-i!*" (How! Old Man!) said Ap-si, and to our surprise, he returned the Blackfeet greeting in that language, replying, "*How, man-i-kap-iks!*" (Young men!) and added, "Whence come you? Have you seen my son?"

We answered his questions, and he continued, speaking very

good Blackfoot, but rather hesitatingly and with an often strange accent, "I parted from him here, from him and his companions. They went to make war against the Sioux, promising to return and meet me here. We waited, I and my people, waited long, but they did not come, so we moved back into our own country."

"Where is that?" Ap-si asked.

"Up on the backbone of the world."

"Oh, you are a Kootenay, then?"

"Of course. I thought you knew. I am Back-in-Sight. You must have heard of me. I married Flyer, you know, sister of your chief, Big Lake. But now where do you think my son can be? Why doesn't he return?"

The old man moved uneasily; the light faded from his eyes. After a moment or two of evident mental distress, he said, "That is the trouble. I don't seem to remember things well. Sometimes I think that he left here last moon, and sometimes it seems that it was a winter, maybe two or three winters ago. But he will come all right; he will come before long. I must be patient. I must wait. Perhaps he went a long way off."

"Yes, that's it, he must have gone a long way," Ap-si said, soothingly, and to me he whispered, "Very crazy, isn't he?"

"Well," he again addressed the Kootenay, "the big camp is down on the river. Big Lake is there, and will be glad to see you. Come with us and rest a few days, and then you can return here and wait for your son."

The old man readily agreed to do so as soon as he could put up a sign or marker of his trail. This he did by laying on a boulder an arrow he seemed to have carved for the purpose, and weighting it in place with a rock. The shaft pointed southeast, in the direction of the big camp.

"There! If he does come, he will follow, and he will find me with the Blackfeet," he said, and then was childishly eager to start at once.

We picked up the traps, went down and packed our outfit, and as the Kootenay had no horse, we told him to ride the pack animal, putting most of its burden on our own horses.

It was probably eleven o'clock by the time we struck out across the plain from the creek, and we rode fast in order to make the river and home that night. Little did Ap-si and I think what was to happen before we arrived there.

On the way Back-in-sight was by turns silent and talkative, and rational enough except for the strange delusion about the son whom he was never to see again. All went well with us until we were about two miles from the breaks of the river. Then, topping a low ridge, we almost ran into a party of men on foot, fifteen of them, also heading for the river—a war party, of course. The instant poor old Back-in-Sight saw them he gave a cry of delight, said something in his own language we could not of course understand, and urged his horse—our horse, rather—down the hill at full speed toward the enemy.

"Come back! Come back!" we shouted. "They are enemies."

He paid no heed, so we followed, trying to head him off; but the packhorse was the best of the three animals, and neither of us could even get up alongside of him.

The war party had stopped the instant they saw us, and stood, guns ready, to meet, as they thought, our charge. Ap-si and I wheeled off to the right, giving up the chase; it was folly to rush into the range of that silent, determined, waiting band. The old man kept on and on, shouting and waving his gun; and then when he was almost upon them, they raised their weapons and fired.

The gun dropped from his hand, he bowed over almost double for a second, then pitched headlong to the ground. The horse stopped, staggered, and also dropped.

Wheeling again, we rode along about three hundred yards from the party, and emptied our rifles at them, but without any apparent effect. Nor did their random shots come anywhere near us. Again we turned, and this time headed for home, pushing our horses to the utmost limit, until, just at dusk, we arrived in camp and told our tale.

In less than twenty minutes several hundred men had mounted their war-horses, and led by Ap-si, on a fresh animal, were rushing in the gathering night up through the breaks on our back trail. We saw no more of them until the next noon, when they came charging back into the valley, singing the song of victory, and holding aloft on sticks fifteen scalps. They had destroyed every one of the Assiniboin war party, and thus was the poor old Kootenay's death avenged. Big Lake and his woman brought in the remains and buried them.

"He has found his son at last," they said.

17

A Council and a Chase

Originally published in *The Youth's Companion*, July 3, 1919.

Our trade with the Crows at the Flatwillow post was even heavier than we had hoped it would be. Consequently, Eli Guardipe had to send Skunk Cap, the half-breed medicine man who had induced the Crows to trade with us, to the main post on the Missouri to notify Joseph Kipp that we must have more ammunition and trade goods without delay. When the old man returned he brought interesting news.

The Blackfoot hunters had seen a white buffalo cow in the breaks of the Musselshell River and had pursued her until their horses were winded. When last seen she was far in advance of the rest of the herd and was running with undiminished speed toward the Snowy Mountains. Many of the Blackfoot hunters were moving out on the plains with their lodges and families, hoping to find and kill the

'LET US JOIN THEM!' HE CRIED. 'LET US ALL, ALL THE PRAIRIE PEOPLES,
GET TOGETHER AND WIPE OUT THE WHITE SKINS!'

sacred animal. Big Lake, their head chief, sent word that he was
coming to visit the Crow chief, Gray Bull, hoping that by their joint
efforts they could avert any trouble that might arise between men of
the two tribes hunting in the same country.

Big Lake arrived the next day with several minor chiefs of the
tribe and rode straight through the camp to the lodge of the Crow
chief. Just as the Blackfoot dismounted from his horse, Gray Bull
stepped out of his lodge and embraced and kissed him, and then said
in the guest's language:

"I am glad to see you here. My lodge is your lodge, my food is
your food, all that I have is yours. Come in and let us feast and
smoke together."

Then Gray Bull greeted the minor chiefs and led the way into his
lodge, where he pointed out a seat to each one; Big Lake sat beside
him on his couch, the others nearer the doorway. The women began
to prepare the feast of broiled, dried buffalo tongues and stewed

dried serviceberries. The host filled his big stone pipe and as a token of esteem passed it to Big Lake to light. The Blackfoot blew the first puff of smoke skyward, and the second puff toward the ground.

"*Hai-yu! Spuhts-uh mut-tup-pi,*" he said reverently. "*Hai-yu ni-ksis-tan an-on.*" (Oh! Above people. Oh! Our mother [earth]. Now pity us all.)

He took a few whiffs and passed the pipe to Gray Bull, who after smoking it went to the extreme right of the semicircle, and from there back without a pause to the man at the extreme left, who resumed the smoking.

Ap-si and I, as befitted our humble rank as warriors, had seats near the doorway. Presently the women had the feast ready—a dish of tongue and berries, and a bowl of hot soup for each one. The Indians never ate ravenously, shoving the food down with both hands, as I have seen some white men do. Instead, they took their food slowly, masticated it thoroughly, and made the meal an occasion for talk and laughter. It is true that they had no forks, but they cut the food deliberately, and into small pieces.

The Crows and Blackfeet gathered round the lodge fire were handsome men. Almost without exception they were tall and slender and wiry, and their hands and feet were models for a sculptor's chisel. Their faces were of pleasing contour. Their eyes, which were large and clear, expressed a high order of intelligence. Their heavy, long hair was neatly braided. They were dressed mostly in buckskin and buffalo leather clothing; some wore blanket togas, and others buffalo robes, on the flesh side of which they had painted in striking colors the pictorial record of their brave deeds.

As I sat there watching them I remembered what [George] Catlin had said: that the Crows and the Blackfeet were the most beautifully and romantically dressed of all the American Indians. And against that these Northwestern people numbered among them some of the finest gentlemen he had ever met. He was right: they were gentlemen, not from training, but by instinct. And gentle they were at home, to one another and to their families, although in war they were terrible foes.

When the feast was over and the big pipe had been refilled and lighted, Gray Bull said to his guest:

"Did a party of Cheyennes carrying the peace pipe visit you some time ago? No? Well, they came to us just before we moved over here from the Yellowstone."

"Ah! Ah!" everyone exclaimed, showing great interest; and Big Lake quickly asked, "What said they? Why did they visit you?"

Gray Bull was silent for a moment; nervously rubbing the palm of one hand on the other, he gazed into the fire. Then suddenly he straightened up, and his eyes flashed as he replied: "They came with a message from the chief of the far-down-the-river Parted Hair people (the Sioux), from Sitting Bull himself, asking us to join them and the Cheyennes in one great war against the whites. The Cheyennes had agreed to it, they said, and they were going on to the Snakes, the Nez Perces, Pend d'Oreilles, Kootenays, Crees, and then to you."

"And what did you reply?" Big Lake asked with intense eagerness.

"I told him that we had never made war against the whites," Gray Bull replied, "and that I could see no reason to do so now. They gave reasons why we should join them. 'These are Sitting Bull's own words, ' said they, 'and his message to you: Not satisfied with the firewagon trail [railroad] that they have built across the plains to the south of us, the whites are building other trails in the eastern part of our country. They have made treaties with us, which were written in black water upon white stuff like thin hide, so that the words should last and there could be no denying them. But they might as well have been written on the surface of the flowing river: every promise they have made they have broken. They have acknowledged that certain lands are ours, and then taken them away from us. They have agreed to make us certain payments, but we have received nothing. They have made us move westward, and westward, and again westward until we encroach upon the hunting grounds that are yours. They follow us, coming in ever greater numbers with their cattle and pigs and sheep, and their women and children, to make their homes on our land. They kill our buffalo by the hundreds and thousands, not for food and clothing, but to save the grass for their evil-smelling stock. Now, the time has come for all this to be ended: we must fight them; we must kill them off, else our children will all die from want of food.' "

When Gray Bull had finished, everyone was looking solemn, and there was a long silence. Then one of the young Blackfeet chiefs hurled out his opinion:

"Let us join them!" he cried. "Let us all, all the prairie peoples, get together and wipe out the white skins! We have never paid them for what they did to us at the Bear River. Have you forgotten that, my brothers? Let me tell it again: Day was just breaking. That good, kind chief, our brother, Heavy Runner, and his people still slept. They had no reason to be awake and watchful for they had done no wrong. It was their last sleep. The soldiers crept to the edge of the bank and began shooting into the lodges. Those not killed or crippled in their beds rushed out, Heavy Runner in the lead, waving a writing given him by the white chiefs, which said that he was a man of peace and a friend to all white people; but it made no difference. He fell with many bullets in his body, and all but five or six of the rest fell with him.

"You remember that there were only a few men in the camp, for most of the hunters had gone north after a big buffalo herd. So our people made no defense, fired not one shot. One after another they fell—men, women, boys, and girls. And then the soldiers came down into the camp, and with the spears at the end of their guns, they jabbed holes in the bodies of the wounded, in the little infants clinging to their mothers' breasts, and ran here and there stabbing the young girls and boys who were trying to conceal themselves in the brush. Have you forgotten that, my brothers?"

"Away out there in the Sand Hills the shadows of thirty-three men, ninety women, and sixty children and babies cry out to you for vengeance. Now is the time to take it. Let us heed these words of the chief of the Parted Hair people. My father was shot down there on the Bear River, my mother and my young sister were speared to death there. Oh, you great chiefs! I beg you to do what this Sitting Bull asks."

That was a very solemn moment. When the chief ceased speaking he was sobbing, and everyone there was deeply affected by his words. I forgot that I was of white blood, and a fierce longing possessed me to join these people in a war against such heartless murderers of women and children. But there were wiser heads there than mine. Big Lake spoke presently and his voice was low and tremulous:

"Arrow Topknot, my young brother! Many times we have talked about this. We have long sought a trail to the wiping out of the great wrong that has been done to us; but there is no trail. There is no way by which we can get rid of the sorrow in our hearts. We cannot fight soldiers who murder women and children. While we were out warring against one band of them, another band would find our camp, and we should return only to find the bones of our families and the ashes of our lodges."

"You speak truth," was Gray Bull's comment. "It is useless to war against men who kill women and children."

"These Parted Hair people were always liars," said another, "and I don't see why we should believe the words of this Sitting Bull now. The white men of the far-down-the-river are naught to us. They are not killing our game; they are not making homes on our land. True, some of them do live away back in our mountains, where they dig and sweat in search of yellow rocks, but let them do so; they and their rocks are naught to us."

"It matters not to me what you all do!" Arrow Topknot cried. "I am going to join these people in their war against the whites. I shall leave for the Cheyenne camp as soon as the north-flying webfeet bring news of approaching summer."

He kept his word, and was never seen or heard of again. If he was not killed while on his way to the Cheyennes, he probably lost his life in the ensuing Sioux wars, which culminated in the memorable Custer massacre.

Gray Bull refilled the big pipe, and, when it was going the rounds once more, he started another subject. "About this white buffalo," he said. "Did your hunters wound her?"

"Those who saw and chased her had no chance to do so," Big Lake replied. "They say that she has the cunning of a wolf and the swiftness of an antelope. The wind was favorable to the hunters, blowing strong and steady in their faces, yet she seemed to sense their coming. Before they rode out of the coulee and showed themselves, she had left her grazing and her sleeping brown brothers, and was trotting toward a ridge nearby. They no sooner showed their heads above the level of the plain than she broke into a swift run. All the time she had been going straight away and had not turned her head; so how could she have seen them? There is a mystery in that. The animal must have powerful medicine."

"Well, then, we must all make medicine," said Gray Bull. "Strong prayers must be said; rich offerings must be made to the gods."

The Blackfeet had one motive in pursuing the cow, the Crows another. The Blackfeet wanted her hide, faultlessly tanned into a soft robe, to present to the sun; the Crows wanted it merely for what it would be worth to them in trade. The beliefs of the Crows I never understood well; their chief god was Ancient Wolf. But this I do know: their religion, or, in other words, their philosophy, was of a very low order compared with that of the Blackfeet, with its beautiful and mystic rites.

A great commotion and the wailing of women in the upper end of the camp suddenly terminated the feast. Boy-like, Ap-si and I rushed out of the lodge to learn the cause of it; the chiefs followed in a more dignified manner. We came to a lodge surrounded by a crowd of people. Inside someone was groaning from intense pain. Two women, between sobs, were explaining to the gathering what had happened; but neither Ap-si nor I could understand them. Following a messenger who had been sent for him, Skunk Cap came pushing his way through the crowd, holding aloft his sacred staff, to which were tied bits of fur, feathers, and bones of animals from the arctic region, where the medicine man had once been on an expedition. He went inside, and instantly there was a hush; the groaning ceased. Then the women broke out crying again, and we heard, too, the deep-voiced wailing of men. We knew what that meant: the sufferer was dead.

Skunk Cap came slowly out of the lodge, and, seeing us and the Blackfoot chiefs, explained what had happened: Old Man Star, the dead man, and three other hunters had found the white buffalo somewhere west of camp and chased her. Instead of running straight away the animal had begun to circle to the south, and Old Man Star, cutting across, had intercepted her and, riding up close, had aimed just behind her shoulder. Either the nipple was clogged or the cap faulty; the charge failed to ignite, and the cow, suddenly whirling straight about, struck and disemboweled the horse, and then hooked and tore open the side of the falling rider. Before the other hunters could get a shot at her, the animal was off again.

We all turned and went over to the fort, where Eli had called a feast for the Crow and Blackfoot chiefs. It was the opinion of all that

SKUNK CAP CAME . . . HOLDING ALOFT HIS SACRED STAFF

the white buffalo was a powerful medicine animal and that con-
certed action must be taken in order to kill her. After some discussion the chiefs decided to send messengers to call in all of the
Blackfoot hunters. The plan was to have the whole force of the two
tribes surround the country where the buffaloes were and then draw
in to a common center, so that, whichever way the animal turned,
she should find hunters facing her. Meantime, no one was to be
allowed to hunt.

The Blackfeet began to come in the next day, and two days later
all who had left the Missouri in quest of the white cow were
encamped just across the river from our fort. The Crows were very
hospitable; they gave numberless feasts and smokes and dances for
the entertainment of their visitors. The young men of both tribes
spent hours over their toilet, washing and combing and braiding
their hair and painting their faces; then, putting on their best clothes
and hanging a fine shield or a plumed war club to their wrists, they
promenaded through the camps, and stood posing here and there,
hoping to be admired by the girls. The girls, however, always pretended that they did not see them, although at any gathering of
those demure maids you could have heard a discussion of the attire
and general appearance and the character of every one of the youths.

In the evenings a dozen different dances were going on at once:
Sioux dances, victory dances—in the pauses of which the partici-
pants would tell of their deeds—women dances, in which the maid-
ens, duly chaperoned, danced with the young men. Most impressive
of all was the medicine-pipe dance, in which some zealous old medicine man led a long, winding column of stately dancing men and
women, who alternately prayed and sang praises of the gods as they
wove their way through the great camp. These rare meetings always
resulted in a number of marriages between members of the two
tribes, and the formation of individual friendships that even subsequent wars could not break.

The morning of the great hunt came, and soon after sunrise the
chiefs of the two tribes rode out of camp at the head of their hundreds of hunters. The Crows went southwest, then west, and then
northwest; at frequent intervals a man dropped out, until a line was
formed from the Musselshell to the southeastern point of the Snowy

Mountains. Twenty miles north of them the Blackfeet made up another line from the river round to the mountains. It had been agreed that when the sun marked the middle of the day they should all start to close the circle.

Ap-si and I had our posts several hundred yards on either side of Skunk Cap. Some time after we started to close the circle we began to see increasing numbers of buffaloes and antelopes, wolves and coyotes, and even some elk and deer, which the riders at the westerly end of the line had scared out of the foothills. All of the animals were on the move, but as yet none showed any particular alarm except the antelopes. A long, stringing band of those timid and wary creatures would fly away out of sight in one direction only to reappear soon heading in another.

Before another hour passed, the thousands of game animals within our ever-narrowing circle were milling. Some swept past us to our right, others left, circling and circling in a vain attempt to find a gap in the endless line of riders.

The antelopes were the first to break through the line of hunters. Running so fast that their feet seemed scarcely to touch the ground, a bunch of several hundred of them flashed between Skunk Cap and me.

They went out unharmed, for we had no thought of shooting at them. Soon great herds of buffaloes began to break through the line. They no longer tried to avoid the hunters, and we frequently had to put our horses to top speed in order to get out of their way.

It was not until the circle had contracted to a diameter of about four miles that I got a glimpse of the white cow. She was running some distance in advance of a buffalo herd, and, overtaking another herd that was running more to the southwest, she was soon lost to view in the midst of it.

Half an hour later I saw her again. The circle was now very small, and she was leading the last band of buffaloes within it. Five Crows, mounted on unusually fast horses, were in close pursuit. The white buffalo's brown mates scattered to the right and the left, and as our part of the circle now sped forward to meet her I saw that the race was between Big Owl, the Blackfoot who had been on my right all the morning, and a Crow who was riding a powerful black horse.

The cow swerved to the west, and then turned due north, a move that brought both men directly behind her. To their rear the plain was covered with riders converging to the chase; most of them had no hope of getting the animal, but of course everyone was anxious to see the finish.

Big Owl and the Crow were both about the same distance from the cow, and, crouching low over their horses' withers, they urged their mounts to top speed. Behind them the other hunters set up a great shouting, as each urged the man of his tribe to greater speed. Had the cow not been rushing here and there for a long time within the ever-narrowing bounds of our circle, even those swiftest riders could not have overtaken her; but as it was they closed in steadily. Both were now holding their guns ready to raise and fire, and each was watching the other, afraid to risk a long shot and miss, and yet wanting to fire the first and fatal ball.

Ap-si, riding near me, was fairly whimpering with excitement. At last the two riders were close enough for a fatal shot; they did not seem more than ten yards behind her, with Big Owl on her right flank and the Crow on her left.

Suddenly the Crow threw up his gun and aimed; but he could not fire before Big Owl had his aim, too. The reports were almost simultaneous. The cow flinched, and I knew that she was hit; she ran on for a few paces and then collapsed, falling over on her right side.

A moment later the two men sprang from their horses beside the body. Both began talking loudly and then angrily. The Crow pointed again and again at the bloody wound in the animal's shoulder and cried:

"See! It is in my side! My gun did that! It is my animal, not yours!"

"No, no! That is where my bullet came out! I killed her! Go away! She is mine!" Big Owl shouted.

"You go away! She is mine! You are a liar!" The other shouted, making the sign for the forked, or lying, tongue.

At that the Blackfoot began hastily to reload his gun, and the Crow followed suit. In another moment they would be shooting, and I realized with a shiver that that would mean a terrible fight between us and the other tribe. Already the Blackfeet were shouting to Big Owl:

"Kill him! Kill him! She is your animal—you shot her!"

Skunk Cap was the first one of us to reach the disputants. He

BEHIND THEM THE OTHER HUNTERS SET UP A GREAT SHOUTING, AS EACH
URGED THE MAN OF HIS TRIBE TO GREATER SPEED.

sprang between them from his horse just as Big Owl was fitting a cap
on his rifle and flourished his ever-present sacred medicine staff
before their eyes.

"Don't you dare shoot, either of you!" he roared.

Big Owl was wild with rage. He tried to push the peacemaker
aside and to raise his rifle, but Skunk Cap jerked the weapon out of
his hands and, turning, struck the Crow's gun with his staff; he was
just in the nick of time: the Crow pulled the trigger, but the charge
went harmlessly into the air. The rest of the hunters were now arriving on the scene; the older men were all for a peaceful settlement of
the affair, the hot-headed young men all eager to fight.

Big Lake and Gray Bull came up none too soon. Each of them
scolded and threatened his people, and in a moment or two the big
crowd became silent. The two chiefs then spoke a few words together
and stepped over to the dead animal. They examined the wound in
her side and cried out loudly, each in his own tongue:

"Here the bullet went in!"

At that a joyous shout went up from the Crows.

Big Owl called to those near him, "Quick! Help me turn her over!"

It was quickly done, and again the two chiefs bent over and examined a wound that was plain to be seen in the right side, exactly opposite the other one.

"Here also went in a bullet," they announced after a moment, and this time the Blackfeet gave a mighty shout of exultation.

"I am ashamed of myself for getting angry," Big Owl said. "It was all a mistake. This sacred animal belongs half to my Crow friend, there, and half to me. Ask him what he will take for his share?"

Skunk Cap immediately put the question, and the Crow quickly answered, "Thirty horses."

The Blackfoot dropped his head. "Thirty horses," he said in despair. "I have nowhere near that number."

At that a hundred voices broke loose: "I give you one," "I give you five." "I give you ten." The offers seemed numberless.

Probably more than five hundred horses were offered to Big Owl with which to purchase the Crow's half of the white cow; but three or four of Big Owl's relatives made their way through the crowd and talked with him a moment, and then he turned again to Skunk Cap.

"Tell him that I and my family will give him the thirty horses," he said.

"I am glad," the Crow replied in signs. "Go to work and skin your animal."

I stood and watched the beautiful cream-white hide roll back from the skillful knives of the hunters. The work was soon completed, and then the tongue was taken out to be dried and presented to the sun with the tanned white robe at the great religious festival of the coming summer. Big Owl then spoke to his chief, who, stepping out beside the carcass of the cow, made an impressive prayer to the sun.

The Crows stood and listened respectfully. When Big Lake had finished, there was a general mounting of horses, and we all rode homeward in the gathering dusk.

All the way across the plain our course was enlivened by song. My companions were happy, for they had secured for their god the gift that they knew was most acceptable to him.

18

The Story of Pita

Originally published under the topical title "More Memoirs of a White Indian" in *The Youth's Companion*, March 14 , 1912.

One November evening Pita (Eagle) sat in his grandfather's lodge, listening to the talk of the old man and his aged visitors.

There had been a council at the agency that day. The inspector had said, "Truly, there are no buffalo left. You can no longer hunt over the plains; you will no longer be allowed to make war on your enemies, nor may they raid your country. There is but one thing for you to do, my friends; you have now to follow the white man's road. Like him you must build houses, fence land, put up hay, and raise cattle and horses; and in this new work you shall have help. The Great Father bids me to tell you that he will give you cattle, tools, wagons, and harness."

This counsel did not agree with what the great medicine man, Low Horn, had been telling the Blackfeet for two years. He had assured them that the buffalo herds had been driven away by the

HE . . . PUT ON THE CAP, AND SAW THE BEAR . . . RUN TOWARD
HIM, OPEN-MOUTHED. (ILLUSTRATION BY H. C. EDWARDS)

white men in order to starve the Indians. Low Horn pretended to be making medicine to bring back the buffalo. The people had only to give him food, a few horses, and other presents now and then, and he would certainly succeed.

"I, for one," said blind old Heavy Bow, Pita's grandfather, "no longer believe in Low Horn. I do believe what this looks-into-things man told us today. His advice is good; his offer generous; but, alas! Of what avail will it be to the aged, to those who are blind like me?"

Pita was as despondent as a youth of sixteen can be. After the visitors were gone, he rolled himself in his blankets and thought harder than he had ever done before. On him devolved the welfare of his widowed mother and of his blind and aged grandfather.

The next day he saw a party of cowboys ride into the agency and stop at the trader's store. Why could he not become a herder of cattle, too? He could break horses; he could throw a rope with skill. But how could he obtain a saddle? His own was a poor affair of rawhide with an elk-horn bow. White men, he knew, did not furnish saddles for the men they employed. He stayed in the store until the cowboys departed; then he went home and laid his plans before his mother and grandfather.

"I am going to be a cowboy," he said, "but first I must have a saddle. I am going up to the mountains to catch some beaver with which to purchase one. You, grandfather, must lend me your traps and your gun, and you, mother, make me some warm moccasins."

The Blackfeet are a people of the plains, and never venture into the Rockies except in large bands. To them the stupendous cañons and dark forests are the abode of malign gods. Wind Maker, the fierce animal a hundred times as large as an elk, stalks along the crest of the range; he works his huge ears like fans, and causes the wind to blow gently or fiercely, as he chooses. More than once he has created such furious blasts that the luckless hunter along the cliffs has been lifted up and hurled to his death in the bottom of a cañon far below.

In the bottomless lakes and rushing rivers live the Underwater People, ever watching to draw the unwary Blackfoot down to his death. At night ghosts of the mountain people, the Kootenays, the Stonies, and other enemies who died there, wander in the forests, shoot sleeping Blackfeet with painless and invisible arrows, and give them an illness of body against which the most powerful of medicine men are unable to cope.

Therefore the mother cried and old Heavy Bow protested against the boy's plan. Nevertheless, the next morning Pita mounted his pony and set out. The hardiest white hunter would not have dreamed of going at that season of the year with such a meager outfit as Pita carried. An old buffalo robe and a blanket were his bedding; he had three pairs of moccasins, four beaver traps, a small tin kettle, a cup, some matches, a long smoothbore, cap lock gun, some ammunition, and a knife.

Pita thought that he had a lavish supply of necessities. He carried no food. Had he not a sack of small shot with which to kill grouse? And for a deer, an elk, or moose—one of the big, round, heavy balls dropped in the barrel on top of the charge of shot instantly converted the gun into a powerful weapon of death.

Very near the great mountains looked; two-thirds of their height was already white with winter snow. But Pita rode all day in order to reach them. He stopped for the night in the edge of the forest bordering on Two Medicine Lake, and picketed his pony in a little open park near by. Gathering a lot of dead wood, he built a small fire, skinned and broiled a pair of grouse he had shot during the day, and ate them. Then, breaking a lot of balsam-bough tips, he made a couch.

But he did not sleep; the unaccustomed forest noises frightened him. He rose and replenished the dying fire, and then prayed long and fervently.

All night he sat before the little fire, praying and dozing. At last daylight came, and with the rising sun his fears vanished. Without hunting for a breakfast, he saddled his pony and rode on into the mountains, until, about noon, he came to a small prairie just below the upper lake of the Two Medicine River.

In the pines beside the stream stood an old "war-house," a lodge or teepee of poles thickly thatched with balsam boughs. It had been built long since to shelter a war party of some mountain tribe on the way to or from a raid into the country of the Blackfeet. Pita took possession of it, rethatched it, gathered a lot of fuel, made a soft couch of evergreens, and then, late in the afternoon, set out with his traps to look for beaver signs along the stream.

He had seen many grouse during the day, but hungry as he was, had refrained from shooting them because he did not wish to alarm the larger game whose footprints were fairly plentiful in the trail.

While he repaired the war-house, Pita had sung the song of Ancient Coyote, chief of hunters, which every good Blackfoot sings before setting forth in quest of meat, for it brings good luck. He hummed it under his breath now as he stealthily slipped along through the timber bordering the creek, and it brought him luck. Off to the left he heard a branch snap. He stopped to listen, and suddenly a great dark animal, with enormous head and wide-palmed antlers, stepped into an opening, stopped, and looked toward him.

He had never before seen a moose, but he knew that this was one. Also he knew that at that season of the year the bulls were of uncertain temper. Yet he was not afraid; he had killed buffalo and other game of the plains.

Slowly, almost imperceptibly, he began raising the gun to his shoulder. The bull shook his head, stamped the ground with an immense forefoot, his wicked, pig-like eyes gleamed, his hair rose straight up along his back. The gun was now in position. Taking careful aim at a point just back of the shoulder, Pita pulled the trigger. With the explosion, a great cloud of smoke filled the air. Hastily springing to one side, the boy reached the shelter of a large pine just as the bull charged past the place where he had stood. Then the animal stopped and turned. It saw the boy, made one last effort to reach him, and then fell heavily to the ground.

Here was meat in plenty—a thousand pounds and more. Pita skinned the animal and worked until dusk cutting up the meat and packing it on his pony to the war-house. He hung it in the trees, safe from the depredations of all night prowlers. Then he build a fire in his rude home, piled the doorway full of fuel, and feasted on rich portions of the meat, which he broiled over the cottonwood coals. But with the night his fear of the unseen returned, and again and again he prayed to the gods—mostly, though, to Ap-pi-stu-to-ki, the white man's God. "I have started in to follow the white men's road," he said to himself. "Surely their God will aid me."

The next day, after pegging the great moose-hide on the ground to dry, Pita began beaver-trapping in earnest. He found plenty of "slides," the paths over which the beavers dragged their cuttings of willow and cottonwood branches down the banks into the stream. Down in deep pools he saw great piles of wood which they had sunk for food when the snow should become deep and ice covered the surface of the water. Pita had never trapped the animals, nor had he any of the scent which trappers prepare in order to lure the cunning animals to their death; but he set his traps in the water at the foot of the slides, two hands deep, staking them out, and walking in the edge of the stream instead of on the shore.

The first night he caught one beaver, with dark and heavy fur, worth at least six dollars at the trader's store. In the evening he figured out, by placing twigs in rows of six each, that ten such skins would buy the saddle, for which the trader asked sixty dollars. But four nights passed before he caught another; and after that seven nights before he got the third—and that a little one born in the spring, and not worth more than two dollars.

Then more blank days ensued. Try as he would, changing his traps about from one slide to another, he was unable to catch another of the animals. But from the signs he knew that they were abroad every night, and more than once he found a trap sprung and contemptuously drawn to one side of the place where he had set it.

Although he had plenty of fat meat, Pita began to grow thin, partly from his fitful sleep at night, and partly from his great anxiety to succeed in his undertaking. Winter was now rapidly coming on. Day after day black clouds obscured the mountain peaks, and the snowline came nearer and nearer the valley. He knew that at almost any time a great storm might set in and drive him back to the plains.

Taking up the traps one morning, Pita set out to explore a branch of the river coming in from the south. Following it for some distance, he came to a dam made by the beavers, and in the upper end of the pond he saw a large "house," the conically piled sticks of which rose breast-high above the water. Three of the traps he set at the foot of freshly used slides. Then, removing his clothing, he waded out to the house, neck-deep in the icy water, and set the fourth trap at the entrance to the house, which was almost at the bottom. He was obliged to dive in order to do it, and having no stake, he fastened the long chain to a large piece of beaver cutting. Then, shivering from the cold, he hurried ashore, hastily got into his clothes, and went on up the stream, instead of homeward, to see if there were any more beavers on the little stream.

Before long he came to the snow-line, and keeping on, he presently saw some huge tracks in the snow, tracks like those made by a bare-footed person, except that for more than a hand's breadth beyond the toes extended the impressions of claws. He knew at once that it was the trail of a grizzly bear, not only because of the size of the tracks, but because, had a black bear made it, its short, curved claws would not have cut the snow more than a finger's width beyond the toes.

Pita's heart seemed to rise and throb in his throat when he saw the tracks. Involuntarily he cocked his gun and scanned the forest with wide eyes.

A grizzly! More dreaded even than human foes was this terrible animal. Pita had heard tales of its ferocity, of its unprovoked attacks on innocent berry-pickers, on people travelling quietly through the brush of the forest and timbered valley. He himself had once seen a grizzly succumb only after its body had been riddled with the bullets of a dozen hunters. Moreover, there was the mystery of the animal. The Blackfeet believed it to be part human; believed that its ghost had power to torment the slayer of its body, to take vengeance even on the person who handled and dried the skin. The medicine men dared not even call the animal by its right name, *kyai-yo*; they said *pahk-si-kwo-yi* (sticky mouth) instead.

Pita turned and cautiously retraced his steps, looking back fre-quently to see if he was pursued. Well he knew the value of the big animal's furry skin—thirty, forty, perhaps even fifty dollars at the trader's store, but he had no thought of getting the needed saddle by attempting to kill this chief of the mountain forests. He had found a new trapping-place; surely he would get enough beavers from the pond to supply his need.

Impatient to see his traps, Pita was up and out very early the next morning, and hastened to the pond. One after another he examined those along the shore, and found they had not been disturbed.

He waded out to the one he had set in the entrance to the house. It had been pulled away to one side, and sprung! Half-heartedly he reset it. Again ashore and in his clothes, shivering, weak from loss of sleep, he cried out in his distress:

"O you, gods of my people, and you, God of the men whose road I am trying to travel, have you deserted me? Must I indeed give up this plan of mine?"

He went back to the war-house, cooked and ate his morning meal of fat moose ribs, and sat by the little fire, trying to think wherein he had failed to set the traps right. He had followed his grandfather's instructions carefully. All day he brooded over his ill luck, and at bedtime he vowed to all the gods: "If there is no beaver in my traps in the morning, I will follow the trail of the grizzly. I will kill it—or be killed."

As usual, there was no beaver; the traps had not even been disturbed. Pita carried ashore the one he had set at the house, dressed himself, and collected the three others from the slides. He dropped them at the foot of a tree and went on up the stream.

He came to the grizzly's tracks; they looked much older than the day before, and were lined with crystals of frost. Old as they were, they caused Pita to wish that he had not made his vow; but it was too late for wishes. The gods had heard him, his father's shadow, away off in the Sand Hills, had heard him; there could be no retracting of the words; there was nothing to do but to go on, perhaps to victory, or perhaps to his death.

The trail led away up the north side of the valley. Following it, Pita presently came in sight of a great mass of boulders—some of them as large as a house—which in ages past had broken from the cliff that still towered above them. Outermost of the huge blocks were two that leaned together; the space between them formed a low, dark cavern of unknown depth.

In front of it Pita saw that the snow was trampled and discolored. The sides of the cave were white with frost. The track he had been following went straight to the place, and he could not see where any trail went away from it. This, then, was undoubtedly the bear den, the place the animal had chosen in which to sleep away the winter months. Stealthily, slowly he retreated, walking backward until he could no longer see the cave, and then he sat down on a snow-covered boulder to rest and to think.

After a while he rose and went homeward, picking up his traps by the way. He did not sleep that night; from dusk to dawn he sat huddled on his couch, trying to think of some way in which to get a shot at the bear without too great risk to himself.

By the time that daylight came, he had decided upon a plan of action, but he had little hope of success; he believed that he was going to certain death. After eating a little boiled meat, and soaking some strips torn from his shirt in marrow fat of the moose, he went out and strode grimly up the valley of the beaver-pond stream. On the way he selected a slender stone of a pound weight, and tied the greased strips to it.

There was a steep slope from the stream up to the foot of the big boulders, bare of trees or any other cover. When Pita arrived at the base of it, he paused for a moment. There was no sign to denote that the bear had been out since the day before. The frost on the wall and roof of the den seemed to have deepened. Pita could see a faint drift of steam rising from the mouth of the place and changing into light frost in the cold air. Without doubt the bear was back there somewhere in the darkness.

The wind, just a faint stir of it, was blowing up the valley. Pita went on with it for some distance, then turned sharply to the right, climbed up to a level with the boulders, and came back. There was nothing to be seen on this side of them. They seemed to be joined together in one huge rock. Cautiously, slowly, he stole along the side, turned the corner, and, leaning forward, peered into the den.

He could see nothing in the darkness, but the rank and unmistakable odor of bear greeted his nostrils. Pita drew back, and praying once more for aid in his desperate undertaking, took a bullet from his pouch and put it in his mouth. He placed a cap between the fingers of his left hand, and poured a heavy charge of powder into the palm of it, leaving the thumb and forefinger free to grasp the fore-arm of his gun.

Ready now for the almost instantaneous reloading of the piece, he struck a match, lighted the grease-soaked rags, and hurled the hissing mass into the rear of the den. It fell on a pile of rubbish, dried weeds, grass, leaves, and twigs, of which bears generally make their winter beds, and set fire to it. Beyond the blaze a huge bear slowly and stupidly rose, as if still half-asleep, and blew its breath sharply through its nose, just as pig does when alarmed or angry.

Twice, three times, it did this, and then, with a deep roar, it sprang past the growing blaze and came bounding toward the mouth of the cave. Pita sprang back and brought the gun to his shoulder. Although he had been nerving himself for this crisis, it was only by the greatest effort of his will that he did not turn and run.

Out came the great bear, and paused, uncertain which way to go. At that instant Pita fired. The animal roared with pain, but what it did for a moment Pita could not see because of the dense powder smoke. As soon as he fired, he hastily poured the charge he was hold-ing into the barrel, struck the piece sharply to make it settle, dropped the ounce ball from his mouth on top of it, put on the cap, and saw the bear rise from the blood-stained snow and run toward him open-mouthed.

Again he fired, and as the bear again roared, he turned and ran down the slope. He heard the animal coming behind him, and then—he was struck a terrible blow on the thigh which hurled him high in the air. When he came down, his head struck a rock and he knew no more.

When he regained consciousness, there was a sharp, throbbing pain in his head and he was shivering from the cold. His thigh ached and smarted. He sat up and saw the bear lying motionless so close that he could reach out and touch it.

He rose and examined himself; blood was trickling from a gash in his head, and also from his thigh, where the bear's claws had lac-erated the flesh and ripped open his blanket legging. But what mat-tered a few hurts? The bear was dead; he had fulfilled his vow; he could buy the needed saddle. With tears streaming down his cheeks, his heart was full of thankfulness for his narrow escape. He lifted his hands toward the heavens and gave earnest thanks to the gods. Then, recovering his gun and loading it, he sharpened his knife on a stone and skinned the big animal.

The Works of James Willard Schultz

My Life as an Indian: The Story of a Red Woman and a White Man in the Lodges of the Blackfeet. New York: Doubleday, Page, 1907. Reprint. Boston: Houghton Mifflin, 1914.

With the Indians in the Rockies. Boston: Houghton Mifflin, 1912.

Sinopah, the Indian Boy. Boston: Houghton Mifflin, 1913.

The Quest of the Fish-Dog Skin. Boston: Houghton Mifflin, 1913.

On the Warpath. Boston: Houghton Mifflin, 1914.

Blackfeet Tales of Glacier National Park. Boston: Houghton Mifflin, 1916.

Apauk, Caller of Buffalo. Boston: Houghton Mifflin, 1916.

The Gold Cache. Boston: Houghton Mifflin, 1917.

Lame Bull's Mistake: A Lodge Pole Chief Story. Boston: Houghton Mifflin, 1918.

Bird Woman. Boston: Houghton Mifflin, 1918.

Running Eagle, the Warrior Girl. Boston: Houghton Mifflin, 1919.

Rising Wolf, the White Blackfoot. Boston: Houghton Mifflin, 1919.

In the Great Apache Forest: The Story of a Lone Boy Scout. Boston: Houghton Mifflin, 1920.

The Dreadful River Cave: Chief Black Elk's Story. Boston: Houghton Mifflin, 1920.

The War-Trail Fort: Further Adventures of Thomas Fox and Pitamakan. Boston: Houghton Mifflin, 1921.

The Trail of the Spanish Horse. Boston: Houghton Mifflin, 1922.

Seizer of Eagles. Boston: Houghton Mifflin, 1922.

The Danger Trail. Boston: Houghton Mifflin, 1923.

Friends of My Life As an Indian. Boston: Houghton Mifflin, 1923.

Sahtaki and I. Boston: Houghton Mifflin, 1924.

Plumed Snake Medicine. Boston: Houghton Mifflin, 1924.

Questers of the Desert. Boston: Houghton Mifflin, 1925.

Signposts of Adventure: Glacier National Park as the Indians Know It. Boston: Houghton Mifflin, 1926.

Sun Woman. Boston: Houghton Mifflin, 1926.

William Jackson, Indian Scout: His True Story Told by His Friend, James Williard Schultz. Boston: Houghton Mifflin, 1926.

Son of the Navahos. Boston: Houghton Mifflin, 1927.

Red Crow's Brother. Boston: Houghton Mifflin, 1927.

In Enemy Country. Boston: Houghton Mifflin, 1928.

Skull Head the Terrible. Boston: Houghton Mifflin, 1929.

The Sun God's Children (with Jessica L. Donaldson). Boston: Houghton Mifflin, 1930.

The White Beaver. Boston: Houghton Mifflin, 1930.

Alder Gulch Gold. Boston: Houghton Mifflin, 1931.

Friends and Foes in the Rockies. Boston: Houghton Mifflin, 1933.

Gold Dust. Boston: Houghton Mifflin, 1934.

The White Buffalo Robe. Boston: Houghton Mifflin, 1936.

Stained Gold. Boston: Houghton Mifflin, 1937.

Short Bow's Big Medicine. Boston: Houghton Mifflin, 1940.

Note: Several of the preceding titles were reprinted in other editions over the years.

The Posthumous Works

Blackfeet and Buffalo: Memories of Life Among the Indians. Edited by
Keith C. Seele. Norman: University of Oklahoma Press, 1962.

Why Gone Those Times? Blackfoot Tales. Edited by Eugene Lee
Silliman. Norman: University of Oklahoma Press, 1974.

Floating on the Missouri. Edited by Eugene Lee Silliman. Norman:
University of Oklahoma Press, 1979.

Many Strange Characters: Montana Frontier Tales. Edited by Eugene
Lee Silliman. Norman: University of Oklahoma Press, 1982.

Bear Chief's War Shirt. Edited by Willard Ward Betts. Missoula,
Montana: Mountain Press, 1983.

Recently Discovered Tales of Life Among the Indians. Compiled and
edited by Warren L. Hanna. Missoula, Montana: Mountain
Press, 1988.

Blackfeet Tales from Apikuni's World. Edited by David C. Andrews.
Norman: University of Oklahoma Press, 2002.